SILENT AUTUMN

by
Gary Gentile

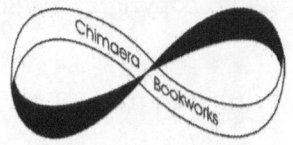

Additional copies of this book may be purchased from
the same address by sending a check or money order in
the amount of $15 U.S. for each copy (plus $3 postage
per order, not per book, in the U.S. Inquire for ship-
ping cost to foreign countries). Alternatively, copies
may be purchased from the author's website, and paid
by credit card:

http://www.ggentile.com

The front cover photograph was taken by the author.

International Standard Book Numbers (ISBN)
1-883056-22-5
978-1-883056-22-3

Original copyright - 1988

Printed in the U.S.A.

Chapter 1

"And the meek shall inherit the Earth."
— *Bible*, Old Testament

The hotel was old — probably late twentieth or early twenty-first century — and most of it was above ground. That was why the rates were so cheap. Dane's room was not even hermetically sealed. During the night he had to get up and don his gas mask, and breathe oxygen from the last o-bottle in his possession. With the regulator set to trickle feed, he survived the night with a minimum of discomfort.

He woke up coughing and choking, scrabbling for the telecom set with blued, slightly anoxic fingers. He punched the receiver button and, gratefully, the incessant buzzer stopped bleating. "What is it?" he asked, in a cracked voice. "My wake-up call's not for another hour."

"I'm a who, not a what." The speaker's tone was slightly nasal, or metallic, more a matter of poor reception than the caller's respiratory inflammation. "We don't get calls from computers down here. We're strictly human."

"Neanderthal, I think, is the word." Dane pulled the clear plastic mask off his face, threw aside the covers, and sat up on the edge of the sagging mattress. The speaker heterodyned as his mouth got too close to the microphone. "Sis, I thought we already said our good-byes."

Her first words were lost in a high-pitched whine. "— in such a huff, I thought we should talk once more before you left."

Dane rubbed sleep out of his eyes. "Didn't we cover everything? You can have the estate, all one hundred twenty-seven beach site acres of it."

"Stop being facetious."

"Not every home has its own walk-in cesspool. Sis,

the land is worthless. It was strip-mined decades ago. And the pollution control equipment in the house is outdated and beyond repair. It needs a new cracking unit, a new carbon filtration system, a new circulator. Hell, all the intake valves need replacement. And the place leaks like a sieve. Like this antiquated flophouse. I've got enough benzene compounds in my lungs to start my own laboratory."

Dane's sister paused before replying. "I take it you didn't sleep well again."

"I haven't slept at *all* since I landed on this godforsaken planet. And you haven't helped any."

"Dane, don't start *that* again. Just because we have a higher sense of morality than you free swinging floaters — "

"Your sense of morality is not high, it's stuck on the ground with cement boots. I can't believe you people. I only asked for a quick — "

"*Dane!* I don't want to talk about it."

"That's the problem with you walkers. You never want to talk about anything."

"I called, didn't I?"

"That was to talk me out of something. If you really wanted to help, you could have given me a — "

"*Dane!* I'm your sister. Mother and Dad didn't bring us up to do those kinds of things. At least, not together."

"But what's the big deal? You didn't have any qualms about rubbing my back. Then, when I asked you to nib — "

"That's enough! I — don't — want — to — talk — about — it. Now, I'll wait for you in the lobby, and we can discuss some *other* things on the way to the port. Can you get dressed and be down here in fifteen minutes?"

"What do you mean? I'm already dressed. You didn't think I'd take off my e-suit in this vaporous miasma, did you?"

"Afraid of bedbugs?"

"Hell, nature didn't evolve anything that could live

in this goo. It's a hell of a way to solve the cockroach problem."

"You could have slept at my place."

"Lying next to an untouchable female is more than I can bear. And this whole crazy planet has got me so rattled that I forgot the gravity was the same in the upper floors."

"Oh, quit your complaining and get down here so we can have a bite to eat before you go."

"Sis, this glop that you call food isn't even processed. Hell, it might have been walking around on four legs the day before yesterday. I'm not eating again till I can get something out of a squeezetube."

"How about a cup of home-grown coffee?"

"Nothing that came out of the ground is going past my lips. Now, I hate to cut you short, but I've got to have some oxygen before I become cyanotic. See you in five."

Dane switched off the telecom, replaced the mask, and adjusted the regulator. The sweet scent of pure O_2 wafted up his nostrils, reminding him of home. He breathed deeply as he padded to the broad window. The anticorrosion coating was fogged with miniature pinpricks, obscuring the view. In any case, from the penthouse he could see only slightly more than from the ground: colorful, mobile rainbow patterns that danced prismatically through the swirling ether. During a clearout — a temporary atmospheric translucency — he made out the fuzzy, orange ball of the sun.

He shook his head slowly at the gloomy montage. He crossed the cramped room and peered into the mirror. Dane's normally bright green eyes were dulled and bloodshot. The chronic irritation of airborne impurities had taken its toll. Worse, the sludge that erupted from the spigot looked and smelled like plumbing effluent. He would not consider washing his hands in the stuff, much less taking a drink.

He lifted the gas mask, pulled off a plastiglove, licked his index finger, and rubbed matter out of the corners of his eyes. He resealed the folds on the environmental suit, but so as not to look like a nerd in the hallways, he took a few deep breaths and packed the mask in its shoulder holster.

The elevator clanked and clattered on an outmoded cable system. Dane shuddered to think how weakened the steel wires might be from leaching chemical corrosives. On the lower floors, passengers crowded into the car and pressed Dane against the back wall. His anxiety increased until he broke into a sweat. His skin crawled. Just as he was about to faint, the car reached ground level.

"Out! I'm getting out! Excuse me." Dane elbowed through the solid packed humanity, and burst into the lobby gasping for air and fighting down nausea. The doors squeaked closed behind him, and the car continued its descent into the bowels of the Earth, where most people lived and worked.

"You certainly don't look like a hotshot spaceman now."

Breathing hard, Dane focused his eyes on the white-haired, slightly bent old woman in front of him. Her smile added more lines to her face, but her melodic voice, undistorted by electronic garble, belied her age.

Dane slowed his heaving chest. "I think I've got claustrophobia." His sister shook her head. "You never had it as a child."

"Yes, but now I'm used to looking out of a window and seeing millions of bright stars and an infinity of space. I'm *not* used to sharing a storage cabinet with half the human race."

"You always did love to exaggerate."

"It's called hyperbole, and it's a perfectly acceptable form of grammar. But in this case, it's no overstatement. How can you people live like this?"

"Dane, you just spent a week lecturing me on how the floaters are so in touch with their fellow man."

"I was talking about feelings, not skin. I have no room for this herd existence."

"I think you just contradicted yourself, but we'll let

it pass. I took the liberty of calling a cab."

"Why not go by tube?"

"Because the tube doesn't go there."

Dane squinted both eyes at her. "Sis, are you telling me you that can't get there from here?"

She laughed a matronly, condescending chortle. "No. But the route is so circuitous that it would take half a day to get to the port, what with waiting for interconnections."

"How can you use the word day in a place that never sees the sun? Half a rev here feels longer than a Martian year." Dane scoured, and glanced around at the empty lobby. "Great city planning. Now you know why ground-based communities are a thing of the past. How far's the garage?"

She hesitated, and pursed her thin lips. "Dane — uh — this hotel doesn't have a garage."

Dane's eyebrows shot up with comprehension. "You mean we've got to go out into that — that — heat and fog and molecular coalescence that you call an atmosphere?"

"It will only be for a moment. The cabs are pressurized."

"Great." Dane wandered across the empty lobby. Outside the picture window, a maintenance crew dressed in full atmosuits, and connected by lifelines, appeared out of the pea-soup smog. The leader dragged his thickly-gloved hands along the crumbling hotel wall. The o-tank on his back carried a week's capacity of oxygen — a workweek, that is: three four-hour days. The pressure bottles were specially coated against sulfur dioxide, hydrogen fluoride, chlorine, and other compounds that formed active reagents in the air, and that pitted metal surfaces, melted plastic, and *ate* cloth. The tanks might last six months before failing a hydrostatic test. "But, Sis, I don't have radiation lining."

She fondled the purple pleats of her own e-suit. "You should be wearing a duraform underneath, instead of disposables."

"I didn't expect to have to go EVA."

"Cut the space lingo, Dane. That's solid ground out there."

"If it's so solid, why does it move?"

He could not hear the slurping of the maintenance crew's battle boots, but he saw the knee-deep impressions as the leader broke trail. Brown condensate drooled down the coated plate glass, ran in rivulets along the oozy ground, and slowly filled the monstrous tracks with green slime.

"There's a platform for the cab, so you won't get your feet wet."

"I don't care about getting them wet. I'm worried about them dissolving in toxic waste."

"Oh, Dane. Stop exaggerating."

"It's not exaggeration. It's — "

The ready light flashed on and a buzzer sounded, announcing the arrival of an aircar. Dane sidestepped to the door, looked out onto the platform, but could not see a thing through the yellow haze. Then a cloud of dust hit the window, and kept pummeling the surface with flying grit until the airjets were switched off. As the cab settled down to the mucuslike surface, only the boxlike silhouette was visible in the churning, natural smog.

A bank of floodlights flashed on — not infrared penetration beams but antique incandescents. The backscatter off suspended particulate matter obscured the cab behind a myriad pinpoints of light.

"Yea, though I walk through the valley of the shadow of death, I shall fear no evil." Dane yanked out his gas mask and pulled it down over his head.

Sis donned her own mask. "You still remember some of your early catechisms."

"Not many of the words, but most of the thought." Through the polarized lenses, he could barely make out the rusted and deeply etched aircar. After a moment of study, he connected enough undissolved paint flecks to read the inscription on the door: Independent Cab, No. 69. The eroded middle "e" looked like a "c", and the adjacent p, n, and d were completely eradicated. "Wonderfully descriptive. Cabs are as independent as their drivers. How do we know this one's for us?"

His sister's voice was muffled by chemical filters. "Most people here are visiting the Plex. We'll be the only ones going to the port." The Underground Museum Complex was as large as a small city, and only one of many. Its Area of Specialty was Grecian times, transport, and merchandise. "And cabbies don't help out with baggage. They only drive cabs."

"Overunionization. Something we don't have to worry about on the platforms, where people specialize in generalization." Dane rubbed his chest pouch. It was full of dentdisks whose information could be dumped through any platform computer terminal. Everything else he owned was compdexed on his IDcard. "We're proud of our lack of possessionism, and our individual ability to take care of ourselves."

"Mechanical slavery."

"Automatics help, but mostly its attitude." Dane winked, and tapped his temple. He checked the reserve on his o-bottle, cinched down the mask straps, felt the seals along his face, and fitted the hose connections. The mask worked without oxygen input, since the filters were electronically enhanced to keep out all dangerous fumes and noxious gases, but it did not arrest odors.

Sis entered the first compartment of the triple airlock and waited for her brother to join her. "Come on, Dane. Stop exaggerating. We'll only be in the open for a few seconds."

"A good whiff of unburned hydrocarbons makes my stomach contents try to escape the container. And the only thing worse than retching inside a mask is — hell, there isn't anything worse."

They cycled through the consecutive locks until they were outside, and running. Dane was only halfway to the aircar when his skin started itching as the acidic atmosphere invaded his e-suit through micropunctures. The pH level precluded the existence of animal life anywhere except in underground zoos.

Ozonides and peroxides had long since killed off all vegetation except the hardy and inimitable lichens of the temperate north and south poles. He could not even envision a time when teeming cattle roamed wild in herds of dozens, or even scores, across open range land. Long gone were the days when one could stand on a mountaintop in the Rockies and see hundreds of meters in either direction.

He reached the aircar first, and fumbled with the door latch. Differential pressure kept the hatch tightly closed. He pulled hard enough to break the seal, but the handle came off in his hand. He stared at the broken plastic for a moment.

"Don't know your own strength."

"It's this insufferable atmosphere that's — "

"Hey, Mack, doncha know air costs money?" the cabby shouted over the intercom. "I don't got enough bot-o to fill the countryside."

Dane slipped his fingers around the overlapping lip, and pulled the hatch open the rest of the way. He allowed his sister to enter. Then he jumped inside, pulled the hatch shut, and dogged the clamps. He dropped the briefcase on the seat between them. After ripping off his mask he held up the dislocated handle. "I guess courtesy went out the window with clear days and sunny skies."

The cabby rolled her eyes. "Okay, Mack, I'm sorry I yelled. It's been a rough night. Everybody's payin' in cash." The compressor cycled on and gently puffed bottled oxygen into the rear cubicle. "This hack ain't been overhauled in a month, my credit balance is low, and I ain't had time to get to the bank with this scrip. What is it with you tourists?"

Dane unzipped the front of his e-suit, pulled out a treated handkerchief, and wiped the back of his neck, where perspiration was reacting with chlorine gas. The stinging slowly subsided.

"I was told that each city's got its own compterm system that wouldn't recognize my IDcard."

"Sure, but we got universal adaptors. Stick your

card in the slot. The reader digitizes your scramble and locks it in memory. Later, I can dump it through a decoder and have the funds transferred when the exchange rate is quantified."

Dane inserted his card. "Why doesn't the Tourist Bureau advertise it?"

"Don't get enough visitors to make it worth repro-gramming. People don't come to Earth, Mack, they leave it." She jabbed a stubby finger toward the insulat-ed ceiling. "One way." When the two compartments equalized, the corpulent cabby slid open the plastiglass barrier. She smoothed back short, slick hair and ran a roving eye up and down Dane's body, lingering in cer-tain areas. "Hey, where's your baggage?"

"I'm traveling light."

"You're gonna be traveling a lot lighter in them clothes." Even though she had turned off the intercom, her voice retained a metallic clink.

"I didn't plan on going EVA — I mean, outside." He glanced at his sister, sitting in the far corner. Her smirk was communication enough without words. "Where I come from, the air is constantly recycled and purified."

Already, his cheap vinyl shoes were deteriorating, and the frail synthetic jumpsuit was dissolving. Nylon and polypropylene could not withstand the rigors of normal Earth atmosphere.

"I'm a floater."

"Don't take a genius to figure *that* out." Her lecher-ous eyes studied him with the intensity of a biochemist examining a slide through a microscope. "The cabcomp said the pickup was headed for the port, and there ain't no other reason for a body to be goin' there less you're ridin' a torch. A local would've used the tube. Cheaper. Goin' far?"

"The other side of the galaxy. I'm a pilot — Exploteam."

"Hey, that's something I always wanted to be when I was kid. You know, blastin' off to other worlds, seein' different planets, toolin' one of them stardrives through the Universe. I wish I coulda been a pilot 'stead of a cabby."

"I may end up being a cabby if I don't catch my flight," Dane said sternly. "They don't wait for latecomers, you know."

"Sure, Mack. I'm sorry. It's just I don't get to see many floaters. They never leave the platforms. Sneer at us that lives on the Earth."

She revved up the airfoil jets, and the cab rose on a thousand columns of siphoned chokedamp. Directional deflectors aimed the turbulence aft, so forward and lateral visibility remained a good twenty meters through the electronic cracking system that was implanted in the windshields. The vehicle accelerated slowly and smoothly, and in a few seconds the outdated hotel was lost in the smog.

"Excuse me, Miss Information, but that's not true. Floaters are neither pretentious nor condescending. We like to think of ourselves as free thinkers. The only thing that differentiates floaters from walkers is their place of abode — and, of course, the reasons for their choice of culture."

"Hey, I ain't no philosophy major, so you're talkin' way over my head. You understand any of this, grandma?"

"I beg your pardon!" Sis's jaw dropped, and her face sagged as if she had suddenly got caught in an amusement park's five-gee accelerator.

"I said, do you understand what your son is talking about?"

Dane tried to stifle his smirk, but failed admirably.

"I happen to be his sister — his *kid* sister."

The cabby stared wide-eyed in the mirror. "Gol-ly. I'm sorry, ma'am. I thought — " Her brow pinched over cowlike orbs. "Hey, wait just a minute. Are you tryin' to pull my leg? He ain't a day over thirty, and you're sixty if you're a day. Now I know you floaters stay younger lookin' cause of low-gee sleep, but you definitely ain't her older brother."

Grinning broadly, Dane brushed carbon soot and fly ash off his pants legs. "I'm afraid it's true."

The cabby glanced at her tracking screen. In the era of effluence, roads no longer existed: they were too difficult to keep in repair. Nor were there any vehicles with wheels, tires, and the numerous mechanical rotating parts. She returned her gaze to the mirror. "Is this one of them jokes where you're half siblings, or something?"

Sis chafed in her corner, and stared out the window at a passing fumarole.

Dane adopted a mien of seriousness. "I'm sorry. I don't mean to poke fun at you. There's no attempt to hurt your feelings. It's just that — " He glanced at his sister, and fought back a smile. "My time is contracted."

"Mack, according to my contract, I got diff'rent rates like half time, double time, and time and a half. What kinda time contract you got?"

"No, you don't understand. I'm talking about subjective time versus objective time."

"Is that anything like overtime?"

"No, it's more like undertime." Dane saw her pursed lips and scrunched up cheeks, and went on quickly before she could rebut. "The stars are too far apart for conventional atomic drive ships, both in terms of fuel consumption and human lifetime. Ramjets pick up fuel on the way (scattered hydrogen atoms in interstellar space) and by spatial translation make the trip at FTL speeds."

The cabby rolled her eyes. Deft fingers touched keyboard sequences that changed the imagery of the optically-enhanced display screen that served as a visual steering pane. Electronic monitors, mounted on the roof, collected data and created a new comphanced image. "Forget the special translation and just talk plain English."

Dane waved his hands in the air, as if warding off a cloud of smoke. "Okay, never mind all that. All you need to know is that star trips take years in obtime, but only weeks in subtime. Time flux during acceleration and deceleration is compressed, without biological progression or conscious awareness."

"That's as clear as air."

Dane clapped his hands. He looked askance at his sister. "Sis, help me."

"You got yourself into it — Sonny."

"Come on, Sis. Act your age — "

"Maybe you should act *your* age. Your obage, not your subage."

"How can I act something I'm not?"

Sis leaned forward and leaned on the back of the front seat. She looked at the cabby's image in the mirror. "What Methuselah here is trying to say is that while he's spent forty years gallivanting around the Universe, he's only grown ten years older. Physically. Mentally, he's going backward."

"Huhn?"

"Sis, you're confusing her."

"Oh, but I'm making a lot of sense to me. Dane, you're not only younger than my own son, but in true-life experience you're less mature. *He's* grown up and got a family. And you're still out there making hay and seeding oats in space."

The cabby winced. "I thought floater food was tank grown organic chemicals — "

"My sex drive is commensurate with my biological age. You may be past your prime, but I'm just reaching mine."

Sis slapped the faded, pockmarked upholstery. "I will not talk about sex with children."

"I don't have sex with children, only consenting — "

"You know what I mean!"

Dane fingered his still-brown hair. "Yes, you mean that you've grown older while I've stayed young. And it bothers you."

"It's the memories, Dane. We grew up together. We played together."

"I tried to play with you yesterday, but you wouldn't let me."

"*Stop it!*" Sis thumped back in her seat. She stared out the window and bit her thumb nail. Tears trickled down her cheeks.

"Sis, I'm sorry. I didn't know — You walkers keep

everything inside, as if your thoughts and feelings are deep, dark secrets."

"Some things are sacred."

Dane slowly shook his head. "No, nothing is sacred. That's the first thing you learn in space. Every individual is part of an organism, like the cells of the body. You communicate osmotically. You're separate, without being secret. You talk, and you listen, and you share. Everything is out in the open: your likes and dislikes, your goals and ambitions, your strong points and weaknesses. That way you don't suddenly erupt with pent-up anger when someone touches an invisible sore."

"I can't be that way. I don't want people knowing what I think, or how I'm feeling."

"Why? How can it hurt you?"

Sobbing, "I don't know. I just — don't."

Dane handed her his handkerchief. "Sis, I know it's difficult. I grew up in the same environment. And I still carry some of it with me. I always will. But when I went to space, I studied the floater's ways. I adapted. Not just because I wanted to get along; because I came to realize what they already know, what they learn since birth: that this is the course of human development. From now on, our evolutionary changes will not be physical, but cultural."

Sis pinched her lips, and dabbed her eyes. "I know, Dane. I know. I'm just too stuck in my ways to change."

Chapter 2

"Children must be taught *how* to think, not *what* to think."

— Margaret Mead

Sandy saw her mother waving from outside the padded cubicle. She waved back without thinking, and the resultant motion flung her sideways in a leisurely pirouette. The children laughed at her unintentional antics. When she alighted next to a padlight, she gripped a rubberoid handle and stabilized her position.

"Okay, now you can see what happens when you lose your concentration in freefall."

The preschoolers giggled. Ten of them hovered about in different attitudes, rotating slowly or kicking wildly. Some of the less adventurous clung to wallgrips as if they would fall off the edge of the world should they let go.

"Now, children, please steady yourselves so I can perform our last experiment of the day. Slide your feet under the bungees like I showed you. Here, Tommy, grab my hand."

The little boy reached out, and Sandy pulled him toward the wall. He worked his fingers along the padding until they located a grip, then bent almost double as only tots can do, and hooked the stretch strap over his instep. The rest of the class swam with exaggerated motions until they were all clinging to the white foam like hanging bats. A dozen and a half heads bent upward from the six walls as Sandy detached herself with a gentle push and drifted very slowly across the cubicle.

Her mother waved again, but Sandy only winked. She was on to her tricks, by now.

She took a squeeze bottle out of her tummy pouch and held it out so all the kids could see it. "This is full of water, plain H2O. Normally, you put your lips around the nozzle and squeeze, or suck, so you can take a drink. But, watch what happens when I squirt it into the air."

Sandy applied a slight pressure. A glistening drop of water appeared on the tip. As she continued to collapse the plastic sides, the bubble expanded until it was the size of an orange. She whipped the bottle aside, and the wet globule floated freely: a perfect sphere in the absence of gravity.

"The water stays together because of what we call molecular cohesion. Each molecule hugs the ones around it, so they can't run away. Now watch what happens when I poke it."

She jabbed it with the plastic tip. The dancing, shimmering surface sent the children into paroxysms of laughter. When the oscillations died down, she punched it again. Each time she did, the ball took up a symmetrical undulation that kept the tots snickering.

"Okay, now let's make another one." Sandy squeezed an equal-sized water ball through the nozzle. "*Now* watch what happens."

She slipped the bottle into her pouch so both hands were free. She corralled the two spheres and pressed them together. They touched, flattened at the point of contact, and bounced apart.

"This is called surface tension. Because the molecules are hugging, each ball is surrounded by a kind of invisible force field which won't let anything else in."

Sandy bounced the balls together several times, to be certain that she had their attention. Then she slammed them hard. Instead of springing apart, the two globes merged into one large one. The children cheered.

"Unless we convince them to be friends. Now all the water will stay together — " She had to shout over their babble of astonishment. " — until enough force is applied to break the little molecules apart."

She cupped the water like a baseball and hurled it at a wall. It burst apart amid the screams of the children. A thousand tiny beads ricocheted around the cubicle as in a three-dimensional billiard game. High-pitched voices squealed. Some tots ducked a splashing, others snatched at recoiling globules.

"Okay, boys and girls. That's enough for today. The circulators will take care of most of the water, and the rest will evaporate." Already, micropores in the foam were inhaling the loose liquid. Sandy waved her mother away from the port, and pushed open the hatch. "Now, remember, no flailing, or jumping from grip to grip. Float slowly. Follow the green arrows along Path 4 until you reach the gravity ramp. And go straight home. If you get lost, ask anyone how to get where you're going. Or put your IDcard into a compslot and someone will come and get you."

She touched hands with each child as he or she left, and smiled at each reiteration of "Goodbye, Sandy."

In z-gee, most of Sandy's short, dirty-blonde hair floated straight out from her scalp. "Mother, you know you disrupted my class."

Barbara smiled, showing a mouthful of perfect pearly implants. She exchanged a peck on the cheek with her daughter. "I thought I could catch you off guard."

Sandy closed and secured the hatch. "I should have known better."

"The way I figure it, you've got to grow up before you can grow old."

"You'll probably live forever." Sandy picked a wall and tagged the grips long enough to propel herself along.

Barbara took a parallel track. "Thanks. Sandy, don't you have a physics class this afternoon?"

"I'm supposed to, but I changed it. I've wangled some extra comptime on the Probe 297 observations. I put out a memo to have the students read up on black hole hypotheses, and we'll go over it tomorrow."

"How do you keep up with such a hectic schedule?"

"I enjoy it. And working with these kids is actually a break. They're response is so astounding, they're minds so malleable."

"Ah, so it's power you want."

"Mother, I know you're teasing. I'm not going to let you psych me. It's a big Universe out there, and the fewer mental reins they have, the better they can cope with their future."

"So when are you going to have a child of your own?"

"Soon, I think. I really do want to have a baby and settle down — for a while, at least. But I think I'm on to something."

Barbara kept up effortlessly in z-gee. "I know you are."

The first landing offered a slight touch of gravity. Sandy jumped onto the padding and sailed into the air, calling over her shoulder. "Mother, have you been peeking into my program again?"

"I couldn't help it. You know I did my first work on neutron stars. Just because I've spent the last thirty years charting quasars and nebulas doesn't mean I've forgotten my first love."

The gravity became stronger at each subsequent landing. Soon, they skipped with practiced ease in long, languorous arcs. As they got further away from the central axis, the Settlement's rotation induced artificial gravity through increasing centrifugal force.

Sandy's hair began to fall evenly over her head, barely covering her ears. "Do you know something the computer doesn't know?"

"Of course not, dear." At half-grav, Barbara took the barrette off her ponytail, and allowed her golden blonde tresses to cascade about her shoulders. "But I know something you haven't collated yet."

"About SC-209?" Sandy had a mind that soaked up information only slightly slower than a mainframe. She did not remember every object in the Stellar Catalogue, but she had a good working knowledge of most ongoing projects. "I only started the compcull yesterday."

"And already it has produced results. You little genius, you practically told the computer what it was going to find. It didn't have to do anything but cull out the obvious and compare what was left."

Sandy stopped and faced the older woman. "Oh, Mother, are you serious? You mean my intuition has come through for me again?"

"Dear, your intuition *always* comes through. I've learned to count on it. I don't know whose gene pool I tapped into when you were conceived, but the sperm bank has yielded good dividends for both of us."

"You're too modest. There's more of you in me than anyone."

"And you are even more modest. As scientists, we both know that intuition is intelligence inspired by sub-conscious deductive reasoning — "

" — multiplied by the square of one's experience," Sandy finished. She started walking lightly, with the gravity up to seventy-five percent. "How can I forget? You won't let me. Semantics aside, how close were my calculations?"

"Sandy, you're the most calculating female in the System. When you decide on an answer, you always pick the formula that will produce it. Shall we go to my cube and tap in from there?"

"If you ever decide to become a grandmother, please don't spoil my children like you spoiled me. Space helmets weren't designed for kids with big heads."

They exited the cylinder's spinning diagonal endcap onto the one-grav living area. In design, the *Heinlein* was like most other B-15 platforms, with a length of just over fifteen kilometers. The inner curvature comprised over sixty thousand square kilometers of surface area, complete with rolling hills, trees, gardens, lawns, twisting paths, flowing creeks, and living cubicles, all lit up by sunlight channeled in through mirror panels. By looking straight up, one could see the gaily-colored roofs of the antipodes, two kilometers away.

A ramp took them below ground to the commuter level, where they caught a lengthwise veyor. The gondola zoomed along its track, switched onto a right-angled path, and dropped them off at Barbara's lower entrance. Upramp, natural sunlight streamed through plastiglass windows into her spacious living quarters.

"How about if I nuke some water?"

Sandy pulled an extra chair in front of the cube-comp terminal and keyed instructions. "Tea for me."

Barbara put water in the microwave oven, and prepared two cups: she was having coffee. "You know, that neutron star at SC-60 was a lot smaller than this, and a lot more powerful. We could have surrounded it with the ramjet deflectors — damn near did, with that hotshot at the helm."

"And almost got baked in the process."

There was a lot more to a neutron star than pressure. In addition to crushing protons and electrons into neutrons, which bunched together in a state of atomic collapse, the rotating stellar mass radiated intense levels of energy.

"Oh, microwave emission wasn't as much of a problem as the magnetic field — Dane dipped so close to the pole that the electron stream wiped out our computer memory. Fred was able to reprogram the peripheral circuits from shielded backups. Would you like sweetener with this?"

"Honey — just a touch." Sandy studied a screen full of figures and formulas. As she leaned back in her seat, the blue formfoam molded around the gentle curvature of her spine. She took the steaming mug from her mother. "That's still the greatest experience of your life, isn't it?"

"Next to childbirth, dear, but every bit as memorable. You don't know what it has meant to me, having gone down in the history tapes as the one who verified, through hard evidence, that pulsars were indeed neutron stars whose magnetic axes intersected with our direction of observation. But this enigma you're working on — I don't understand it. I don't even know how you found it."

Sandy sipped her tea. "I don't understand it either. The probe was several hundred parsecs away when it picked up a weak pulse. The reason we can't observe it directly is because, first, there's a gas cloud in our line of sight, and second, because the polar alignment is forty-three degrees out of phase. The pulse veers off at an angle. It was just dumb luck that the probe detected it on an angular sweep. And actually, what triggered its sensors was the gas cloud excitement. It's got properties of an impending nova that could blow itself through the white dwarf stage right into a neutron star. We can't get more specific data because it's a solitary, so there's no gravitational influence."

Barbara shook her head. "But if it's a solitary, how can that be? It would have to have a close companion with which to interact. Where else could it draw off enough hydrogen to initiate the fusion reaction in the accretion disk?"

"That's only one puzzle. It seems to be collecting hydrogen at the surface. Yet, it's got an iron core surrounded by a broad layer of less heavy elements. Look at the stats." Sandy turned the pedestal so her mother could see the monitor from her chair. "Cobalt, nickel, potassium — unidentified hydrocarbons. Hmmnn, traces of practically the whole periodic table. Mother, it's a new phenomenon — some kind of halfway stage. I think it's a neutron star in the making."

Barbara turned away from the screen. "You've reached that conclusion from pure intuition, not from any evidence that I've seen. I'll grant you it's something outside our experience, but no more."

"Mother, what else could be spinning that fast? I know it's no thirty pulse-per-second body smaller than the *Heinlein*, with a million times the density of the Sun. But a pulse every four-point-zero-three-seven hours isn't exactly slow."

"On a cosmic scale —

"This is a stellar mass, one-point-four-four Sols."

"Chandrasekhar's limit."

"Right on the nose. Now, picture this super-dense core sucking in its own radiation zone while the outer integrity of the star remains intact. Because it must conserve its angular momentum, the core spins faster as it contracts, but the visible chromosphere lags behind. For some reason, there's enough hydrogen left in the photosphere to spark the fusion reaction that blows the thing into a supernova. Or, for some other reason, the slow compression goes beyond the simple white dwarf stage, with enough pressure for atomic collapse. All the evidence points in that direction. How it got that way is another question — one for which I'd give anything to know the answer."

"So, you think it will either shrink all the way to neutronium, or blow itself up in a supernova explosion?"

"Or both, depending upon how its mass is distributed at the ultimate moment. And it's going to happen soon. Cosmologically speaking, of course. It might not be for another million years."

Barbara stared through the steam over her mug, and watched the still scrolling display screen. "Or it could go off tomorrow."

Sandy shrugged. "But wouldn't you love to have a device there to tell us what triggers it?"

Barbara smiled at her daughter, nodding. "You seem to have the preliminary physics already worked out — at least in light of the available data. So, what's going on in that devious mind of yours? You called me up for something, and it's obviously not advice."

"Perhaps I just wanted to impress you with my deductions."

"You never have before. You have too much self-confidence. No, you want something from me. Parent schemer that I am, I just haven't been able to figure out what."

"Mother, are you sure — I mean, do you think — uh, would you mind terribly if this turned out to be something really big? Would it bother you if — well, your daughter — made a discovery more important than — Of course, it may turn out to be nothing. The probecomp could have gone haywire, or the telemetry might be affected by transmission errors — "

Barbara laughed out loud. She put down her mug, and with a sweep of her arm, drew Sandy close to her breast. "Dear, I have at least that much confidence in myself. I'm not afraid of being upstaged or overshadowed — especially by my own flesh and blood. I love you, and I want the best for you."

"I love you, too, Mother. I just wanted to be sure that you didn't feel — I mean, I didn't want to hurt you. Also, I guess, I wanted your approval."

"I've always tried to let you have what *you* wanted, not what *I* wanted you to have. So if that's all you're worried about — "

Sandy cast down steely-gray eyes. "No, there *is* something else." Blonde brows, electro-arced to thinness, launched into a wrinkled forehead. "Oh?"

"Mother, you know about Brunel's new ramjet? The Galactic Odyssey Model One?"

"The fully automated version, that's going to put human crews out of business? Sure, he's been keeping it in the news for years. It's almost ready for space trials, isn't it?"

"According to Fred, it *is* ready."

"Fred? Fred who?"

"The one and only. You and Dane flew with him to the neutron star."

"What a coincidence. I haven't heard from him in years until just the other — " Barbara's brows now plummeted as low as they had been high. "As a scientist, I'm always suspicious of coincidences."

Sandy pulled back. "Mother, this time I'm innocent. It just so happens that he sent out a memo through the astrocomp. Since they're getting ready to test the GOmod-1, they're accepting proposals for investigation. And I think I've got a shot at it."

Barbara's brows returned to their normal arch. "You know, I think you have something there. And I couldn't even compete with you." Ever since she confirmed through statistical computer scenarios that quasars were galactic-sized explosions with artificially induced red shifts, her research had been balked by technological considerations. She shrugged, and tilted her head. "It's going to take something more than a ramjet to reach a quasar in my lifetime. And your proto-neutron star is just far enough away to make it a perfect test cruise for Brunel's GOmod-1."

Sandy gave her mother a big hug. "I knew you'd agree. Now, the question is, do you think you can get Fred to exert some influence on Brunel?"

"You don't think your project will win on its merits?"

"Of course I do. But there's nothing wrong with stacking the deck just to make sure."

Barbara laughed heartily. "Dear, I wonder if intrigue is a genetic trait."

"I think it's learned, not inherited. But whichever it is, I got it from you."

"Plus some. All right, I'll send Fred a gram." Because of the time lag, interplanetary calls were not usually made live, but by transmitted computergrams. "I'm sure it was your proposal that prompted his contact message. Okay, if you're sure that's what you want, I'll see if this little lady can still pull a few strings."

Sandy sighed. "When did you ever stop?"

Chapter 3

"He who knows himself is wise; he who knows others is genius."

— Unknown

"Look at that! Look at that!"

Brunel held the clear plastic squeeze bottle in front of the foodtech's startled face.

"Sir, I — "

"You idiot, you should know better than to shake a liquid in z-gee."

The woman cringed, lost her grip, and cartwheeled slowly across the central computer room, looking like a shrunken Alice lost in a house full of holovision screens.

"Sir, I'm not feeling — "

"Where were you brought up, for god's sake? On a planet?" Brunel pointed at the chocolate fluid. "Every school child knows that in weightlessness the slightest jostling causes air to mix with a liquid. And without gravity, without an up or down, there is no surface, no way for air to rise and escape."

The woman put a hand up to her mouth. "I really must be excused — "

"*No.* There is no excuse for incompetence, nor room for mediocrity on a Brunel project. If I were to imbibe such a colloidal concoction, the muscular action of the stomach and intestines would force trapped air out of solution with deleterious side effects which, beside causing discomfort, are not socially acceptable. You follow me?"

Drifting helplessly, the foodtech's anguished face was now upside down with reference to Brunel's. "Sir, I — think I'm going — to be — "

"Get her out of here before she — "

Brunel was cut off by two comptechs who shoved off from their consoles and pushed him out of the way.

One clamped an emergency vacuum bag over her face, the other dragged her away from exposed electronic circuitry.

"Get her out!" Brunel actuated microthrusters in the chair to which he was strapped, and skillfully brought his tumble under control.

A soft-spoken, barely audible voice said, "It would seem that she had a digestive problem of her own."

With two deft thruster manipulations, Brunel swung around and hung motionless. "Fred, if that is intended to be funny, I do not care for your brand of humor."

The tall, emaciated man smiled benevolently. "I don't think you've ever been branded with humor."

Under the scraggly beard, Brunel's face was red and puffy: not so much from anger as from a prolonged life in weightlessness. Without gravity to pull blood and other fluids to the extremities, fluids tended to migrate to the upper body. His eyes were bloodshot as well. "Fred, if you were not such a damned fine engineer, I would have gotten rid of you years ago."

Fred showed a mouthful of teeth. "I know how much I can get away with."

Brunel bent his head back and inhaled deeply through dark, flared nostrils that made his nose look like the business end of a double-barreled shotgun. "Sometimes I think you know too much."

"My greatest asset."

Brunel grimaced. He tapped the chair's telecom button. "Have some more refreshments delivered. And for god's sake, get a foodtech with a modicum of common sense. You follow me?" To Fred, "We have twenty thousand workers on this platform, all supposedly from floater stock. Where do people like that come from?"

"I suspect from a biological function that is as universal as the digestive process, but socially acceptable and a lot more fun to perform."

"Your wit is growing thin on me, and I tolerate it only because you must have some useful information to impart. Otherwise, you would not have come to share my company."

Fred remained smug. "Correct on both counts. Your deductive reasoning has not been impaired by senescence."

Brunel glared silently. He suddenly became aware of the absolute silence of the central computer room. He was surrounded by scores of one-meter screens and a dozen larger ones, each being monitored by comptechs with jobs to do. Yet no one at that moment was bending fingers to keypad.

"What are you all gawking at? Get back to work!" Looks alone got the message across.

"You really shouldn't raise your voice at the workers."

"In one-third atmospheric pressure, it is all I can do to be heard." In lesser density air, even a shout sounded like a whisper from ten meters.

"It takes a long time to fill with air a forty kleter cylinder that measures five kleters across, with a volume of — "

"Spare me the arithmetic." Brunel waved his hand past his ear. He thrusted his chair to a six-screen console and latched the arm extensions into the counter top. His hands worked two keyboards at the same time, and he watched all six screens with trained peripheral vision. "Just tell me why you are here — physically. You could have phoned anything that you wanted to say. I don't understand why people bother to travel any more."

"Despite technology, people still enjoy human contact. They'd rather make love than watch it on the holly."

Brunel's normally ruddy face froze in a mask of horror. He stared sideways at Fred, who was floating next to the console. He bit off each word with a deep-throated growl. "This time you have gone too far. When your jokes become a personal assault against my — "

"I apologize, Brunel," Fred interrupted, gritting his teeth. "I didn't mean to imply — "

"Forget it. Just tell me why you're here."

Fred stammered. "It's your grandson. Your great-grandson."

"I have forty-seven. To which one are you referring?"

"Forty-eight."

For a moment, Brunel was nonplussed. Black, bushy eyebrows pinched together. "Your mathema — Oh, was it Wilma?"

"Not for another month. This was Beatrice."

Brunel touched his keyboard. One screen switched from tabulated numbers to a catalog of names: children, grandchildren, greats, and great-greats. He scanned the multiple lists, and noticed the date after the latest addition. "Right you are. I would have missed it. Hey, there is a girl in there I don't recognize."

"She was born last week. You were pretty busy with the solar inertial attitude jets and the momentum control gyros."

"Fred, you do have your positive qualities. I will send them both congratulations." Brunel's fingers flew across the keyboard with lightning speed. "Done. Was there anything else?"

Fred steadied himself with one hand and tapped a code sequence with the other. "Yes, I thought you should take a look at the spin differential analyses."

"There is nothing wrong with them. I did the work myself."

"I wasn't implying that you had made a mistake, just that you should authorize a test for the torque converters."

"They do not need to be tested. *I* designed them. If anything is wrong, it would have to be from material standards. And for that I rely on *you*. Take care of it yourself. I am more interested in cross-phasing the spikes on the GOmod-1's inertia pump."

Except for the Selkirk FTL drive, the greatest technological boon of the century was the force that enabled multi-gee acceleration. Even the Selkirk drive was useless without it. Without the pump pulling a starship forward at the same speed at which it was being pushed from behind, all its components — organic as well as electronic — would be crushed flat into nucleic acid or disconnected plastic polymers. Since the inertia pump derived its power from the ramjet intake, it could only be used on vehicles moving with enough speed for the magnetic collectors to fuel it. It could not induce artificial gravity in a stationary object without the possession of enormous hydrogen reserves. If the system was perfectly balanced, with half the fuel feeding the stardrive and half feeding the pump, internal stress was neutralized. The ship sailed in freefall condition.

"By a coincidence, that's the other item that I came to talk with you about."

"The pump?"

"No, the Galactic Odyssey. I've had some interesting proposals from astros who want data on everything from planetary nebula formation to interstellar gas emissions."

"How boring. Astrophysicists always seem to have their heads in the clouds. I refuse to send the GOmod-1 out on any mission that can be accomplished by lesser craft. I want it to prove itself. You follow me?"

"Perfectly. And, as a matter of fact, there is one fascinating concept that might possibly meet such criteria. Have you heard of Prof. Mettleson?"

"The one you shipped out with on your final space jaunt?"

"Her daughter. She, too, is an astrophysicist. A full professor, but not yet a doctorate."

Brunel wiped the screens free and leaned back in his chair. "I do not even know my own children; you expect me to know the children of others?" Surrogate fatherhood was an accepted practice, and women who wanted a specific genetic heritage often chose certain individuals to sire their offspring. He waved his hand by his ear as a gesture of 'forget it.' "What does she have that is so intriguing?"

"Besides her mother?" When Brunel did not respond, Fred elaborated. "She's got some readings from a deepspace drone that could lead to something quite revolutionary. I can't vouch for her facts, since they are beyond my comprehension — "

"Nothing is beyond your comprehension, except modesty. Please continue."

Fred looped his foot through a springgrip so he could type with both hands. One screen activated and displayed a comphanced graphic that looked like a see-through orange with a peach pit in the middle.

"This isn't a true optical recording, but her interpretation of the data. That hard central core is a very dense, rapidly rotating stellar mass which — "

"Excuse me, Mr. Brunel?"

"It is just Brunel." Gruffly, "What is it? Surely you can see that I am busy?"

"I'm sorry, sir. I'm new here." The young foodtech held out a tray full of squeezetubes of varying colors. "I was dispatched with a selection from our menu."

"Did you shake them up like your predecessor?"

"No, sir. I was very careful, sir."

Brunel took a brown tube, held it up to the light, harrumphed, and stuck it in the upper breast pocket of his utility vest. "Thanks. That will suffice." When he waved him off, the lad retreated with short bursts from a jetpack. Brunel inserted a straw in the nozzle, and stuck the flared end in his mouth. He sucked slowly. "I hope you can make this nontechnical — and fast."

"I can explain only what I can understand." Fred hit a string of numbers which sent the three-dimensional graphic display into a spin. "What Prof. Mettleson is proposing is a prototype in stellar evolution which, depending upon mass, leads to either a white dwarf or a neutron star."

"That is elementary astronomy — high school stuff. I did not say I was totally ignorant. I know at least as much as Chandrasekhar in the nineteenth century."

"It was the twentieth, but nevertheless — What we seem to have here is a stellar object that may be a white dwarf surrounded by a red giant. Or, if you will, a red giant star with a white dwarf core."

"Is that possible?"

"No. It was just an illustration. I meant that the core

of this stellar object is extremely dense and extremely hot, while the outer skin is as tenuous, and as cool, as a red giant. The center is rotating rapidly and sending out weak microwave pulses, but the outside moves relatively slowly. This is an unstable condition which Prof. Mettleson thinks is something in the making: it may go nova, or supernova, any time. Her — supposition — is that the shrinkage of the additional mass may make it go super."

Brunel nodded, and pursed his lips. "A thought-provoking concept. How does she think this — stellar object — got the way it is?"

"She doesn't have enough evidence. But she seems certain that a close observation will prove not only how it reached such a state, but what it will become."

"Hmmnn." Brunel studied the figures in the corner of the screen. "Do we have mass readings?"

"Approximations." Fred tapped the keyboard. "Core, and total. The difference — "

"I can subtract. And depending upon which way she blows, it might even leave nothing but a nebulosity. Fascinating."

"That's what I thought."

"Fred, with all due respect, you have too much imagination for an engineer."

"Thank you."

Brunel sucked thoughtfully on the straw, keeping a continuous stream of dark fluid trickling into his stomach. "How old is she?"

"Undoubtedly third generation. Certainly less than six billion years."

"I meant the young lady."

"Oh. Thirty-two."

"Has she ever left solside?"

"No. But what dif — "

"If she wants to make a close observation, she would have to go there, would she not?"

"But, the GOmod-1 is intended to replace human observers. The time lag — "

Brown liquid flowed into Brunel's mouth in a slow,

continuous stream. "Quite right, the overall program is pointed toward completely computerized scientific stations that can record and transmit every bit of observable data. You did not think that I was going to send the first one unmanned, did you?"

"Brunel, I — "

"Of course, you have been busy with the final touches on the B-40, and start-up construction of the sister platform. Fred, what would happen if we sent the GOmod-1 on patrol and it did not return? We would have no way of knowing what happened to it, what went wrong, what changes or improvements to make. No, the first one needs a human crew. And, in order to guarantee appropriations for launching a fleet, the prototype must prove worthy of the expenditure."

"But, I hadn't counted on — that is, I'm not sure that Dr. Mettleson — "

"I thought you said that she was still a professor?"

"I meant her mother. I don't think she — "

"Mettleson the younger is a big girl now. She does not need her mother's permission to stay out overnight."

"No, but this is a long hop — "

"Only in obtime. She can make the whole trip between periods. If she is as smart as you make her out to be, and as interested in this project as she should be, she will jump at the opportunity to go. It will undoubtedly mean a full doctorate for her. No more teaching ignorant students, just pure research."

"Yes, but, you can't send her out there alone?"

"Of course not. The test flight will require a pilot and a systems maintenance engineer, just as all other star journeys."

"Should I contact Exploteam for a crew?"

"Fred, there is only one man in the System I would trust to pilot my baby. Your long-time buddy."

Fred rolled his eyes.

"Do you think he is willing to take the chance?"

Fred hesitated a millisecond and a half before replying. "Does the red giant glow?"

Chapter 4

"Earth is the cradle of mankind, but one does not live in the cradle forever."

— Konstantin Tsiolkovski

"Mack, if you'll pardon me for intrudin', I gotta go along with your sister. I was born on the good Earth, and it'll always be home to me. I like havin' more under my feet than two meters of radiation shielding."

"You're missing the point entirely." Dane rubbed condensation off the side window. "The difference between us is not venue, but outlook."

"Okay, so your platform windows look out over the stars. I got a holly on my wall that does the same thing. But my window ain't gonna break and let in the vacuum."

Dane rolled his eyes. *Holograms are not the real thing. And you don't let in vacuum; you let out air.* "But we've got room to breathe, and infinite space in which to expand."

"Okay, so we got a pollution problem — "

The understatement of the millennium.

"We just dig down and don't let it bother us."

The ostrich complex.

The aircar lurched, then went into a slide. The cabby pulled the throttles on the blowers, and lifted the vehicle higher off the ground. Blue foam splattered the windshields. The cab skewed with a sickening, slinking motion.

"Dane — " Sis placed cupped hands to her mouth.

"Nothing to worry about, ma'am. A little turbulence is all."

The primary terrestrial modification brought about by intensive industrial contamination was the melting of the polar ice caps due to a global rise in temperature. Besides submerging twenty percent of the world's land mass, and increasing atmospheric pressure, the process self-amplified beyond the point of criticality: Earth went into a greenhouse cycle. Pressure begat temperature which begat tempestuous winds.

"Got some drifts up ahead."

As the air became more acidic, soil and rock dissolved into soggy, riverine chemical mudflows. Mountains shrank in avalanche. Airborne catalysts caused crystallization in the upper atmosphere. Particulates gained weight with agglutination and fell in the form of hot, smoky microspheres: sewer snow.

"Looks like a smowstorm comin' our way."

Automatic balancers shifted pressurized air to the rear venturis. The aircar maintained a relatively even keel as it climbed the steep pitch. Kicked up dust and falling foam covered the aircar like a shroud. The cabby kept her eyes glued to the gauge readouts on the computer display.

Sis emitted a deep-throated grumble that presaged trouble.

"Hell. Where's the vacusiphon?"

"This is an aircar, Mack, not a spaceship. Got barf bags in the console."

Dane rummaged through the convenience compartment. "It's empty."

"So be inventive."

He pulled out his gas mask and shoved it in front of his sister's face just as she emptied her pouch.

Ten-meter drifts alternated with deep bowls, pumping the aircar up and down like a hydraulic piston. The cab rocked wildly in unsynchronized zephyrs. Spume lashed violently at the windows, whipping the plastiglass with a bubbly blue froth. The overworked balancers got out of cycle, causing the floor to pitch and yaw with stomach churning irregularity.

"Hang in there. This might get a little rough."

Sis groaned. Dane cinched her safety harness a little tighter. She gagged a couple more times, then went into the dry heaves. Dane's hands swayed with the motion of the cab. He wielded the now-full gas mask like a waiter with a tray full of long stemmed goblets dodging a dancing dinner crowd.

The engines whined down, the rolling motion ceased. Thick, bluish suds drooled down the windows. The howling outside continued, but the worst of the wind passed overhead.

"This cab can take more than you can, but why fight it? Besides, your sister looks a little green around the gills."

"I feel like a squeezed lime." Sis pushed her brother's hands away. He stared at the mask full of digested victuals, looked around for the disposal, and dropped everything into the stainless steel chute. He slammed down the lid. "Cycle it."

"The Air Guard's got rules about land dumping. I'm not allowed to eliminate anything outside a proper receptacle unless I scrub it first."

"They'll never notice it out here."

The cabby punched a keyboard function. The droplock expunged the mess out the bottom of the air-car. "Just testing, Mack. I do it all the time — everybody does. But I don't want to get turned in by some offworld environmentalist." She dropped a freshmint pellet into the circulator and cranked up the fan a notch. "The big companies and industrial corporations just pay the fines, but an independent can't afford to be illegal."

"Doesn't make any difference. They should have started working on the pollution problem right at the beginning of the Industrial Age. Now it's too late."

Sis wiped her mouth with the handkerchief. "Thanks for stopping."

The cabby's flaxen jowls puckered. "We're sitting in a trough, and I got the risers on low power to keep us from sinking into the smow. It'll blow over soon, then we'll make a dash for it."

Dane nodded admiringly. "You handle this machine well."

She swung her seat around and faced her passengers. "Ain't as glamorous as flitting through the asteroids, but I like it. And it's nothing like exploring the stars."

"Stellar trips aren't as romantic as you think." Dane breathed easier in the cooler, fresher-smelling air. "As long as I've been with the Team, I have yet to find a planetary system. All the stars I've seen are either old maids or grandmothers: some never had planets, others have long since lost them. Virgins are as hard to find in space as they are on Earth."

"What difference does it make? You ain't ever gonna live on planets again. Not as long as Brunel keeps making them platforms. And with all that space out there, I don't even know why you bother lookin' for stars."

"Ah, but to build a platform, you need material. And to make it thrive, you need power. That means, ideally, you need a solitary star system full of planetoids. That puts a severe limit on location, because most of the stellar mass in the Galaxy exists in the form of multiple star systems. We never find planet-sized bodies among them because the complex gravitational perturbations are too great for long stability."

"But I see it on the holly all the time — all them pretty planets with rings and colored clouds. Like Jupiter, and Saturn."

"That's the problem. Those gas giants are more like stunted suns than large planets. I've found a couple of those. But in our state of technology, they're useless. Anyway, what really fascinates me is pure scientific investigation into the nature of — "

"Excuse me for interrupting, but you do have a ship to catch."

Dane paused with his mouth still open, and stared at his sister. "Are you trying to get rid of me?"

"No, but I've come this far — mentally. I don't want to have to psych myself up for another parting on tomorrow's shuttle."

Dane patted her leg in a brotherly fashion — well below the thigh. "You're right. Besides, the Prof seems to think there's something hot up there besides a nova." Turning to the cabby, "Can we move slowly in this storm?"

She swiveled toward the control console. "Better

than that. We can follow this trough for a while until the dunes peter out, then catch a tailwind and roller coaster to the port."

"I don't think I like the roller coaster part," Sis moaned.

"Won't be too bad if I accelerate the gyros, but fuel consumption goes way up. Oh, well, I'm due for a core change anyhow." The engines strained for a moment, but the cab did not budge. The digital throttle readings increased with each tap on the vernier key. "Gotta break the suction." The aircar surged upward with a plop, as if launched on a spring, then settled down with several smooth bounces.

"Ooo-oo-ooh."

"It's okay, Sis. It's over."

She gulped.

Foam continued to pound the windscreens. The aircar's forward motion was detectable only by the fluctuating speed indicator. "So what's so important about baby planets? You like short horizons, or something?"

Dane shook his head. "No, they're more cost effective. We need a practical way to supply structural matter in the form of heavy elements. Why do you think we use the Moon for raw materials? The Earth's at the bottom of a six thousand kleter gravity well, and the cost of orbiting anything other than people is prohibitive."

"Forget it, Mack. You floaters are way over my head. If I — "

Dane heard a pop, the sound of tearing metal, then the hiss of escaping air. Alarms and flashing red lights erupted all over the aircar.

"Hull breach!"

The cab was equipped with all the mandatory safety devices prescribed by the Air Guard: radio distress beacons, survival suits, oxygen storage bottles, sealing tape, and solvents. Dane pulled a patch bag from the emergency kit, ripped it open, and punctured an orange locator ball. As the smoke was sucked out of the hole, identifying the breach site, he took out a wad of soft putty, and slapped it over the tiny perforation. Suction held the temporary patch in place as it melted into a gluey mass, and solidified. The hissing slowed, and stopped.

"That temppatch ought to hold it for a while."

"Quick thinking, Mack."

"Just reflex. Sis, are you okay?"

"I will be as soon as we get back underground." Her subterranean pallor was unaffected, but her eyes were as big as portholes. "I hate the outdoors."

The aircar lurched forward. "Sorry, Macks, but I ain't sparin' the nukes. This damn ole hack is fallin' apart, and I don't fancy walkin'."

The aircar buffeted, but not as badly as before. The ground was flat, and the wind unidirectional. The cabby concentrated on her instrument panel, and did not talk until the proximity signal illuminated. She halted in front of the garage door, barely visible through the swirling smow and smog, and waited for clearance. She glanced in the mirror at her charges.

"I know how you feel, ma'am. If I didn't need the work, I wouldn't be here myself."

"Surely you can find another job," Dane said.

"What? Punching a keyboard?" The ready light blinked on, and the gasket sphincter expanded. "It's not the job I need, it's the work."

The overlapping folds of rubberoid yielded to the forward motion of the aircar, and formed a pseudosheath around the duraplastic body, letting as little external air as possible into the locking chamber. Once the leakage was evacuated and cycled back outside, the inner airlock opened and the cab was conveyed on a moving belt through a chemical scrub and into the docking bay.

"I get enough dole money for not havin' kids to live pretty good. But a woman's got to do something productive with her life. She can't just sit around all day and watch soapventures on the holly."

"A marvelous attitude. One which will get you past the Settlement exams, if you ever decide to go for it."

"Gol-ly. You really think I could? I mean, you think

they'd let me live on the platforms?"

"Why not? All it takes is initiative. If you want to expand your horizons, and explore your full potential, go for it. With your driving skills, there's a lot of equipment you could pilot."

"No one's ever told me that before."

Dane punched some numbers on the paycomp, and extracted his card. "That's not the only tip I'm giving you. Use it well, and thanks for the ride." He pushed open the hatch, and pulled his sister across the seat.

The cabby's grin revealed a missing front tooth. "Hey, thanks a lot, Mack. Maybe I'll look you up."

Dane pointed to the box. "You've got my stats."

As soon as they were out of range, Sis said, "You are disgusting." Dane did a double take. "Huhn? What're you talking about?"

"You know what I mean."

"No, I don't. Not unless you tell me."

"I'm not blind. I can read body language."

"Where I come from, we use English. Now what the hell are you talking about?"

"Excuse me while I wash a foul taste from my mouth." She ducked into a women-only private room.

Dane stood there for a moment, shaking his head. Then he entered the adjacent men-only room. He ripped off his e-suit and tossed it into the disposal chute. Still wearing his lightweight disposables, he stepped into a stall for an electromagnetic shower. He emerged feeling brisk and clean, free of alluvial deposits.

In the deserted corridor, he called information on his wristrad and noted directions and departure instructions. As he should have expected, his flight departed from the other side of the port.

"Well, what are we waiting for?" Sis walked right by him.

He caught up with her just as the secondary entrance portal unsealed to admit them into the port proper. "Sis, I don't feel like playing guessing games. If you have something to say, then say it."

The crowd and the din were intense. The corridor was lined on both sides by tube exits, and throngs of people buzzed along like angry bees whose hive had been disturbed. The port was a nexus for intercontinental subspace hops. Dane grabbed onto his sister's hand, lest they be permanently separated by the mob.

"Let's take a veyor," Sis shouted. She led him through the concourse of pushing, shoving people.

A solid pack of humanity blocked the slidewalk conveyor, and it was several minutes before they managed to slip into a gondola. Dane slid the door closed, and plopped into a hard seat. He inserted his IDcard into the compay slot. The monitor blinked "unacceptable."

"Damn, it doesn't recognize — "

Sis removed his card and inserted her own. "I'll pay for it."

Dane keyed his wristrad, and punched in the coordinates. The gondola still did not move. "What's wrong?"

Sis studied the flat screen between them. "The route has seventeen intersections along the way."

"So?"

"The onboard computer can handle only one direction at a time. You've got to key in each segment individually."

"That's what happens when you don't build from the vacuum out. Platform veyors have only two directions: lengthwise and around. You can get anywhere with only one interchange. You key in the final co-ords, and the computer does the rest."

"Many Earth ways are quaint."

"Backward is the word." Dane transferred the first set of numbers from the wristrad memo circuit. The gondola swiveled on its track and moved slowly away from the terminal. "You may as well tell me what your problem is, because I'm going to keep asking until I get an answer."

"It's that woman," she blurted. "You were playing up to her right in front of me. And I saw the eyes she was making at you."

Dane burst out laughing. "So what? She seemed like an intelligent person. Stuck with her Earthly upbringing, of course, and with walker patois, but very skilled at her job and full of initiative."

"Is that all a woman means to you."

"No, but it's a good beginning. What's your hang-up? Beside your Victorian mores, that is."

"She's fat, for one thing. And lecherous, too. She's crude, she's aggressive, and she's missing a tooth."

"I'm missing four. Had them replaced with implants. Forget about cosmetics, Sis, and look at people for who they are. Fancy wrapping paper doesn't make a good gift."

"Dane, I just don't understand you anymore. Ever since you left home to become a shuttlecraft pilot — "

"Navigator."

"Whatever. You — you've picked up so many strange ideas."

"You think it's strange not wanting to be tied down by a piece of property? You want me to live someplace where the water table's so low that the ground's cracking up?"

"It's not just property — it's the homestead."

"Sis, you can't keep living in the past. I don't need objects, or mementoes, to keep alive my feelings for Mom and Dad, or my childhood. I need only my heart, my memory — something I carry with me always. If you want to hang onto a piece of useless land, you do it. *I'm* going to the stars."

"Oh, Dane, don't make it sound so final."

The gondola halted. Dane programmed the next leg of their journey. "Sis, we're never farther apart than the closest telecom. That archaic hotel's got the only set in the System without a visual hookup."

"I'm not just talking about not seeing you again, or aging another five years while you age one on your next traction trip. I'm talking about you, and the floaters, losing their ties to the past, to their ancestors. I'm talking about roots."

Dane groaned. "Oh, no. Not that again."

"Dane, history is important."

"No. History is interesting. It's not important. All you historians think — "

"I'm an archaeologist."

— the past is so holy, that we're going to learn great lessons by studying our previous mistakes. But all that's behind us. It doesn't matter where we came from. It's where we're going that counts. And while you're down here digging up the past, I'm up there making the future."

"We're not just cataloguing the errors of our ways. We're discovering things about mankind we never knew before: his beginnings, his direction, his purpose, possibly his end."

"Man doesn't have a purpose, he creates his own."

"Typical floater philosophy."

"Floaters don't have philosophy any more than they have beliefs. We're realists. We accept what we find, seek out what we don't know, study what we don't understand. We don't create concepts or fantasies to believe in, because we choose to live without the comfort of self-delusion."

"Oh, how can you be so hypocritical?"

"Typical walker defense. Sis, I'm not saying this to hurt you. I'm not attacking you. I'm merely venting my thoughts, a floater's privilege. This Spanish galleon that your research group is excavating is a fascinating project, I admit that. And I know you get a lot of personal satisfaction out of the involvement. But, in the big picture, who really cares how many strakes are in the hull? How is that going to change the course of human destiny? The past serves no purpose. It's just another piece of useless trivia for Museum Earth. Get your head out of the past and face the future. Stop looking over your shoulder, and concentrate on where you're going."

"But we're finding so much: tools of the times, implements, utensils, navigational equipment, personal items."

"Your emphasis is totally misplaced. People are important, not their artifacts. And what are you going to do next? Raise this silly wooden hull, then have to conserve it and put it in a moldy museum where it will need constant maintenance? Hell, half this damn planet is devoted to curatorial work. Every other person is either a historian or an anthropologist or a conservator or an archivist or a compcat assistant. And *that* is a published statistic, not hyperbole. The Earth has become one gigantic, underground mausoleum. And for what?"

"So the people of the future can come back, and see what they're all about."

The gondola halted again. Dane punched the seventeenth transfer coordinate. "But we don't care. We're moving on. We're leaving this aerosol planet to those who made it that way. And I'm living where I don't have to worry about pollution ever again."

Sis stifled a sob. "Oh, Dane, here I am an old woman, and you're still a starry-eyed kid who refuses to grow up. But do yourself a favor. The next time you're out there among the stars, far away from home, remember that just because we're too small to see, we're still here. Think about us, Dane. Just take the time to think. There's more to life than running away like a sailor going to sea. And remember what home is like."

Chapter 5

"For the generations as yet unborn, prevention is the imperative need."

— Rachel Carson

Since nearly all spaceport traffic was interatmospheric, the departure chamber for the geosynch transfer shuttle was practically deserted. A few people sat in observation-communication booths, talking in hushed tones with those already on board, and a bored clerk stared with heavy-lidded eyes at his holovision.

Dane dropped his IDcard into the compscan slot. "Whew. I thought I was going to miss my flight. Traffic was heavy, and I'm not used to this fossilized veyor system."

The clerk turned his head, but did not raise his eyelids. "Been held up by a flare. Hafta wait till it blows over before it can take off."

Broiling pollution flares were not uncommon. The increased density of the atmosphere, due to the proportionate number of high molecular weight compounds, was especially susceptible to plummeting, rapidly moving low-pressure systems. The relative vacuum within the circulating air mass often built up to multiple cyclonic speeds. Besides halting all forms of aviation, when storm centers touched the surface, they caused external buildings to explode, and decompression sickness in people caught outside.

It took but a microsecond for the computer to scan Dane's IDcard and transfer funds from his account. When the card popped up, he returned it to his chest pouch. "Which way?"

"Only one way from here. Follow the signs."

Dane squinted when he saw the docking bay arrows pointing along a dimly lit corridor. "Looks dark."

"Power outage. Microwaves can't get through stratospheric precipitates."

"You'd think with all those beaming stations in orbit you'd have enough electricity to keep a few lights on." Still shaking his head, Dane sauntered along the narrow corridor. It curved in a large arc and angled downward, crossed a few intersections, went through a construction site where the facade had been ripped away to expose rough hewn, granite walls, and eventually led to a rotary airlock.

His IDcard served as a pass to the boarding connection tube. At the shuttle's hatch, a computer monitor offered seating instructions. With the passenger compartment practically empty, Dane had no difficulty locating a porthole couch. He immediately switched on the convenience computer and keyed for a refreshment menu. He scrolled through a few screens to see what was available, punched in his choices on the alphanumeric pad, then inserted his IDcard for the debit charge.

As soon as the computer knew where he was, the screen flashed a seek message that was on hold. "Hi, Hot Pants. Awaiting desperately your arrival. Salon 3. Will have hot tea and honey, Honey. Mettleson."

He snickered on the way to the self-service kitchen to collect his meal.

"Mr. Gerrace?"

Dane eyed the stewardess. "You have me at a disadvantage, madam."

"What?"

Dane laughed. "Sorry, I've been watching antique movies all week. It means: you know who I am, but I don't know who you are."

Her smile revealed two perfect rows of plastiteeth. "Alice."

"At your service, Alice. And please, only computers use my last name."

"And the news service."

"So, you know who I am."

She nodded slowly. "The captains extend their greetings, and would like to know if you'd care to join them in the control cabin."

"That's the second best offer you could have made."

"It's as much as I'm allowed — I'm on duty."

"And when are you off?"

"During layovers."

"Would you like to layover during layover?"

She handed him her IDcard. Dane took out his own, as well as his infopad. When he placed the two cards in it face to face, personal statistics and locator information were exchanged immediately.

Dane returned her card, and gave her a peck on the cheek. "I'm meeting someone as soon as we dock, but maybe later."

Alice returned his kiss. "I've got my children waiting, anyway. I'll get in touch when I'm available. You may take your food pack with you."

"Thanks." Dane collected his foodtubes and liquid containers and stuffed them into his pouch. He strode forward and, when he reached the control cabin door, announced his presence by slipping his IDcard into the annunciator slot. The door opened with a hiss, and a compuphone uttered, "Welcome." Dane walked in with a smile on his face. When the pilot and navigator turned their couches around, he said, "Good morning, ladies."

The redhead looked like a teenager, her face sprinkled with tiny pimples which modern medicine had yet failed to cure. "How do you do, sir?"

"Glad to meet you, sir." The brunette might have been older by a month.

"You can sit there."

"Thank you, but, Dane will suffice. I'm honored at the invitation."

They all touched palms and announced names. Dane sat in the starboard observation couch and perfunctorily strapped himself in.

"It's our pleasure."

"Sure, to have the great Dane Gerrace guiding the way?"

Dane held out his hands as if warding off a bulkhead in a zero-gee fall. "Hey, I'm no back-couch driver.

I'm just along for the flight. It's been a long time since I've been in the c-c of one of these babies."

Shirley laughed. "Oh, they retired the Synchrodyne models before I was born. This is a Symsystems Three. Not nearly as sophisticated as the *Phantom Jackal*, of course."

Dane winced. "How do you know so much about me?"

"We don't *live* on Earth, we just ferry people there." Rhonda swiveled back to her console and responded to flashing compqueries by touching her keyboard. "Everyone in the business knows about Ace Gerrace, from mineship operator in the Belt to tugship captain. You could have had a plush job running excursion ships interplanetary, but you chose Exploteam."

Dane cleared his throat. "I saw it as a way to eternal youth."

The shuttle jerked forward as the towramp started to drag it from the docking bay to the launch silo. Only a few emergency lanterns fought back the darkness of the cavern.

"Hey, where're the rest of the passengers? Most of the couches were empty."

"Immigration is down to a trickle, and we don't get may tourists." Shirley keyed her comprompts. The shuttle was programmed to fly itself, leaving pilot and navigator as supernumeraries who merely handled fine controls. "They're talking about making this an every-other instead of a daily."

The huge airlock cranked open and admitted the shuttle to the silo. All visual ports were blacked out against the effects of corrosive atmosphere: three minutes of such exposure, time after time, could eat right through the strongest plastiglass with unhappy results. External cameras telemetered images onto comp-screens.

"So where are you headed this time?" Rhonda asked.

Dane shrugged his shoulders. "They want to give me a solside berth in administration — possibly even head of the Board of Directors."

"They've been trying that for years."

Dane leaned forward against the straps. "Hey, is there anything about me that you ladies don't already know?"

They laughed. Rhonda winked a lid full of lashplants. "You're name's always in the newscomps."

Shirley adjusted her headrest while the automatics took care of the countdown. "Rumor has it that you're going out after another neutron star. Isn't that how you got the name Hot Pants?"

Once in position, powerful hydraulics lifted the craft to a vertical attitude. In the after compartments, the cushioned passenger couches pivoted on their gimbels. In the nose, the entire control car rotated so smoothly that the inclinometer was the only indication of movement.

"You're baiting me, aren't you? You're just teasing me."

"You'd better flatten your couch for takeoff."

The overhead dome split open, admitting thick, external smog that glowed blue from hydrocarbon content.

"All right." Dane pressed a button, and servomotors slowly stretched out his couch from chair form to acceleration couch mode. "But I want some answers. I'm old enough to be your grandfather, and I demand some respect."

Rhonda initiated the firing sequence. "Oh, Dane. Obtime doesn't count. In subtime, you're probably only a decade older."

Dane opened his mouth, but the roar of nuclear engines burst through insulated bulkheads and drowned out any squeaks he made as he was pressed into the formfoam. At top acceleration of three gees, Dane's body sank into the cushions. The takeoff was so smooth that he felt no vibration. "A real suave execution. I'm impressed."

"Dynamic pressure buildup was minimal."

Shirley added, "Polymerized foam, floating engine

mounts, and synchronized nuclear generation. Welcome to the future, grandpaw."

Dane burst into gales of laughter. "You girls are too much. I might have to put you across my knee and teach you a few tricks."

Shirley checked the automatic guidance controls. "I've never done it that way, but it sounds interesting. Wait till we get through the inversion layer. Sometimes lightning strikes knock out our onboard computers, and we have to be ready to go on full manual."

Dane kept his eyes glued to the viewscreens. He saw nothing but a rainbow blur until they rose above the troposphere. When the air thinned behind them, he was hypnotized by the serpentine, varicolored cloud motion: like a gyrating oil slick. Much higher, just before engine cutoff, he glimpsed the sun on the horizon: a coruscating arc of chromatic aberration, so beautiful, but so deadly.

Then came silence, and weightlessness.

"Okay, ladies. Thanks for the show. Now I'm ready to eat." He returned his couch to a sitting position, and dug the foodtubes out of his chest pouch. "A week of Earth fodder and I'm ready for some real cuisine. Something that doesn't taste like insecticide."

"Sounds as if you didn't enjoy your stay."

Dane sucked on a tube full of orange paste. "I knew what it was going to be like. Besides a ground fixation, walkers have enough phobias to fill a texttape. And they talk about days down there as if they can tell the difference without a timer. My nephew didn't even know what a suntan was. Food is a dirty word, and they won't even think about sex. Man's greatest gift is his intellect and his ability to communicate, yet they converse with hidden innuendoes, roundabout euphemisms, and archaic body language. They're like kids with tacks in their shoes: they're in too much pain to think about what they're doing. My own sister wouldn't give me a romp in the — " He gulped, goggle-eyed.

Shirley spun her couch. "What's wrong?"

Dane swallowed quickly. "You haven't detached the

externals."

Rhonda glanced at her screen, scrolled, and studied the readouts. "We've got another thirty seconds before the automatics kick them off."

"But, they'll never make it to the ground. They've got too much IV."

Rhonda raised her rerouted eyebrows. "Of course not. Their initial velocity is the same as ours. If we detach them too soon, aerodynamic drag will ruin their trajectory. How else are we going to keep them from falling back to Earth?"

Dane was nonplussed. "When I was on the milkrun, we dropped them into the Pacific."

Shirley laughed out loud. "Dane, that hasn't been done for decades. We're not allowed to discharge pollutants into the atmosphere."

Dane humphed. "A fat lot of good that'll do. That's like not throwing trash into a sewer. So what do you do with the stuff?"

"All waste debris goes into close solar orbit." A muffled whump was accompanied by the veering off of the propellant tanks, viewed through the side screens. "There they go now. Auxiliary engines will give them a push downstream. We don't have the power to put them *into* the sun, but at least they're out of the way."

Electronic filters dimmed the great, yellow ball. In space, sunlight meant power and energy and life: a place of unimaginable volume where pollution could never exist. Jets of smoke appeared from the shuttle's directional control rockets, but they soon disappeared in the vastness of solar vacuum.

Dane extracted a fluid tube and took a long draft. "Things certainly change when you're on slowtime."

"One thing that hasn't changed is your reputation. So tell us, Hot Pants, how *did* you earn your name?"

Dane groaned. "In all my galactic missions, I have yet to make an important contribution to the colonization effort, or a significant discovery of practical value. And my only claim to fame has to be vilified by a base epithet."

"Don't be so modest," Rhonda cooed. "You've visited every kind of star on the Hertzsprung-Russell diagram, and even a few that aren't."

"And have more years in slowtime than anyone this side of an event horizon."

"Okay, okay, okay. I can see you're really intent on making me work for my passage." Dane slurped at another foodtube, a green one that was labeled spinach. "It was on my third or fourth trip. The astros had located an unnamed binary with perturbations unaccounted for by the two visible stars. Figured the shiners were swinging around a dark companion. It was a long way out, but — what the heck — time was on my hands. Besides, I was interested in cosmology and stellar evolution. I volunteered. Babs Mettleson was head of the astroteam that discovered the anomaly — the best in the biz. Naturally, she wanted to tag along. We started encounter sessions, and got along best with a young systems engineer named Fred Malkowitz. Nice guy, but a bit of a flake. Knew more about starship subsystems and computer routines than anyone in the System. He'd spend hours tracking down a bug, make the most amazing jury-rigged telemetry repairs, but would forget to put on both socks — or both shoes. We used to call him Derf.

"Anyway, we headed for the wild black yonder. The longest trip ever made — four hundred sixty-seven days in realtime. Still holds the record. We came out of translation next to the densest piece of stellar matter ever encountered, and proved the existence of neutron stars."

Dane paused, and stared sightlessly at the viewscreens. Now they were in space proper, and eclipsed by the Earth. Outside the umbra, the stars shone in full panoply: bright, untwinkling pinpoints against a black velvet background.

"And the Hot Pants?"

Dane shook his head, sucked on another tube. "It was a recent neutron star, and still hot. The system was full of supernova debris, and it was baking our magnetic shields. Figured it couldn't have blown more than a couple thousand years ago. Had enough heavy elements flying around to tip over the atomic scale. I went into orbit closer than the computers advised was possible — I patched the inertia pump through the shield circuits, and put a bandage over the FTL drive. We got so close to that baby that you could see the bumps on her bottom."

Shirley closed her gaping jaw. "Wow, that sounds like a pretty piece of hotrodding."

Dane shrugged. "I thought so, too. But neither of those two jokers ever flew again. Babs collected enough data to keep her busy for decades. And Derf went to work for Brunel, probably the only man in the System with engineering projects that wouldn't bore him to tears."

"Wait a sec, I've got a call coming in from the *Lagrange*." Rhonda typed some code sequences on her keyboard. The display screen filled with spatial coordinates and attitudes. "Shirl, they're putting us on a holding pattern."

The *Lagrange* was the first space settlement ever built: an outdated torus with twin tubes rotating in opposite directions to maintain artificial gravity while canceling centrifugal force. It was cramped by modern day standards, with a maximum ceiling height of a hundred meters. It was somewhat of a white elephant: obsolete, and in constant need of repairs. It housed only a few thousand people, and its sole function was that of an Earth traffic way station: a trade that was slowly dying.

Shirley switched to manual, and keyed retrothrusters. "What's the problem? They can't be *that* busy. No one comes here any more unless they have to."

"They've got extra garbage dumps because of the convention. The Historic Preservation Committee doesn't want the *Lagrange* to be dismantled, and they've been holding demonstrations all week."

"Now I've heard everything," Dane groaned. "Just

because prehistoric man invented the wheel doesn't mean that we have to be burdened with it forever. It sounds as if they've been contaminated by Earth standards. One thing we don't need in space is to turn this wagon wheel into a floating museum."

The six spokes of each wheel served as hydraulivators between the z-gee docking area in the central hub, and the circular tube where daily activity operated at a comfortable one gravity. The incinerator doors opened and expulsed a stream of gaseous material into space, where it would be lost forever.

"They ought to sweep the rest of this place under the rug. The sooner the *Lagrange* is disassembled and vaporized, and consigned to the solar reaches, the sooner they can move in one of the L3 platforms. The *Asimov* and the *Clarke* have been going in circles around each other for so long that they're getting dizzy."

Rhonda leaned back in her couch while Shirley jockeyed the shuttle. "Yes, it's getting crowded around here. With the limited number of stable parking orbits around the Earth, more and more people are talking about moving out to the Trojans."

Dane said wistfully, "By the time I get back from this hop, the first one will be completed, and another will be under construction. If I decide to settle down, I might live there myself."

"You mean the great Dane would consider the sedentary life?" Shirley laughed. "Then they'll have to call him *mun*-Dane."

"Okay, ladies. You can let me out here. I'll walk the rest of the way."

Another cloud of garbage exhaust burst into space before they were given the go-ahead to proceed. Rhonda computed the rotation-matching trajectory, and Shirley put the shuttle into a match spin. The vehicle slowly closed on the central hub of the *Lagrange*.

"And when I *do* get back, I'll be the same age. And maybe you two will be old enough to stop playing with dolls and start playing with men."

Chapter 6

"For mankind as a whole, a possession infinitely more valuable than individual life is our genetic heritage, our link with past and future."

— Rachel Carson

Dane felt fine in freefall not because he was so used to the condition of weightlessness, but because of nausea inhibitors which coagulated the fluid in the semicircular ear canal. It was the sloshing of this fluid that caused spacesickness. But as soon as he reached the outer ring of the platform, which was spinning fast enough to simulate Earth gravity, he began to feel sick again.

"Hi, there, Love." A hand sank into his gluteus, and squeezed with uncommon strength. "Did you miss me?"

Dane swallowed, and stammered, "I guess so. I must have walked right by you — "

"That's not what I meant." Sandy pouted with both hands on her hips. "I haven't seen you for weeks and — " She climbed up onto her tiptoes and kissed him resoundingly on the lips. "I've missed you."

Dane swallowed again, and managed a weak smile. "Oh, of course. I missed you, too. It's just that I'm not feeling — "

"Come on, I've got just the thing for you." Sandy took him by the hand and led him to a table overlooking the Earth. "The message said I'd have the tea and honey waiting — and here it is." In a lower voice, conspiratorially, "And I slipped in the anti-n medicine, too."

"I thought the message was from your mother."

"I planned it that way. I wanted to surprise you."

Dane sat down and gratefully sipped at his tea. "I'm duly surprised — and enchanted. I'm just a little off center now."

"Coriolis force?"

Dane nodded. "I know it's optically induced, but I

swear I can feel the movement. Every time I pick up my foot, I can see the floor move before I put it down again."

Sandy smiled. "If you'd been born in space you'd be used to it."

"If I'd been born in space, I'd be used to a lot of things."

Blonde brows peaked. "Typical walker roundabout talk. You're not slipping into your old ways, are you?"

Dane laughed. "Touché. Would you believe that I just had this same conversation with my sister, only the roles were reversed?" He took another sip of tea. "Her favorite statement is 'Don't listen to what I say, understand what I mean.' "

"Thank god we've gotten away from all that language charade. So, what did you mean?"

Dane looked up from his tea and did his best to maintain eye contact, despite the feeling of discomfort in the pit of his stomach. "What I meant was — that I always feel — awkward — when I think about you — and your mother — in a nonprofessional way."

"Do you mean sexually?"

Dane stared down at the swirling wisps of orange that passed as the Earth's upper atmosphere. "Yes — I mean sexually."

"But we've had sex before, and it never seemed to bother you."

"All my floater training tells me that I'm not supposed to keep it in, but sometimes I forget — and I do."

"Is it because you've had sex with my mother?"

"Partially, I guess."

"But, what's wrong with that? You're very fond of each other. And you've known each other for a long time."

"I know. I — know. It's just — "

Sandy reached across the table and held his hand, softly, tenderly. "Come on, Dane. Please tell me. You know it'll make you feel better."

Dane nodded with exaggeration. "You know I was very close to — Babs. Practically in love, I should say.

We got along terrifically — all three of us, during that last hop together. But, we each had different goals, we were moving in different directions. She wanted to study the stars, I wanted to go there to see them. So, we were right for each other, but our timing was off. Now I've changed. I'm prepared to give up the star search, ready to settle down. Now I realize what I passed up. And there's no going back. Your mother's older — not that she's too old for me — but she's — that is, her outlook has — matured. Different. She's — grown up. While I've stayed the same mental age."

"She still loves you."

"Oh, I know that. She's told me. But we're at different stages in life — separated by thirty years of subjective time. In growth, she's twice my age — and twice as wise." Dane grinned broadly. "But still as sexy as ever."

Sandy laughed, and sipped her own tea. "That's my mother. But I still don't understand the problem."

Dane shrugged. "It's not a problem, really. It's just a — a slight feeling of strangeness. My feelings for her are only a few years old — hers for me are a few decades. Now that I'm actually considering the acceptance of the Board of Directors position — and not for the power it will give me — I wish things were different. That's all. And seeing you — look so much like her. I guess — "

"Lamb Chops, in today's extracentury life extension, that's a common situation. You have to look at people as individuals, not as a complex familial relationship. The only reason you have trouble dealing with it is because you haven't fully integrated floater philosophy with walker upbringing. You still equate — "

" 'The simple but satisfying act of sex with the deeper feelings of the psyche.' I know that. I've studied all the texttapes on the subject. But there's still that corner of my mind that has trouble accepting it."

Sandy nodded. "Sure, Dane, I can understand that. And don't ever let anyone tell you that you haven't made a marvelous adaptation. Most walkers can't adjust to the cultural shock of an open system of morality, and the lack of facade in human relation-ships."

Looking askance, Dane tilted his head.

"Now, on a more personal level. How does this affect our present arrangements?"

Dane sipped his tea. "I guess — you always hit the nail on the head, don't you?"

Sandy winked. "That's part of my upbringing. So, I'll take the risk. Would you rather not have sex right now?"

Dane bit his lower lip. "I guess — I was hoping to spend some time with your mother. You know, to talk things over. I just — "

"Dane, it's okay. Now that you've aired your feel-ings, you'll know what to say to her. And you'll be see-ing her soon. So, how do you feel?"

He tilted his head, and nodded. "Like I've just been psychoanalyzed by a loving, and lovable — and sexy — woman. A woman I've seen grow up from the time she was an infant. You know that's why I feel so strange around you. It seems as if one day you were a little girl, then, a couple of hops later, you were a teenager. Sud-denly, you became a full-grown woman —like your mother. Anyway, I feel great. I always feel great when I'm with you."

"I'll bet you say that to all the gals."

"If I do, it's only because it's true." Dane produced his IDcard and tapped it on the table. "In any case, I could use something to eat."

"Later." Sandy winked, and stuck her IDcard into the compslot. The menu flashed on the screen facing her. "Let's have lunch first."

Dane inserted his card. He gazed at his screen, and scrolled through the bill of fare.

"Hey, mister. Can you help me?"

Dane looked at the six-year-old with tousled hair. "Sure, son. What's the problem?"

The boy pouted, his lower lip curved out and down. A tear rolled down one cheek. "I lost my card."

"That's nothing to fret over." Dane picked up the

toddler and plopped him on his lap. "Let's see if we can find it for you. But first, a greeting." He held out his hand. "Dane."

The boy offered his palm. "Gil."

"Okay, Gil, here's what we do. First, we clear the screen. Then we enter the user sequence. We'll do a search scan. Either you left your card in a slot, or you dropped it and someone picked it up and inserted it for you. Can you type your name?"

Gil pecked the keyboard with rigid index fingers.

"Good. Now hit the command key." The green display vanished, and another appeared in its place. "There you go. Your card is in message sender number 1108, sector four, east corridor three, intersection seventeen. Do you remember leaving it there, or shall we call up a locator grid?"

Tearfully, the boy nodded. "I called my mom. I was hungry."

"She wasn't home?"

Gil shook his head.

"Okay, then let's go back to the food menu. What are you having?"

"Fourteen, twenty-seven, and one-zero-two."

Dane moved the cursor and winked at Sandy. "The kid knows how to read."

"No, my daddy told me the numbers for burger, French fries, and carb."

"You're smart, anyway, Honey." Sandy rubbed Gil's forearm. "Would you like to eat with us?"

Gil shook his head. "I better go home and wait."

"You know how to collect your food?"

He nodded. Dane let the boy slide off his lap. "Thanks, mister. You too, miss." He ran off, his tears gone.

"A carbonated drink sounds good. In fact, I think I'll repeat his order. Plus a fresh apple." Dane punched in his choices and removed his card. "Have you ordered?"

Sandy nodded. They got up and walked to the dispensary. Three hot trays slid out of their recesses. Gil put the wrapped package in his stomach pouch, zipped it shut, and smiled at them. Then he ran out of the cafeteria. As he passed through the hatch, Dane heard singing on the other side: a familiar old western Earth tune with the words changed to "Home, home on *Lagrange*."

"They're still at it."

Dane took his tray and followed Sandy back to their table. "Who's at what?"

"The Preservers. They're marching throughout the whole platform trying to evoke sympathizers for their project."

"They're too much like walkers: saving every bit of their past as if it had any meaning to the future." Dane bit with gusto into the soyburger. He pointed down at the crystal floor beneath them, through which the Earth hung like an angry, fiery ball. "You know, they still eat *animals* down there? You'd think they never heard of vegederivitives or synthextracts."

Sandy gnawed a fresh peach. "The *Lagrange* may have outdated synthetic extract equipment, but they import the best fruit that ponics can grow."

Dane looked at the stamp on his apple. "From the *Simak*. Now there's a platform whose hydroponics are the best, and whose people are as pastoral as they come. So, tell me about this almost neutron star you've cooked up."

She inserted her IDcard and hit a code sequence. "I can show you a few facts and figures."

"When it comes to figures, yours is the best. *Are* the best."

She poked him in the ribs with her elbow. "This is not a three-body problem, but try to fake some interest." She filled the screen with computations, and launched into a brief description of her findings. "So, we have no idea what this stellar object is, or how it got to its present state. It doesn't fit any known solar evolutionary pattern — or, our data is way off base."

Dane shook his head, and nibbled on a French fry. "It's not even in the same ballpark. This stellob couldn't have evolved naturally, unless there's something about degenerate matter that changes physics. How can you have two such vastly different rotational speeds so close together?"

"You can if the two are not gravitationally interactive. Suppose you've got two areas of extreme density: a central core, and a shell. The core is spitting out the microwave beam, and the shell is — I don't know — thick enough to prevent even high-energy particles from escaping. You'd have this stellar object — this stellob — emitting like an ordinary sun from its core, but the shell would be catching it all. The core spins extremely fast, with white dwarf speed. The shell spins more slowly, but as more matter is accumulated, the more it would shrink and the faster it would rotate. Momentum and centrifugal force would keep the shell from collapsing into the core."

"But what's the in-between doing? You've got a two AU diameter shell surrounding a hundred kleter core." The Astronomical Unit was the radius of Earth's orbit about the Sun. "Where did all the heavy metals come from?"

Sandy shrugged her shoulders. "That's what I'd like to find out. So, what do you think?"

Dane switched off his monitor. He stared off to the side, through the plastiglass flooring. Due to platform rotation, the clear, bright, cratered surface of the Moon now floated in place of the Earth. Behind it, stars filled the background like holes in a brilliantly backlit tapestry. "You're Doppler calcs show the shell moving at about ten Earth revs. It's too slow for a star that size, with that mass. And the damn thing is practically room temperature."

"Except for the core, which is extremely hot and super dense, and is spitting microwaves from the poles."

Dane rubbed his chin. "Have you considered that riding a pulsar beam may be detrimental to your health? To say nothing of your genes. The closer we get, the more intense the radiation. I'd like to go down in history with you, but not with a glowing half-life."

Sandy flicked her hand in the air, and squealed, "Dane, I'm not about to make a mistake that simple. The stellob was detected by remote probe. It points away from Earth, otherwise it would already have been in the catalogue. No, the real problem is instability. We don't know how to categorize this thing, but the collapse from a red giant to supernova, when it begins to happen, is very fast."

Dane winced, and looked at her askance. "How fast is very fast?"

"Theoretically?"

"No, your best estimate."

She said emphatically, "Very fast."

"I see. So, if we don't get fried on the way in, we may have the opportunity to become stellar matter for the next generation of stars."

Sandy shrugged. "You probably won't know it, though."

"You fill me with confidence." Dane pushed away the plastic wrapping debris and took a bite of his apple. "So, where is this anomaly?"

"Toward the Core. XL axis, 27 tilt."

"How far."

"Far."

"Now, wait a minute. How much time are we going to lose — "

"Brunel's new GOmod-1 should cut the hop in half. It's — "

"How — far?"

Sandy took a deep breath. "Four hundred ninety-seven days — real time." Dane raised his eyebrows. "That's farther than I went with your mother."

"One way."

He came half way out of his seat. "That's almost three years!"

"Two point seven two, to be precise." Sandy pushed her disposables into the chute in the center of the table, and chucked in the peach pit. "I hadn't actually planned on a manned hop, but when Brunel offered the use of his new starhopper — "

Dane eased back down, and slumped against the backrest. "I don't know. I thought — a short hop, then take up permanent residence — I don't know."

"There'll be a bonus — "

"I don't need the money. It's just that — things are suddenly so unsettled. On Earth. With this Board of Directors position. With — "

Sandy placed a warm hand on Dane's. "Things always change. That's the nature of life. Especially in the Settlements. Anything that stays static, stagnates. Like Earth."

"I know. But — "

"Besides, you won't be without close companionship. At least one crew member will be a sexual partner of your liking."

Suspiciously, "Who?"

"Me."

Dane's head jerked up. "What? Sandy, you've — "

"Never gone on a hop before. Never had any inclination, really. But this is a phenomenon that I want to investigate first hand. And with you as the pilot, it's the perfect opportunity to — to spend some time together."

Dane rolled his eyes.

"I have to tell you something. I used to look up to you as — oh, I guess, as a father figure. You weren't around all that much, but somehow I always felt — close to you. Then, when I went through puberty, those feelings of fatherly love turned to feelings of mature love. But you were always taking off, going out on another hop. I used to get the feeling you were avoiding me. But that first time I seduced you — "

"That wasn't fair." Dane fidgeted with his apple core, trying to find another scrap of pulp. "I — I just couldn't get over your — your sudden sexuality."

"It wasn't sudden. I grew up just like every other girl. Only you didn't see the interim stages because of your Odyssean wanderings. Besides, if I hadn't taken the initiative you never would have made any advances. You still stumble around with walker dialectics."

Dane held up his hands in mock defense. "Let's

stick to the issue at hand. What makes you think I'd accept an assignment with you as astronomer?"

"Would you rather my mother go in my place?"

"That's an unfair question, intended to obfuscate the issue."

"I love teasing you. You respond with such — animation."

"Stop with the walker tactics. Answer the question honestly."

Sandy puckered her lower lip in direct imitation of the little boy Gil. "You wouldn't leave me out of the revelation phase of my own discovery, would you?" When Dane's face remained adamant, she went on, "And besides, we have a fixed history of harmony. We get along well personally, socially, and — of course — intimately. We'd have no hang-ups in encounter training. I defy you to find even a reasonable doubt as to why we shouldn't embark on this great adventure together."

Dane's expression was still clouded. "I can't think of anything on the spur of the moment, but I'll give it some thought. I'm sure I'll come up with something."

"When you do, please give me a call. I'll bet I can soften your resolve."

"That's what worries me."

Chapter 7

"We cannot escape from the past, but neither can we avoid inventing the future."

— Rene Dubos

The odor of fresh brewed coffee lingered for the barest moment before being sucked into the ventilator system. Dane rolled out of bed and slipped into his jumpsuit. A quick e-m shower realigned his pores. An inhalation of dental mist cleaned his teeth and freshened his breath. He joined Alice in the kitchen.

He encircled her from behind, buried his face in her neck, and gave her a resounding smack. "Are the kids up, yet?"

Alice twisted and returned his kiss, planting her red lips on his cheek. "No. They're on a shift three schedule, and only got home from school a couple of hours ago. I'll let them sleep while I do some chores. Then we'll have shift two together. Coffee?"

"Love some." He stuck his IDcard into the kitchen compslot, and typed his breakfast choices on the countertop touchpad. The central computer debited his account, credited hers, and updated her inventory. Compressed foodbars dropped out of the delivery chute below the storage cabinet. Dane popped them into the microwave oven for heating and expansion. "Do you know that on Earth they still cook?"

Alice carried her own breakfast to the table. "Oh, yes. They even make meals from scratch."

"And from flesh and blood. They have some very strange customs."

"Did you think they were strange when you lived there?"

Dane laughed, removed his food from the oven, and joined her. "No, I guess not. But I didn't know any better. You know, whenever I go back, and see how illogical the entire planetside community operates, I wonder how platform people were ever able to get their feet out of the mud. Walkers are so mired in their roots that most of them would die if they were replanted."

"That's why the shuttle service is being cut back. There aren't enough free thinkers willing to leave the ground anymore." Alice snugged the housecoat about her middle. "Walkers are so consumed by their veblenesque society that they can't break the mold. It's sad in a way. They live solely for the value of their physical possessions. They just can't comprehend an information society which places its importance on knowledge and data retrieval. They never have the opportunity to grow out of their childhood materialism — they continue to collect toys as long as they live."

"Yes, and storage becomes a major problem. I'm glad I left all that behind."

Alice sipped slowly. She leaned her chair back until it assumed a forty-five degree angle, and locked it in place with a touch of her long-nailed finger. "Dane, don't you ever have feelings of — nostalgia?"

"Sure. Until I get a whiff of the air." Dane spooned out the oatmeal that filled his bowl. "But you know what's worse than living in the ground like a mole, where you can never see the sun and the moon and the stars? Worse even than the chemical pollution and atmospheric contamination? It's the cultural corruption. And I don't mean that the people are bad, despite their antediluvian attitudes. The problem is that they're — misguided. I guess they cling to the past because it's the only hold they have on their basic humanity. Instead of changing their outlook, they seek ways of rationalizing their atavistic behavior. They convince themselves that their civilization is the result of prehistoric tribal influences which are indelibly imprinted in their genetic makeup. They can't understand that change is no longer a matter of natural evolution, but of intellectual choice. I tell you, they really boggle me sometimes."

Alice nodded as she sipped on her coffee. "Yes, I know what you mean. Being a shuttle stewardess has significantly broadened my insight into walker psychology. I have so much opportunity to talk with those who *are* able to break free of the mold. And they're very much like you: willing to change, and unable to accept those who can't."

"Sure, I know my viewpoint is biased. It always will be. But, Alice, they have holly down there, and the Settlements pipe down programs all the time. They know what it's like up here. For all of man's history, he's been star struck: an explorer willing to risk everything to discover new lands, new thoughts. What's happened down there? How did the wanderlust get lost?"

Alice shrugged. "Perhaps when they lost visual contact with the stars, they lost sight of them as well. Or, perhaps, all throughout mankind's evolution, there have been only a small clique of people who were the visionaries, while the masses of humanity have been followers, and malingerers. Perhaps only that select spearhead is what we perceive as the true inquisitors. To put it in perspective, think about how many people in the System today would be unwilling to leave it should the opportunity arise to emigrate to other stars."

Dane winced one eye.

"You see what I mean? I'm comfortable here. I live with my children. I like the neighbors and my job and the society that molds it all. I have no reason to move. And I wouldn't. Ever. I'm too complacent with what I have to want to move on to something so utterly alien. Oh, I might transfer to another platform should my vocation change, but that's not the same as the complete metamorphosis involved in shifting horizons and challenging new conditions. You can't see that because you *are* a pioneer. You've come from a point behind me, and you're just as willing to go to a point beyond. You're like a post Columbian exile leaving Europe. Once you've crossed the Atlantic on a rickety schooner, you're just as apt to cross the plains of America in a Conestoga wagon. You'd sneer at people like me: the Pilgrims clinging to their seaside comforts. Why go farther when you've already found what you're looking for?"

"I never looked at it that way, Alice. In fact, I've never taken the time to look at a lot of things. It seems as if I've spent my whole life on the go — always reaching out for the mirage on the horizon instead of for the oasis at my feet."

Alice smiled, nodding. "I didn't mean to imply that there was anything wrong with that. A healthy culture needs people of all sorts — "

"No, I wasn't taking it personally. I'm just saying that you've given me an insight into myself that I wasn't aware of. And that's good — for me — because it will help my growth as I contemplate the subtleties in that train of thought."

"I'm glad I can repay you for your sensitivity of last night."

Dane winced again.

"See, you don't even know that our encounter has already paid off for me," Alice laughed. She stood up and poured another cup of coffee. She held out the pitcher, questioning with raised eyebrows, but Dane declined. "You see, having encounters only with similarly thinking men has gotten me into a rut. I can see now that I've taken a lot for granted. I'd forgotten that Earth still thrives on antiquated mores which we've given up because they are self-defeating. Like the old household system."

"Ah, now I see what you're getting at. Sure, because you've lived on the platforms all your life, you've never experienced firsthand the comparison between the sanctity of walker kinship ties and the floater extended family philosophy. Up here, everyone is part of the same great gestalt. But down there, people are broken up into tiny segments whose only basis for integument is blood relation. Each parent-child domicile is a distinct unit bound by intricate and inexplicable legal statutes, but separated from the rest of society by a perception of distrust. They believe in the bond of law rather than the bond of love: as if two people can be forced to stay together, unhappily, because of dictatorial legislation. They still believe that feelings between people can be forced by contract."

Alice resumed her seat, and crossed her legs. "Yes, and when you're brought up in a system that abhors the loss of personal freedom, you forget that not everyone enjoys that freedom. Then I see someone like you, who had only one mother and one father, and I realize how lucky I was, and how fortunate my children are, to have as parents every adult they encounter. Tell me, was it lonely — being brought up in solitary confinement?"

Dane tilted his head. "I was lucky. I had a sister. Since I didn't know differently, it seemed perfectly natural. You have to understand that even though in modern walker society the localized family structure serves no purpose, for most of man's history it was an integral part of his culture. Back then, you needed a mother who could specialize in child rearing, and a father for protection and food gathering. A million years of habit is hard to break. That's just another part of the past that they cling to because it's too painful to change, despite the obvious advantages. So, they continue to maintain a marriage and divorce system, in which children are possessions of the original parents, even when they separate. A bond seldom formulates with the new partners because the children of the previous marriage belong to someone else. And women still give up their names, and their identities, when they form a new relationship. They never have the opportunity to find out who they are on their own; they always have a male anchor linked to them. Again, I was lucky. My folks stayed together during my upbringing. But they were the last of a dying breed. Without a sense of community values, walker children become alienated. Loneliness is an accepted part of their heritage."

"That sounds awful."

"Kids today just don't know how good they have it. They don't have to be afraid to walk the corridors, they don't have to worry — "

The hatch chime rang, and the ceiling speaker called out melodiously, "Sandy Mettleson."

"That's my lover." Dane rose to meet her.

Alice directed her voice toward the sound actuated tripping mechanism. "Open."

When the pressure switches balanced, the central hatch wheel spun out hydraulically. The hatch unsealed by blasting air through pinholes in the gasket, then swung back against the bulkhead. Each cubicle was a separate, airtight, double-hulled, self-contained chamber.

"Hello, Precious." Sandy exchanged pecks on the cheek with Dane, and held out her hand to Alice. "Sandy."

"Alice." She touched Sandy's palm. "We were just having breakfast. Will you join us?"

"Just had dinner, thanks. I can come back later if — "

"No, it's okay with me. Alice?"

She smiled, and nodded. "Fine."

"We were just discussing how difficult it is to change customs, especially when you're surrounded by the artifacts of your society. It's another reason why they've got to get rid of this antique."

"Tell it to the Preservers. They're staging another march right now." Sandy glanced at her wristrad. "We've got two hours before our shuttle flight, if you'd like to join them."

"Always the teaser."

Alice remained seated. "Yes, Dane's told me so much about you. I can't say I envy your upcoming hop. You'll be gone for three years?"

"Not counting observation time after arrival. We don't know what we'll find, or how long we'll have to stay. We might just leave probes, and pick them up in a few decades."

"Just think. The next time I see you — I *will* see you, Dane, won't I?"

"I'll make a point of it."

"The next time I see you, Tommy and Marie will be teenagers."

"And so will Dane," Sandy laughed. "He's the eternal teenager. So, did you two have a nice encounter?"

"It was good for me," Alice said.

Dane nodded thoughtfully. "She helped me to get over my Earth-visit anxiety — and a few other things. We'll talk about it on the way. Alice — " Dane bent and kissed her on the lips. "Thanks for everything. Love to you and the kids."

"Love. Nice meeting you, Sandy."

"You, too, Alice."

As they stepped into the corridor, the hatch hissed shut behind them. People ambled by on the inwardly curving floor; the curve was barely perceptible due to the unblocked length of the central passage in the living quarters section. Water and nutrient solutions gurgled along in channels, feeding the oxygenating plantforms that helped to freshen the limited atmosphere.

"Everything is all set. Mother is meeting us on the *Ellison*, and you're going to fly us the rest of the way in the *Phantom Jackal*."

"Sounds incestuous."

"Enjoy it. It may be your last time together."

Dane held out his palms. "Hey, my problems are solved. Alice helped me to put my feelings in perspective. Sandy, I'm always a little frayed when I get back from Earth. But this is the last time. I signed everything over to Sis, so there won't be any more ground fixation. My mind is completely free of that. And I worked out most of my mother and daughter conflicts — at least, the conscious ones. I hope I can talk more openly about it with you and Babs. Alice was a great catharsis. I just wish walkers had psychotherapy instruction from kindergarten onward — you just can't imagine how inhibited we are, being raised to keep everything in."

"Praise the walkers who instituted the Settlement program. They had the insight to realize that life in space needed psychological adjustment. But, you ramble in the wrong direction. I was saying that this may be your last time on the *Phantom Jackal*. The Galactic Odyssey model will force all other starships into instant obsolescence."

Dane halted in front of the tube hatch. He frowned as he pushed the call button. "Gee, I never thought of that. I don't know if I like the idea of giving up the old girl . . . "

"Dane!" Sandy whined, throwing up her hands in frustration.

"But, Sandy, we've been all over the Galaxy together. We — "

The hatch burst open in a puff of dust, and with the odor of oxidized oil and burnt grease. Dane swept his hands in front of his face, coughing as he entered the pneumatic passenger capsule. Sandy touched the send button: the tube had only two stops, at the hub and at the base. The hatch sealed itself shut, and slowly the capsule was sucked up the spoke by the evacuation of gas at the other end. The gas was then pumped back down to the bottom for the reverse journey.

"I hate this rattletrap. Why can't people see that this fossil should be buried with the dinosaurs? All shift long the Preservers were singing, as if their cadence could renew such *de*cadence. Don't they realize what a useless impediment the *Lagrange* has become? We have to look to the future, not live in the past. You know what our problem is?"

Sandy rolled her eyes. "No, but I'm sure you'll tell me."

Dane slid one foot through a bungee and held onto the handgrips. As the capsule receded farther from the rim, and the centrifugal force exerted less of an influence, the artificially induced gravity was reduced.

"We don't have wars any more."

"That's a problem?"

"I didn't mean it like that. In the old days, when cities got bombed out, it was those countries that had the most opportunity to gain by recent technological advancement. The victorious nations, whose cities didn't suffer as much damage, struggled along with their antiquated structures because it was prohibitively expensive to tear down and rebuild. The losers had no choice.

"Okay. So, today, we have space battles: arguments over allocation of living accommodation versus public parks and gathering centers. But that's all settled through compstats, and the population ratio within the platform. The only interplatform altercations are trade disputes, and they're settled through arbitration. Nobody fights anymore. Therefore, since we don't lose Settlements through combat, and destruction through natural catastrophe is a practical impossibility, we're stuck with all these outdated museum pieces. We're running out of orbital space for them."

"Sounds like Brunel's idea of moving humanity out to the Trojans would solve the inner orbit crowding problem. We can leave the lunar lagrangian points for the stay-at-homes."

"Except for one thing: if the Space Park Service wants to keep up the first generation Settlements in their natural condition, I don't want my tax money paying for it. Let the hardheads who want to preserve it, pay for it."

Sandy started to float off the padded floor. She let her legs go free, but held onto a grip for stability. "Dane, if I didn't know your penchant for high hyperbole, I'd think you were serious."

Dane burst into gales of laughter. "Sorry. I guess I got carried away by my own fustian. I just love to yammer about trivial grievances. I'm just nitpicking."

"It's good for you. I can see you coming out of your walker-influenced torpor. Not that there's not a lot of truth in what you say. I'm beginning to agree with Mother. We need more outspoken people on the Committee."

The capsule squished to a halt. After an interminable delay, while the safety panel double-checked interface circuits and flashed annunciator lights, the hatch popped open. The pressure had not quite equalized and, caught off guard, Dane was expelled out of the capsule with a burst of expanding air.

Weightless, he sailed across the receiving room, arms and legs flailing, until he hit the opposite wallpad and grabbed onto a suregrip.

It was Sandy's turn to laugh, but Dane grew solemn. "You see? That's what I mean. This hulk ought to be towed to the scrapyard and dismantled." He pointed to the tube entrance. "They're still using balloon switches and bimetallic strips for pressure differentiation, instead of artificial neurotransmitters."

Sandy shook her head. Her short hair had accumulated a static charge in the dehumidified atmosphere and, without the stronger force of gravity, now stood off her scalp like fine brush bristles. Her breasts, also relieved of their ponderous weight, floated up inside her form-fitting body stocking. "Liver Pill, I can always rely on you to relieve the tension of the moment."

Dane gathered himself together, and struck a pose with a leg and an arm enmeshed with bungees. "I never let a lady down."

"Only because you insist on sex in z-gee."

"If it weren't impossible, it would be miraculous. I just hate bouncing away when things get good." He indicated the padded corridor with his free hand. "So, shall we leave this archaic paddlewheel and start our journey into the technological future?"

Sandy nodded. "At least aboard the shuttle, we won't have to listen to the Preservers." She patted her belly pouch. "I've got a card full of hollies."

"And I have a card full of old Earth literature. What do you say we stop plotting the course of the future, and vege out for a while?"

"Do you feel up to it?"

"Is a black hole black?"

Chapter 8

"Genes determine your talents. Society offers the opportunity, within its bounds, to use them. What you make of them is who you are.

— G. G.

The *Ellison* was a troublesome platform. Unlike the *Lagrange*, it did not have the advantage of a geosynchronous orbit. Instead, it was the sole occupant of the L3 position, a libration point of unstable equilibrium on the opposite side of the Earth from the Moon. In addition to being so far from raw lunar materials, and having mass catchers which required chronic elliptic adjustment, the platform tended to migrate away from the primary system. Gravitational attraction was in poor balance.

For that reason, huge thrusters were built into the cylinder endcaps. Automatic signal transponders actuated triangulation circuits which backfed through spatial perception monitors. In conjunction with momentum control gyros, the *Ellison* was constantly on the move as it jockeyed along the longitudinal axis in an approximation of stationary berthing.

When the thrusters burped their nuclear flames, the platform jolted and vibrated with the uneasy motion of a mild earthquake. To the inhabitants, this meant that the floor was liable to move out from under them at any moment. It was an unsettling existence. The *Ellison* was often noisy, and always unpredictable.

"These shuttle pilots really have to know their business. You never know when the *Ellison* is going to explode on you and take off like a wounded lion."

Sandy nodded. Her head lay against Dane's shoulder. "That's why people don't stay there long. They can't take the perturbations. They had to shut down the observatory and turn it into a group therapy center."

The screen showed a cloud of vaporized particulates

streaming from both ends of the fifteen-kilometer-long cylinder. It glowed red at the exhaust pipe, orange further out, then disappeared transparently into the vastness of interplanetary space. Abruptly, the *Ellison's* main engines shut down. The guidance control jets fired a little longer, until the rotating cylinder's axial tilt was re-established. The shuttlecraft advanced on vernier rockets, matched spin, and vectored for coupling.

"It must be disconcerting when the forward motion synchronizes with rotation, and everyone floats out of his shoes during gravity cancellation."

"You're hyperbolizing again."

Dane switched on the intercom so he could listen in on the docking conversation. "That's the way my imagination works. I take in all seemingly impertinent facts, collate them with inconsequential background data, and extrapolate the wildest scenario possible — a truly galactic perspective. It keeps me from going insane on long hops."

"You'd better try another method." Sandy twisted in her seat, and pressed back against the retaining straps until her body rewarped the formfoam. She hit the magnification button, and the camera telescoped back so that the entire end of the *Ellison* filled the viewscreen. The docking sphincter dilated like the mouth of a gigantic lamprey. "Sometimes, you don't see the galaxy for the stars."

Dane pressed the console dispenser for a calcium tablet. In weightlessness, pills cannot be shaken out of a bottle; a plunger pushed out the tablet, and he scooped it out of the air. "How's that?"

"For example, what would you do with a retired space vehicle?"

Dane chewed thoughtfully on the mint-flavored calcium derivative. "Junk it. Cannibalize it for parts. If the components were unreliable, I'd put it on automatic and drop it into low solar orbit and let it vaporize."

Sandy nodded. "Is that how you see the fate of the *Phantom Jackal*, once it's superseded by assembly-line, mass-produced GOmods?"

Dane rankled. "That's a different story. The *Phantom Jackal's* got a lot of life in her yet. And she's been through more clusters and star fields then any other starship in the System. She's a classic."

"So is the *Lagrange*. It was the first Settlement ever built, at a time when Earth's economy was at low ebb and could least afford such a visionary venture. Yet, the people of a hundred nations contributed to its construction, and launched the greatest enterprise in human history. And that means something — to a great many people. Progress doesn't always leave room for sentimentality, but memories are important to some people, especially when certain reminders can evoke such depth of feeling."

Dane frowned, and swallowed the rest of the tablet without letting it melt. Decalcification of his bones was no longer on his mind. "You sneak. You suckered me in."

She perked up the corners of her mouth, and tilted her head. "Of course. I learned how to scheme from an expert — my mother. I used circumlocution: I took you around in a big circle so you could see the situation from a different perspective. Now you can translate your feelings for the *Phantom Jackal* to a relevant position concerning the *Lagrange*."

The viewscreen was set on the widest angle of the remote sensing lens, on the nose of the shuttlecraft. The sides of the cone-shaped endcap slid out of view. The ship proceeded slowly into the docking orifice. A thirty-foot-thick layer of formfoam lined the circular opening. Four extended shock-absorbing columns protruded beyond the blunt, forward end of the shuttle. They collapsed into the ship with pneumatic precision, while the landing pad retracted under the mass and momentum. At the critical moment of recoil, enormous clamps pinioned the shock columns like a praying mantis biting the antennae of an insect. Barely a shudder passed through the titanium hull. The sphincter aperture closed.

Applause rang out through the cabin as the passengers showed their approval of the soft touchdown. Dane and Sandy joined by clapping their hands.

Console speakers blurted, "Please do not unfasten your safety harnesses until the shuttle is locked in place." Everyone immediately unbuckled, and floated out of their acceleration couches toward the forward hatches. Dane and Sandy joined the mob. Several children squeezed over the headrests as they pulled themselves along the outer bulkhead. Men and women jostled along in a snaillike progression. Without any kind of orientation, someone's feet were as likely to be in front of one's eyes as the back of one's head. But experienced floaters did not flail and kick: they kept their bodies and feet still as they progressed along the handgrips.

Once through the hatch into the receiving room, the passengers fanned out along all four walls, gliding quickly from grip to grip. There was an information console for anyone who needed directions or locator data, but most people fanned their IDcards past coderead windows and kept on moving. No time was lost inserting the cards into compslots as in the old model debit machines still in use on Earth, and on the *Lagrange.*

"Now there's a heavenly body I wouldn't mind crashing into."

"Mother!"

"Babs!"

Barbara Mettleson, her slippered feet tucked under wallgrips, held out her arms and hugged first her daughter, then her lover. "I was referring to you, Hot Pants, not this celestial sphere. You look great. You've hardly aged a day since I saw you last year."

"Babs, I've been on three hops since then, and all we did on arrival was drop off surveillance monitors. I *haven't* aged a day."

"How do you manage to keep up on current events?"

Dane hooked his toe under a grip. "I take newschips

and scan them during slowtime. I see you're as young and healthy looking as ever."

"I know, I don't look a day over fifty, even though I'm in my — well, never mind." In zero gravity, her ample breasts floated up like helium-filled balloons. "Sandy, have you been keeping this hunk of masculinity drained, or is there something left for me?"

"His output has been commensurate with his age."

"His subage, I hope, and not his obage."

"Why do I feel like a toy?" Dane mused.

"Because you're so much fun to play with. And you love every minute of it." Barbara ungripped, and spun her body so she floated parallel to the wall. She propelled herself along the white padding. "Come on. I've got a cube for us, but you're going to have to work for it. It's at midpoint. We'll jog along a downstream corridor."

They gripped down one of the two walls reserved for outbound traffic. When the simulated gravitational effect of centrifugal force began to make them heavy, the corridor split apart so that people jumping upward from adjacent side panels did not crash into each other. It was a constant source of headache for travelers who did not follow the directional arrows.

"Why don't we just take the lift?"

Barbara looked at Dane askance. "Why would you take a mechanical conveyance to get some place to go running?"

Dane pursed his lips. "So we can start sooner?"

"You can start right now. As the gravity increases, it will break you in. By the time we get to one-gee, you'll be warmed up."

"Babe, I really don't — "

"I know, dear. You'd rather be molded into a starship-pilot cybernetic interface. But you'll have plenty of time for that — three years at least. For now, you're going to work out your gams."

Dane was already puffing hard, and the wallplant signs were displaying only point six gee. "Okay, but if — I get too — tired cut — "

Barbara's long hair swept from side to side. "Then you'll fall asleep, and Sandy and I can have a mother to daughter chat without your smart-alecky interference."

Dane had to concentrate too much on breathing to make further observations. Once they hit deck level, the easy, downhill loping flattened out. He hardly noticed the spacious beauty of the cylinder, the curving, tree-lined pathways, the blooming flower gardens, the fern-scented atmosphere, the pedestrians strolling in sunlight refracted through great prisms, the loungers lying on the grass, the children on bicycles, the cleverly disguised cubicles, the bridges that crossed the broad, plastiglass windows that let filtered sunlight into the cylinder, or hang gliders cruising through the central core. He might just as well have been dodging machinery in the below-decks mechanical spaces, or touring the production areas. The grandeur of the space settlement was lost to him like the sidewalk was lost to a horse wearing blinders.

He started to fall behind after the first kilometer. After the second, the two women were still in sight, but they were running abreast with shoulders erect and flung back as if they were merely promenading. After three kilometers, Dane veered toward an open archway and ducked down a ramp to the commuter level. He bent at the waist, hands on hips, and gasped for several minutes before he was able to stand upright. He considered going down to the service level for a drink, but opted against it. He jumped onto a gondola and let it whisk him along its track until a point that was half a kilometer before midpoint. Then he struggled up another ramp to the cylinder's inner surface.

"I told you this was where we'd find him."

"Mother, how did you predict with such accuracy exactly what he would do?"

"Oh, I've known this man a lot longer than you have. I've got his course charted."

Dane's face did not crack. "Okay, so you lucked out and figured I'd be a little out of shape — "

"A little! Look at you. You're covered with sweat,

you're chest is still heaving, and I'll bet your heartbeat still hasn't returned to normal. Honey, you need to exercise more than your jaw. If you're going across the Galaxy with my daughter, I don't want you keeling over on her."

"Whenever I feel faint, I'll power down the gravity. Babs, when we get to her precious stellob, we're not going to have to run around the thing. I'll *fly* her on a parabolic curve."

"Mother, he looks more broken up than broken in."

"Nothing a hot shower and a good rub down won't cure. Come on, kids, we'll do it together."

Barbara led them to the cube. The shower and the rub down worked wonders. They all felt better afterwards. The three of them lay on the broad foam mattress, Dane in the middle.

Barbara played with Dane's hair, making curlicues with her delicate fingers. "You haven't seen Fred for a while, have you?"

"It's been years — my time. Must be decades obtime. Gee, time flies when you're going FTL. It seems like just the other rev we were setting out together in the — What was I flying then? The *Light Brigade*? Starships have come a long way since the early revs. The ship was turned into a trainer, until they came out with the holographic simulators. I guess she's ridden off into the sunset by now."

"All the old models were sent into close solar orbit when the split beam intelligence amplifiers were integrated into starship circuits," Sandy said matter-of-factly. "They weren't considered safe any more. By this time, the *Light Brigade* has been reduced to its constituent heavy elements."

"Don't treat her so distantly. I was in love with that ship. How about you, Babe?"

"I was in love with her pilot. I still am."

"I love you, too, Babs. I always will."

"Thanks, Dane. But, you know, charging though the Galaxy on a ramjet steed, and seeing the stars through image enhancers, was not my idea of making scientific notation. I still prefer long-term investigation over short term statistical studies."

"You never did like quickies, even at FTL."

"That's beside the point. I always wanted to be able to plan my future, to direct a course of events that would lead to something meaningful — both for me and for those I love. I can do all that from a solside berth, living in realtime. Now, I think I can do it even better from Brunel's B-40. Do you know much about it, Dane?"

"Only what I've seen in the adchips. 'More air space than ever, so you won't bump heads with your neighbors.' Which I suppose means a bigger diameter. 'No more blinding sunlight or fear of ultraviolet contamination.' Building way out in Jupiter's orbit has *some* advantages. 'Every cube with its own private evacuator.' With the technological advances in productivity, recycling has been on its way out for a long time. It doesn't pay to save waste matter when it's cheaper to vac it and manufacture from scratch. What's he trying to prove, building out there in the boondocks? People don't want to live halfway out of the solar system."

"It's much more complicated than that, and the overall concept is absolutely brilliant. First of all, the Earth-Moon lagrangian libration points are overcrowded. You may be able to squeeze in a few more small platforms, but they won't meet the future needs of human expansion. And they'd have to be like the *Ellison*: mobile units that are always fighting to neutralize the instability of their orbits. Did you hear about the near disaster last year?"

Dane rolled his head. "I must have been away."

"For the lack of a microchip, the platform was almost lost. A computer malfunction allowed it to desynchronize. It started tumbling. With its solar vanes out of alignment, it lost power. If a couple of tugships hadn't been nearby to grapple the endcaps, it might have gone into oscillation. We'd have had an inert cylinder full of floating people and crashing debris."

Dane sat up, pushing Sandy away from his shoulder. He stabbed the air with an errant finger. "And that's because they don't have a backup monitoring system. I'd never fly a starship without one, I don't see why a platform should be any different. I even made a recommendation to that effect in one of my flight reports."

Sandy sat up as well. "Now, you're always making criticisms in your flight reports."

"That's because I have lots of time to think when I'm out there on slowtime."

"But don't you see what you're up against? People are so complacent today, they're not likely to change because of a way-out suggestion. They're stuck in their orbits. Why do you think Brunel's having such a hard time convincing immigrants to move out to the Trojans? People like being close to Earth. They — "

"But why? What's so sacrosanct about a one AU orbit?"

"It's not the distance from the sun, it's the proximity of their home planet."

"Oh, come on, now. Floaters don't give a gram about Earth."

"Not to live on. But it was mankind's manger, his origin, and it possesses deep-seated meaning."

"Not for me. I just got back from there, and I can see it for what it is."

"You're confusing reality with memory. The history tapes show the planet in its glory: with rolling grasslands, great green forests, teeming rivers, sparkling oceans, majestic snow-capped mountains, clean air and crystal blue skies, and life — natural life — everywhere. And because the imagery is pleasant, that's how people perceive it. Why do you think the Settlements are modeled after a twentieth-century environment?"

"Because Earth doesn't have an environment any more. It's one big chemical factory, with people living in test tubes. Down there, a stray solar photon is a rare event."

Sandy shook her head. "You're missing the point. People like having origins."

"You're beginning to sound like a walker."

"I'm just doing it to get your attention. Change is necessary for growth, but some things we covet. Parts of our childhood are precious, and live within us always. We want to keep those memories alive — Mother, you explain it to him."

Barbara laughed. "I don't have to. He understands perfectly. It's you who doesn't understand him. He's only teasing."

Dane smirked. "I never could fool you, could I, Babs?"

She winked at him. "That's because I won't let you. Seriously, though, there are people on the Committee who advocate your viewpoint. The very people who would like to see you head the Committee. You have a vast amount of experience, both as an explorer and as an innovator. You're a very popular guy."

"Are you one of those who has been pushing my image in my absence, trying to get me to concede to taking office?"

"Why, Dane, are you charging me with subterfuge?"

"It wasn't an accusation. It was an acknowledgement of your prowess. You never do anything without a reason."

"None of us do. It's just that I'm consciously aware of mine. I admit that I'd like to see the Committee directed by stronger leadership."

"Why don't you run yourself?"

Barbara shook her head. "No, I don't enjoy the notoriety. I'm a rear-seat pilot. I like to make the computations, and let someone else push the buttons. But I'm aware that we need the strong influence that you could imbue into the Committee. With your backing, the System would be a better place to live, and I'd like to see that. I'd also like to see more emigration to the Jovian sphere. Do you know how much territory it would make available for new colonies?"

"Sure, and I'm all for it. Instead of crowding around this ball of dirt, we'd have the extremely stable Trojan lagrangian points, and all the heavy elements we needed from the asteroids that we'd be replacing."

"You underestimate Brunel. He's got more imagination than people realize — more than even *he* realizes. If you think the B-40 is an engineering feat, you should see what he's got planned for the future. Fred hollied me all about it. Do you want me to play it for you?"

Dane drew his legs under him, and kneaded his aching calves. "Just give me the highlights."

"He's designing a platform with a shield that rotates so fast that the centrifugal force will create nearly perfect angular orientation. It will be permanently stabilized. The *Ellison* will become old wave, a thing of the past."

"Hmmnn, a gyroscope - like a Settlement-sized child's top."

"And that's only a pathway to his other ideas." Sandy squeezed Dane's sore thigh muscles and made him wince. "He's a genius ahead of his time. He's going to revolutionize the entire System. But the details will have to wait until we get there. Fred said he keeps most of his ideas digitized because he's afraid they'll scare people off."

Dane nodded slowly. "You mean the Committee."

"You catch on fast. And let me tell you a little secret here. I think Mother has more up her kimono than her arm. Now, this hop is important to all of us, in a scientific way. But I think she really wants you to meet Brunel, not just to fly his GOmod-1, but to gain some insights into his scheme for the future. Am I right, Mother?"

Barbara only winked.

Chapter 9

"You can be told about a thing a hundred times. It is better to see it just once."

— Ho Chi Minh

As soon as the airlock cycled, Dane unsnapped his plastiglass helmet. "I hate spacesuits."

Barbara followed him in, and cast aspersive looks around the small interior of the *Phantom Jackal.* "And I hate starships." She doffed her headgear and shook out her bun. "They're so cramped."

"And I hate complainers." Sandy faked a whine as she shrugged out of her suit. She stored it in the locker along with the others. Her bodyalls were bright red, and fit her like a second layer of skin, although the stretch material allowed free movement. "I hope you two aren't going to keep it up all the way to Jupiter." After a pause, and two returning grimaces, she added, "You know what I mean."

Dane slipped lovingly into the pilot's seat. He switched on the auxiliaries, but did not lock himself into the cybercircuit. "Babs, there's plenty of room for three friendly people. After all, that's how starships are designed."

The control room was built around the three main viewscreens, mounted adjacently and faceted like three outside edges of an octagon. The pilot sat in the middle, flanked by the astro and the engineer, so that he could see all three screens. Each two-meter square monitor could be quartered twice, making sixteen display windows with access to the ship's entire data base.

When Dane's screen lit up, he switched to visual scanning. The image of the retreating shuttlecab was visible in four of the windows. He typed instructions for connective telemetry. Immediately, one sixteenth of the screen displayed a face with late shift shadow and drooping eyelids.

"We're all aboard, Jim. Safe and sound."

"Then I'm for cube and a bed." The cab pilot dug knuckles into his eyes. "Have a good hop. And bring back that box of silicon chips in one piece."

"I don't plan to change my itinerary now. Out." Dane switched off. He typed in a sequencing code that started the ship's function checks. The various screen slices went through a plethora of numerical processing procedures intended to represent actual flight trajectories. "If you ladies will take your seats, we'll get this bird out of its nest."

Sandy floated into the astro seat and clamped herself in. "Hmmnn, it looks exactly like the simulators."

"It's supposed to."

To his right, Barbara stared at the animated graphics that were evolving and mutating on her screens. "I'm glad the *Phantom Jackal* has been checked out by a real engineer. I might as well be reading hieroglyphics."

"Don't feel bad. I can't make much out of it either. Just let it run through its logic circuits. When it starts looping, you'll know it's on a repeat cycle."

Dane activated the linkage motor controls. The acceleration couch slid into the cybernetic umbilical, where surface contacts interfaced with the crystal lattice network. He pulled the EEG cap over his head; the life support system hooked to the output module and filled the upper left quarter of the screen with diagnostic data.

"Looks like I'm still alive."

He pulled the keyboard close to his abdomen and split the middle to his preset fifteen-degree comfort span. Dane's broad shoulders made a contiguous touchpad awkward: it forced a wrist bend that limited dexterity and increased fatigue. With the separate halves facing outward, he had better control of his typing abilities during the continuous demands of flying. He input specific coordinates.

"If everyone's locked in, I'll raise the sails and start pushing vacuum."

Dane's screen filled with spatial coordinates, then alternated with mascons and gravity wells. The smaller mass concentrations were merely objects to be avoided, but planetary bodies forced gravitational anomalies into the fabric of space-time that generated asymptotic agitation in the stardrive field that could disorient and damage the ship in the same way as an airplane catching a wingtip on a mountainside. They had to move on slow ion thrusters until they were out of range of the Earth-Moon system. Magnetic sails reached out and started stoking solar wind into the electrical accumulators.

"Okay, acceleration here we come."

Dane touched footpads that initiated the drive system. Outside the fuselage, the engine trunnions groaned under increasing stress. The engineering screen flashed systems analyses figures on everything from hull temperature to molecular bonding fatigue. If any of the microprocessing routines sensed danger, they flashed red.

"Is there still time to transfer to a cruise ship?"

"Mother, isn't this exciting?"

"I thought so when I was your age. Now I'm not so sure."

"Come on, Babs. It's just like old times."

"Except that those times are older for me than they are for you."

"Besides, on fusion drive, a commercial flight would take trevs to get to Jupiter." Dane sank into the formfoam as the *Phantom Jackal* passed the one gee mark. He shuddered at the thought of spending ten revs just to go five Astronomical Units: about forty light minutes. "Once we get this baby fired up, we'll be there in hours."

With the pulse beam focused and wound up to full excitement, acceleration increased rapidly. At two gees, with his apparent weight doubled, Dane locked his elbows into the foam pads. Wrist supports left his fingers free to dance across the keyboard. He delighted with the sensation of power at his fingertips. Scrolling viewscreens shouted data which his mind absorbed with trained efficiency. For the moment, he was at one with his machine.

"We're getting heavy now," he shouted with glee.

"How soon can we go on a diet?" Barbara quipped.

Sandy said, "Mascons are clear. We're still getting distortion from Earth, though."

"I can see that." Since she was not an engineer, and the outputting data meant little or nothing to her, Barbara switched her monitors to navigational display. "The *Phantom Jackal* is a lot more sensitive than the old *Light Brigade*, so I don't know how much perturbation she can withstand before translation."

"Let's get Sirius." Dane locked the attitude controls onto the Dog Star, and powered the gyros. Absolute location was now computed from outside the solar system. "Now remember, this is a short hop. We're not going to break quantum mechanics, just bend it a little. Five p-sol will get us there in plenty of time."

"Dane, I don't think I can take any — "

"Is the inertia pump primed?" Dane could just as easily have called the information on his own screen, but since Barbara was sitting in the engineering couch, and needed something to take her mind off her evident discomfort, he gave her the order to check.

"Readout states go."

At their present speed, they would all be dead and decayed before they reached their destination. But at five percent the speed of light, they could make it to the Jovian sphere in less than twelve hours, a little more to the Trojans on an elliptical course.

Sandy called out from her astrophysics display. "Gravity flux is negligible."

At three gees, Barbara was having difficulty forming words. "Dane, I don't need a hysterectomy. How much longer — "

"Get ready to translate." Dane calibrated the inertia pump to simulate a constant one gee. "She's riding high. All primed and ready to go. Let's pay our respects to Selkirk."

Dane trampled the foot pedal and the interlocked

thumb switch at the same time. In the microsecond lag between cause and effect, the onboard computer double and triple checked that all systems were go. Then, it shut down the ion thrusters at the same instant it energized the Selkirk, faster than light, stardrive.

For the briefest moment, Dane felt his stomach wrench itself out of place. His organs did a square dance, while his lungs aspirated orbiting comets whose flaming tails tickled his innards. His mouth filled with viscera, and only by swallowing hard did he keep it all in. His head exploded when his brain was replaced by ball lightning. His spine became a grounded lightning rod. Every ganglion was a charged wire, sending high voltage electricity through every nerve fiber in his body.

It ended so suddenly that the release from three-gee pressure made him feel as if he were floating off the couch: like a power down in translation failure. The viewscreen was flashing messages, but his eyes were too out of focus to read, and his brain too rattled to comprehend. Eventually, he recognized the weight approximation of one gee.

When his guts slid back down his esophagus, he said, "That wasn't so bad, now, was it?"

Barbara reached for a suction vac and vomited into the open end.

"Somehow, the simulators left that part of it out." Sandy deflected a ventilator over her face. The cool air soon evaporated the perspiration dripping down her brow. "Is FTL worse than p-sol?"

"The physics are different, but the physical reaction is the same."

"And after forty years, my tolerance hasn't changed." Barbara sprayed her mouth and throat with aromatic analgesics. "Dane, do you really think this is fun?"

"No, but it feels so good when it stops." When his eyes adjusted to the new reality, he saw that the viewscreen was displaying two magic words: Translation Successful. Silicon wafers carried preprogrammed orders and navigational instructions throughout the ship. Unless an emergency arose, the *Phantom Jackal* could fly itself completely around the Universe. He popped off the helmet and released his body and mind from the cybernetic controls. The ship was on its own.

"Mother! Are you all right?"

Dane sat up, and pushed himself to the floor by Barbara's side. "Babs. You're as pale as a white dwarf." He took her hand in his. "You're trembling, too."

She waved it off with her other hand. "I — I'm sorry. It's just — it brought back all those memories. Why I couldn't — ever — go on another hop. The fear . . . "

"Babs, I know translation is a little unsettling, but — "

"No, I'm not talking about physiological trauma. That's nothing worse than morning sickness." She lay back in the couch, staring up at the overhead. Her eyes were bloodshot; tiny vessels had burst during the acceleration phase. But the tears that formed were not from pain. "It's the utter — loneliness — of space. The emptiness of the Universe."

"Fear of the unknown is nothing — "

"No, it's not that. It's the fear of not getting back; being lost forever in the great vastness of the cosmos; drifting forever through the illimitable void, alone . . . "

Sandy jumped down from her couch, crossed the tiny room, and perched herself on the edge of her mother's couch. "Mother, I never knew you felt that way."

Barbara managed a weak grin. "I don't. I've only felt that way once — when I made that hop."

"But, our preflight encounter sessions never conveyed a hint — "

"And they never would. You see, I discovered something about myself that there was no other way of discovering. I had to experience it before I could know I had it — like not knowing about spacesickness until the gravity has been switched off. It's an idea, a concept, that doesn't enter your mind. So, I found out the hard way. The only way."

"But, Babs, why didn't you ever talk about it — at the time? Or did Fred — "

She shook her head. "Fred never knew. No one really knew. And at the time, I was too busy with my observations to understand my sense of — unease. It's a good thing I had my scientific distractions to keep me sane, or you might have had a basket case on your hands. No, I never figured it out until later. Until I came down from the exaltation of the discovery. Actually, not until after I wrote my papers. Then, the ugly truth descended upon me. Then I began to get afraid. Then I had to reconcile my feelings. And Dane, you weren't around then. You were off on another hop. I — "

"I'm sorry, Babs." Dane squeezed her hand. The tingling that coursed through his veins came straight from the heart. "I didn't know. I never took the time — "

"You had no way of knowing. It wasn't your fault. And that was when I realized how much I was in love with you. You brought me through that hop. Your off-beat humor, your stupid witicisms, your endless jokes, your — open and childlike outlook. Your willingness to reach out for whatever the Universe had to offer, and to hold it in the palm of your hand like a Greek god holding fire. You never felt the pain of the heat, because your mind was awed by the wonder of the flames. You have been a — a great inspiration to me. You have altered the direction of my life. In more ways than you know."

Dane tilted his head from side to side. "Babs, I don't know if I can take all this at once. I wish I knew this before. I might have — "

"It wouldn't have changed you a bit, and you know it. You have nothing to be sorry for. It's just a confession that, in my mind, is forty years too late. You see, even floaters, with their positive philosophy and open upbringing, can bury their feelings to the depth of unawareness."

Dane shrugged. "It's nice to know you're not perfect."

Barbara chuckled. Her tears dried up, and her eyes danced with life. "You see what I mean? It's so easy for you to make me laugh. You chase away my insecurities with such — nonchalance. That's what makes you so precious. And that's why, of all the people in the System, I'm glad you're going on this hop with my daughter. Otherwise, I'd be very concerned about her well-being."

"Oh, Mother. I'm a big girl now. I can take care of myself."

"I know you can. But I thought the same way until I encountered the great unknown. You never know what's inside you. Perhaps you've got more explorer's blood in you than astronomer's."

Sandy pursed her lips. "I've been thinking that I'd like my children to have a little more of that blood, too. I might even choose a man like — well, like Dane — to sire my brood."

Dane backed away to his own couch. "All right, this conversation is getting way out of control. I don't know what you two devious women are up to, but I've got something to say right now. I don't like being used — at least, not without my say so."

"That sounds like walker talk."

"Call it what you want. It bothers me when I become a pawn in people's machinations."

Barbara nodded thoughtfully. "Such as my interference in your Committee nomination?"

"That, too. But that isn't what I had in mind. No, I'm leaning in that direction anyway, so my opposition is merely in principle. What I'm concerned with is the misapplication of personal freedom standards under the pretext of exercising individual rights."

"I'm sure *you* know what you're talking about."

Sandy hunched her shoulders. "And what connection does this have with babies?"

"All right, let me explain." Dane gestured with his hands, something that natural born floaters had no need to do. When a person is raised in a communication culture that specializes in the use of language as the ultimate means to the end of misunderstanding, physical symbolism loses its applicability. "A few years back, between hops, I was walking along the main concourse of the *Sturgeon* when I met a woman I had encountered with. We talked, and decided to re-encounter since I had several trevs of fasttime coming up. Later, when I got to her cube, she introduced me to her son. He was a cute little tyke, full of pep, smart as a memory chip, with enough — Anyway, you know what I mean. So, she very casually introduced me as his — his father."

Dane lapsed into silence. Barbara and Sandy exchanged looks. "I still don't see the connection."

Dane stuttered before he could go on. "Don't you see? He was my son. And she never told me."

Barbara said, "Dane, she's not obligated to — "

"But she could have given me the courtesy — "

"No, Dane. No. That's your walker influence showing through. That child was not yours. He was *hers*. You happened to have supplied some of the genetic material to his makeup, but he didn't belong to you because you didn't contract with her to have him."

"But — isn't that wrong? Don't I have some say in whether or not I choose to be a father?"

"In being a father, yes. In being a sire, no. A father raises a child. All you did was help her to realize her dreams. She chose you, and you should be proud of that."

"Now, wait a minute. I've encountered women before who discussed with me the possibility of my giving them a child. That's different, because they were up front about it. But this woman didn't give me that respect. She just took him from me. She — "

"Dane, this isn't Earth, with its antiquated forms of child support and marriage commitment. You relinquished Victorian sexual mores when you left the ground. This woman didn't take anything from you."

"Babs, she *contrived* the whole encounter, right from the beginning. It was a scheme just to have my child."

"And were you any less because of it?"

"That's not the point."

Barbara slowly shook her head. "Then, I don't

understand. What *is* the point?"

Dane rolled his eyes, and sighed heavily. "She planned her motherhood with clinical precision."

"So? Sounds like a bright gal. Would you have her get pregnant by accident? That would be really stupid. Or do you believe parthenogenesis is the only acceptable method of procreation for women who choose not to form a more permanent relationship?"

Sandy said, "Some women who want children don't necessarily want mates. With a fulltime career, she may not have the time for — "

"You still don't get it."

Barbara said, "Remember your training. Bring out your feelings; don't hide them. Not from yourself. Say what it is that's bothering you. And if you aren't sure, can I help?" She touched her daughter's leg. "Can *we* help?"

Dane glanced around the cockpit, at everything but the two women he loved so much. "She — she — she led me to believe that — she cared for me. That our encounter was more than it was."

"No, you led yourself to believe that. And while it's probably true that she was not in love with you, it doesn't mean that she didn't care about you. You've certainly had enough experience to know that you weren't in love with all the women you encountered. Each encounter develops a bond of its own strength. It's not a predetermined standard."

Sandy went to Dane, and sat on the couch beside him. "Sweetie, you've taken a defensive attitude leftover from your Earth breeding. That woman paid you the highest compliment, and you don't even know it. You should be proud that she chose you among all the others available, both living and in the sperm bank. Perhaps she didn't love you. Perhaps she isn't even capable of that kind of love. But she admired you. She thought so highly of you that she wanted a man like you for her son. That's the positive way of looking at it."

Dane squeezed her thigh. "Thanks. I guess you're right. Both of you. Still, I'd have felt better if she had asked."

Barbara said, "Floaters may consider themselves on a higher plane than walkers, but we've still got a long way to go. Perhaps she *couldn't* ask. But what you can do, is understand."

Chapter 10

"Time is the essence of life, and once spent can never be recaptured. But life itself is ephemeral. Therefore, in human context, time is meaningless because it continues after life ceases to exist."

— G. G.

The shuttlebus operator ran his fingers over the touchpad, and kept a sharp eye on the forward monitors. "I'll be honest with you, Mr. Gerrace. Even though I've done this manually on a simulator without crashing, if the docking computer ever malfunctioned, I'd probably drift till it was repaired. Matching a rotating vector is pretty tricky, despite peripheral thrust deflectors."

Dane held onto the pilot chair headrest, and peered over the pilot's curly locks at the large viewscreen. The lengthwise view of the forty-kilometer-long cylinder bestowed an uncomfortable perspective: the other end of the Settlement seemed to converge on a point. As the bus maneuvered close to the longitudinal surface, it could have been a mosquito buzzing across an elephant's textured hide.

Then the length disappeared, and in front of them was the broad circular endcap. The B-40 spun considerably slower than B-15 cylinders because its longer radius required less rotational velocity to simulate one gee on its inner shell. Still, the shuttlebus had to match two directional equations as the docking bay at the endcap's terminus described an arc.

"You could never do this with a freighter, or a cruise ship. Side thrusters can't move the hull fast enough. That's why we've got a revolving dock loader for the big ships."

Dane glanced at the side viewscreen. A fifteen-kilometer platform could get by on two docking bays, one at the center of each endcap. But the supplies and personnel transfer required for a platform of this size demanded a much larger loading capacity. Brunel had designed a free-floating cylindrical complex in the form of a pistol barrel, except that each cartridge chamber held a space vehicle warped into place by tugships. The asteroid-sized contrivance could then be winched down a central guy cable by short bursts from a low energy fusion drive. Up to five ships at a time could thus be anchored to podbays in each endcap.

"It's amazing what a box full of crystalline solid-state semiconductors can do. But I'll bet if this bus had quicker switching capability, I could program a trigonometric function that would dock it with just its power thrusters."

The pilot harrumphed. "That's why you're a starship captain, and I'm just a bus driver. Besides, this is about as far away as I want to get from good old Sol. You know how many light amplifiers you need to get a decent suntan out here?"

Dane laughed. "Look at the dim side: at least you don't need UV visors."

"Yeah, but it's scary being this close to the heliosphere. We've got special shielding problems because of cosmic ray incursion, to say nothing of secondary X-radiation production. And I don't trust those plasma core shields. Because of the size, there's too much magnetic flux to suit me. Nobody's proved to me these new shuttle shells are doing their job."

"What happens to all the produced ions?"

"Dumped spaceside. They're all out there, zipping around between here and Saturn."

"Out of sight, out of mind."

The shuttlebus ramp loomed in the forward viewscreen. It was still out of phase and moving faster in its circular orientation than the bus. As the distance closed and the vectors coincided, the glide path locked on target with the magnetic pistons. The shuttlebus rolled for centrifugal alignment.

"Mr. Gerrace, the gravity's growing exponentially now. We're almost matched."

"Okay, I'll get back to my seat. Thanks for the front row view."

"Any time."

Dane worked his way forward into the passenger compartment, which was full of EVA constructors and technicians ending their work shift. They all wore spacesuits, and carried their helmets in their hands. On its way in, the shuttlebus had stopped by the orbiting *Phantom Jackal*, deployed a flexible transfer tube, and embarked Dane and the Mettlesons.

Dane eased into the contoured seat between Sandy and Barbara. "Helmets off to Brunel. It's an incredible piece of engineering."

"Full of innovations, too," Barbara said. "Solar panels would have to be incredibly large to fuel a Settlement of this size. Instead, its got magnetic scoops collecting subatomic particles — "

Dane felt himself sinking into the formfoam. "Like a ramjet?"

Barbara nodded. "Except that the collector heads work in both directions, trapping the solar wind as well as cosmic radiation. It converts protons and electrons into reaction mass. The air filtration system works on the molecular level, so any dust in the air larger than diatomic oxygen is siphoned out and automatically ejected into space. And they did away with IDcards: they use whorl patterns instead of codereads for all personal accounting. Instead of wiping your card across a viewing screen, you can touch it with any finger."

"That makes shopping easy."

Sandy pointed to the local viewscreen. A thin, cadaverous face stared out from an enclosed teleview booth. "I think you've got a long-time friend on the line."

Dane quickly touched the flashing annunciator lens. "Fred, you old gun-of-a-sun. How the hell are you?"

"Doing well. I see you've brought the family with you. Hello, Barbara. Hi, Sandy."

"It's nice to see you again."

"Hello, Fred."

Dane said, "Where are you? Is Brunel going to let you out of his sight long enough to meet us?"

"I'm in the dock lounge now. How soon will you arrive?"

Dane felt a grating vibration through the hull. "I think we're here."

"Fine, I'll fade out and meet you in the transfer compartment"

"Gotcha." As the image dissolved into darkness, Dane unsnapped the safety harness. "Good old Fred. It's been so long since we've communicated. And his face had wrinkles." Dane paused for a moment of introspection. "You know, I've got a strange feeling that life is passing me by, and I'm no longer part of it."

Sandy stood and joined the crowd that was pushing and shoving toward the forward hatch. "Slowtime psychosis, or instantaneity perception. I just took a course in it to prepare myself for the big hop. It's defined as 'temporal disorientation caused by the seemingly rapid progress of events in a compressed stream of time, and interpreted mentally as an aberration of observation faculties.' Patients with fevers, or on strong pain medication, experience it as well. As consciousness comes and goes, they see their period of illness as a series of disconnected occurrences which don't make sense in the overall pattern of reality."

"They didn't have courses like that when I started hopping."

"They didn't need them then. You were among the first in the interstellar program. At that time — objectively speaking — psychologists weren't sure how time contraction was going to affect people. The only advice they could offer was that Exploteam members should undergo group self-actualization therapy among prospective teams before each hop."

"You sound as if you're reading that off a texttape."

Barbara said proudly, "She's a quick learner, a high achiever, and highly motivated."

Dane squeezed through the hatch along with the

rest of the mob. "Yes. Gifted like her mother, in too many ways."

"Stop it, both of you. You'll give me a complex."

"Sandy, you're complex enough already. I don't want you catching up with your mother. Now, if you only — Hey, Fred! Over here."

Dane grabbed onto both women's hands and dragged them through the surging mob toward the towering form of the *Phantom Jackal's* ex-engineer. He stood off to one side, wearing a red jumpsuit that was mostly small patches of thread stitching together an endless array of bulging, self-sealing pockets.

Dane strode right to Fred and threw his arms around him. He slapped him hard on the back. "Fred, it's good to see you again. I've been looking forward to this for a long time."

"It's been longer for me," Fred said, grinning broadly. "Obtime moves so slowly."

"So I'm told."

"Barbara, how wonderful to see you." Fred exchanged hugs with her, then held her out at arm's length. "You haven't changed a bit."

"Thank you, Fred. I see you've managed to keep your youthful figure despite the amount of freefall time."

"Living on the Jovian sphere has also diminished the number of times I've circled the sun. I've experienced less years than you, and therefore I'm not as old."

Dane smirked, and shook his head. He glanced at Sandy while he jerked a thumb at Fred. "I would laugh, except he's so brilliant that he can probably prove it mathematically."

"And this must be Sandy." Fred reached out and took both of her hands in his. "You're the spitting image of your mother."

"Not only that, they sound alike, act alike, and think alike. I can never tell which one I'm talking with till I see their hair. The resemblance is frightening."

"It's nice to meet you, Fred. Mother has told me so

much about you."

Fred smiled. "Good things, I hope."

"Mostly."

Fred rolled his eyes in Barbara's direction.

"I only told her the truth."

"But which part of it?"

"Fred, you shame me."

"That's not possible." Fred glanced at his wristrad. "We don't have much time. I told Brunel you were here, so he's expecting us immediately. He doesn't like to be kept waiting."

Dane said, "Sounds like an impatient, imperious man."

"You won't like him. No one does." Fred led them to a tube entrance and pressed the call pad. "Even I don't like him."

"And that's saying something. I always thought you were a direct descendant of Will Rogers."

"Who's that?"

"A twentieth-century humorist whose most famous saying was, 'I never met a man I didn't like'."

"It's a good thing he never met Brunel, or he'd have to amend that statement." The tube hatch opened and Fred led them inside. "Are you still reading Earth literature?"

"What can I say? I like reading books more than watching the holly, and today's creative artists write strictly for the visual media." He tapped his tummy pouch. "I picked up a whole bunch of books from the Central Museum Library on Earth. Enough to last me this hop and several others — if I take any more."

"I heard a rumor that you were thinking of accepting the Committee offer. Is there any truth to that?"

Dane put an arm around Barbara's shoulder and gave her a peck on the head. "Ask my press agent. She seems to think that she can make my decisions for me."

Barbara stuck her arm through a wallgrip. "At this stage in his career, I think he could do a lot more good advising the Committee on the direction of scientific exploration and the aims of technological advancement, than flitting about the Galaxy trying to get his pants warmed."

Dane pointed a finger at her. "See what I mean? She's got my entire future mapped out for me. I *have* to hop to the other side of the Galaxy just to escape her influence."

"What he doesn't know is that the psychological force is the strongest force in the Universe, with an intensity that actually *increases* with distance."

Dane scowled. "The hypothetical fifth force, a source of power defined as 'Absence makes the heart grow fonder.' Another old Earth phrase. Seriously, Fred, I've heard an awful lot about this Brunel. Is he as unmanageable as the holly makes him out to be?"

"He is — rather unique."

"And typical of you to be so oblique." Dane found himself floating off Barbara's shoulder. He slipped a foot and a hand into wallgrips. "Aside from the fact that he's a genius, I've heard he's pretty quirky."

"Delicately put. Yes, he is a genius, and it's been a great privilege to work with him. He sees great concepts as easily as you see these padded panels. And where air is invisible to you except as an intellectual deduction, he can divine molecular interaction. He works a twenty-hour rev, and subliminates during the other four. He has so many plans and projects in the works that it takes a full staff just to categorize them all. And he does not think only on the broad scope. Not only does he have an overview of his inventions, such as this Settlement, but he has perfect recall about its most miniscule working parts. He is absolutely driven.

"On the personality level he is less attractive. He dominates any conversation with bluntness and incision. He accepts no failure of any kind, will not allow incompetence or lack of expertise, and cannot suffer less than total commitment from his employees. No one goes off shift when he is around — they wait until he is out of sight before leaving. But he is so enveloped in his own mind, and his mainframe, that he seldom notices them gone. He knows hardly anyone by name: people are merely devices to him, human rather than mechanical tools to get the job done."

"I can't wait to meet him — or should I say 'it'? He sounds more like a machine than a man."

"His mind works like computer, totally devoid of feeling and with complete attention to synaptic routine. But I wouldn't make any comments — " Fred's wristrad buzzed, and he put it up to his lips. "Malkowitz."

A deep, base voice shouted over the microspeaker with a volume that filled the capsule. "Fred, where the hell are you?"

The hatch opened without a hiss. Outside, in the z-gee area, was a bustling computer center that stretched as far as the eye could see. Tier upon tier of data input personnel stood in front of banks of terminals, monitors, switches, annunciator lights, and touchpads. The entire complex was designed with singular orientation, like a one gee establishment, with catwalks and multiple levels. Most workers maintained a vertical attitude in front of their consoles where, without gravity, it was not necessary to sit in order to relax physically.

"Right in front of you." Fred smiled, and waved.

In the middle of the room, surrounded by a circular array of viewscreens, a bearded, scraggly haired man shouted into a telecom. The voice came out over the wristrad speaker, but not through the atmosphere. "Do not just stand there gawking, bring them in so I can talk to them."

Fred did not acknowledge. He lowered his arm, and said aloud, "We're still under low pressure, so, if he ever gets too irritating for you, just get back about twenty feet. Even *his* voice can't travel that far. And you'd better put on some stippers." He took four pairs of sticky slippers from a pouch within the tube capsule, and passed them out. "He doesn't like people floating around him."

"I can see this is going to be fun." Dane slipped on the single sized, soft material booties and cinched the ankle tab tight. When he touched them to the deck, the suregrip soles adhered silently to the blue carpeting. "I hope it's a short interview."

Sandy said, "I've been looking forward to meeting him. After all, he has given me the opportunity to go on this hop."

Barbara took the first tentative step into the operations room. "Fred had quite a bit to do with it, too. Didn't you, Fred?"

"If you say so."

"You're so humble, it hurts." As he padded along behind Barbara, Dane said in aside to Sandy, "Did I tell you that we used to call him Derf? Not because he knew everything forward and backward, but because — "

Brunel's booming voice drowned out further conversation. "Fred, did you complete that degenerate matter program? I need the calculations for the Jupiter Project. For god's sake, wipe that grin off your face."

Barbara ignored Brunel's loud facade, and extended her hand. "Barbara Mettleson. I've been looking forward to this — "

"I know who you are! You submitted a proposal to send an automated GOmod into the Coal-Sack region. I do not know the details — "

This time Barbara interrupted. "Then I'll refresh your memory — or enlighten your ignorance. The Coal-Sack is a dark nebula in the constellation of the Southern Cross, a vast umbra which blocks out the stars behind it with utter totality. It's long been theorized — "

"I do not care about astro —

"Excuse me, Brunel. I'm speaking. It's not polite to interrupt." Brunel paused with his mouth agape.

"It's long been theorized that the Coal-Sack nebula is a cloud of interstellar dust. But recent spectographic analyses have been inconclusive — in addition to free hydrogen, it shows a concentration of heavy elements in a manner reminiscent of Sandy's stellob. But this is on a completely different scale. My guess is that it's a cluster of several hundred interacting stars in extremely close proximity, perhaps only several light-years across. And for some reason, taken in conjunction with the broad separation of the Coal-Sack from any neighboring clusters or stars, this dark island was formed by an as yet unknown law of stellar physics. It is a cloud dense enough to obscure all the light of the interior stars, as well as broad enough to absorb light entering it."

Barbara smiled, and raised an eyebrow.

Brunel sucked on the straw end of a foodtube that was tucked into his jacket pocket. "Are you quite finished?"

"You may comment before I continue."

Brunel's eyes brooded like binary white dwarfs. "I assume there is a point to all this. Are you trying to outbid your daughter?"

Barbara's smile grew into a smirk. "I am making several points: long term, short range, and immediate necessity. In that order, the Coal-Sack nebula is too far away for a manned flight in our present state of technology. However, I think it is an important phenomenon that needs to be studied, and that may lead to a greater understanding of cosmology, and our place in the Universe. I would like to impress upon you that, when future versions of the GOmod-1 are ready for unmanned exploration, the Coal-Sack region should receive priority."

Brunel typed quickly on his lap pad, and said grudgingly, "So noted."

"Secondly, I know how hard you've been pushing your projects, especially the GOmod-1, and I'm concerned about the safety of a test hop. I understand that you have personal anxieties about its return — that it might be lost in the interstellar void — and I think that precautions should be taken before the flight to insure that its operating systems are functioning properly. I don't want to lose — " She glanced at the three people alongside her. " — anyone, especially those close to me, by dispatching it prematurely."

Brunel folded his arms, and took another suck on his tube. "I can assure you that the GOmod-1 is completely prepared for this flight. I have checked it over myself. In addition, it is in my best interests that nothing — absolutely nothing — go wrong with the GOmod-1, or that any ill should come to its flight crew. If it did, my own position would be at as great a risk. I stake more than my reputation upon a successful mission. May we get on with — "

Barbara kept smiling. "Thirdly, I wanted to impress upon you that your abrasive personality is not appreciated, that I will not allow you to badger me or anyone else in my presence, and that I insist on a less mechanical and more humanitarian approach in the conversations we will undoubtedly have during the course of our relationship. I want to instill a pattern of respect for the human equation, and I demand that you cease your abusive, bullying, dictatorial behavior."

Not a keyboard was touched in that vast, freefall chamber. Not a single program was running. Even the electrons were stunned into stillness. The comptechs who were out of hearing range held microreceptors to their ears, or were keyed into the speaker system on Brunel's console. A pin left floating could have been heard by the stray currents of air that pushed against it.

Brunel was, probably for the first time in his long career, speechless. His foot tube touched the corner of his mouth, but his jaw was slack and his eyes had collapsed to tiny black holes.

Dane stared at Barbara, aghast. Despite the lack of gravity, his heart sank into his stomach like a ball of neutronium. His whole body tingled with explosive anticipation. "Babs. Brunel. Now, we've all been under a strain — maybe working a little too hard, or suffering the aftershock of FTL translation. But let's not slip out of orbit. Why don't we calm down, relax, maybe work out the old muscles to relieve the tension, and take it from there. Brunel, why don't we take a walk around the Settlement, and you can show us the sights — and your engineering marvels. How about it?"

Brunel very slowly unfolded his arms. He gripped the sides of his chair and activated the microthrusters. A tiny jet of expulsed air set him in motion. He rose upward from behind the console, past the stacked monitors. More of his body became visible. But where his legs should have been dangling over the edge of the seat, there was nothing to be seen.

"I find walking difficult, these revs." He folded back the lap pad on its hingeplate. Underneath, there was no lap.

Chapter 11

"The universe is not required to be in perfect harmony with human ambition."

— Carl Sagan

Only the fact that Dane was standing in z-gee prevented him from falling down. His legs were twitching like Galvani's frogs. "Babs, what the hell are you trying to do? Get us keelhauled in vacuum without our suits?"

Barbara smiled pleasantly, as if nothing were wrong. "I don't want Brunel to get out of hand, or take advantage of the situation. I had to put him in his place right at the start."

"Well done, too, Mother. Although, I wish you had warned us."

"I like surprises. But Dane, your comment was decidedly improper. Brunel is naturally sensitive about his disability."

"How the hell did I know that he was a double amputee? It isn't in any of the biotapes."

Sandy said, "Dane, you'd better get your datafiles revised. That accident happened over ten years ago, when he was building the science cylinder at Venus."

Barbara explained, "He was pinched between a shuttlecab and an atmosphere siphon that he was developing. It completely severed his lower body. Zero temp and suit sealant prevented him from bleeding to death immediately. The cab pilot stuffed him into a survival balloon and raced him back to the platform medical facilities. His legs spiraled off into space, and were lost, but the doctors said it wouldn't have mattered anyway: the pelvic girdle was crushed beyond reconstruction. And the lower organs were mangled. The bottom of his chair is a colostomy tank."

Dane shook his head. "I had no idea. I read his public file, and even traced some of the references. But there was no mention . . . "

"He doesn't talk about his physical handicap, and the compgraphs always show him sitting." Barbara pulled Dane along by the elbow. "You must have been away for a couple years around that time."

Sandy kept a firm grip on his other elbow. "I'm sure he'll understand, once you've explained it to him."

"I don't know if I can ever face him again. Maybe I'll just take the GOmod-1 and hop completely around the Universe. By the time I get back the System will be a burned-out cinder, and all will be forgotten."

"Don't even think about it, Hot Pants," Barbara said. "Now, Fred's signaling us, so, let's see if he's mollified his mentor."

Dane walked as slowly as his escorts would allow. He felt like a maladjusted child forced to apologize to his victim. He was not just embarrassed at his unconscionable but unconscious solecism, he was abhorred by the accidental mental anguish that he had unknowingly inflicted.

Brunel hovered at the central panel of a hundred-meter-diameter picture window that beheld the immense interior of the cylinder. The back of the air-chair faced Dane. With controlled bursts, the chair rotated until the bearded master engineer faced Dane with jaw outthrust and eyes ablaze.

"Brunel, I apologize for my egregious — "

"Forget it, Dane. I am well aware of the amount of slowtime that you have logged in the past four decades. Certainly, in the overall scheme of things, my injuries are a minor reference in System files, and undoubtedly escaped your notice. Your locution was less than eloquent, but undoubtedly unintended. Yours, however, Dr. Mettleson, was more pertinent and intentional, and in that respect requires great thought. In a short amount of time, I have given your declarations that thought, and, within certain limitations, and absolving both parties of primary emotional response, I must in the light of rationality admit that your statements have some foundation in fact. I am not used to dealing with people of your caliber."

Fred added, "That's about as close to a proclamation of acquiescence as you're likely to get."

Brunel scowled at Fred. "I do not need an interpreter. I have lost the ability to walk, not to talk." To Barbara, "We must work together if we are to see great projects come to fruition. In order to prove my sincerity, I extend my hand in greeting." He powered the chair toward Barbara, and stopped within touching distance.

Barbara touched his palm with hers. "In my estimation, your greatness has just risen in scale."

"I am happy to learn that you can be as gracious as you can be aggressive." The chair moved sideways, and halted in front of Dane. "And to prove to you, and to Fred, that I do in fact have a sense of humor, I hope that this relationship has not gotten off, shall we say, on the wrong foot."

Brunel's expression did not leaven, but Dane thought he detected a glistening in the engineer's eyes that was of less than solar prominence. Dane could not help but grin maniacally as they touched palms. "Brunel, tack a notch on for me, too."

"Consider it — 'tacked'." The chair vectored toward Sandy. Brunel's hand stretched out again. "My dear, you have your mother's beauty, but I hope you have your own serenity."

Sandy smiled innocently. "Thank you. I just want to say that I stand behind everything my mother says, and does. I'm overjoyed that you chose my proposal among the many that you must have received."

"You can thank Fred for that. He is the one who brought it to my attention. I know very little astronomy or astrophysics, other than what is taught in grade school — and the elementary calculus that deals with it. I have channeled all my energies into my chosen profession, and do not bother cluttering my mind with the impedimenta of other trades."

"I don't know much about engineering, either. I'm simply fascinated by this Settlement: its size, its beauty, its grandeur. And I do appreciate the ingenuity of design. The twin shells with ambi-rotational surfaces is an enthralling idea."

Brunel reversed his chair and spun it around so that he faced the picture window. He moved up to the clear surface. "It is nothing. Simplicity itself. Smaller minds have never looked at the mechanics of living in space with any fluidity. Their dense brains think only of solids. They have no more imagination than a wafer of silicon diodes."

Dane ripped his stippers off the floor, and padded up to the observation window. The computer center was a longitudinal monolith projecting inward from the hub of the endcap the distance of a kilometer. Because rotational stress was almost nonexistent, the guy cables running from the tip of the structure to the platform's circular corner, two and a half kilometers away, seemed impossibly thin and puny. To Dane, in comparison, the cables were as gossamerlike as the strands of a spider's web.

Looking along the length of the cylinder, Dane felt like an ant peering up the barrel of a giant telescope. In the distance, despite the crystal clarity of the air, parks, houses, and public buildings grew indistinguishable from the pattern of wavy thoroughfares. Splotches of color attested to the relief that was too far away to be evident.

Straight down below (or upward, or sideways, or in any direction away from the window) he could discern rooftops and yards and the miniscule moving dots that under magnification would resolve into the heads of people. Yet, there was an indifference, a utilitarian appearance that was hostile, and unmistakable in the absence of life. Without the green glow of Earth, without the touch of home, the Settlement was a metallic desert as antagonistic and as inhospitable as the cold surface of the Moon.

Trees had not yet been planted, grass had not yet been sown, gardens had not yet been cultivated. The barren landscape had yet to be suffused with the organic equation that was so important to the human psyche. Although man's intellect was a product of his own making, his instinct was still very much a part of him. He was unable to divorce himself from the bonds that tied him to the Earth. Every platform in space was a microcosm of the past, a miniature ecology which man, because of his deep-rooted sense of belonging to the land from which he had sprung, carried with him. The sense of community which he felt, as an integral portion of his environment, came about by the constant reminder of his ancestral abode. Vegetation was more than ornament and decoration; it was an anesthetic.

Brunel sucked on a foodtube. "People perceive an object merely as a whole, not as a constituent of its parts. They think of this window as a solid unit — " He tapped the thick pane with his knuckles. " — instead of as an intricate molecular matrix held not together, but apart, by atomic forces which build solid matter out of largely empty space."

He held his hands in front of him, fingers extended and grouped, with the tips touching. "I do not take a rigid cylinder and add a rotating member. This structure is not a hybrid. Instead, I take two separate cylinders, each with only one endcap, and I meld them as one would take two mismatched drinking glasses, with mouths facing, and insert one into the other." He collapsed the fingers of one hand within the fingers of the other, and pushed them into the palm. "I construct bearing points, and I induce movement." He turned his hands in opposite directions. "Differing speeds yield the same centrifugal force on each inner surface."

"Wonderful. Simply wonderful," Sandy said enthusiastically.

Brunel continued to stare over the weightless precipice, like a lord over his creation. "No, it is wonderfully simple. It is not a miraculous achievement. It is elementary engineering: bigger than the B-15's that my father built, but no different."

"Not from where I stand. Whoops. Sorry." Dane rolled his eyes at Barbara, his jaw clenched at his unfortunate choice of words. "I mean, I think it's a fantastic application of sound, scientific principles combined with efficient and economical design."

Brunel looked up sharply. "That is what I said. You have merely defined the term in greater detail. But that does not make the B-40 unique. Oh, the greater dimension imposed topographical changes. I have placed all the farming facilities in the outer shell, where people refuse to live because of the moving inner shell overhead. That freed quite a bit of the inner shell for domestic cubes. Overall, of course, it does not add space, it merely reapportions it. People are so fickle, they may not like the idea of having the agricultural settings out of sight."

Barbara placed her head against Dane's shoulder, but never took her eyes off the sweeping panorama below, above, and around their artificial aerie. "Is it true that you're going to have an open air zoo, with real live animals?"

Brunel typed furiously on his lap pad, and issued subvocal commands into a throat mike, before answering. "Against my better judgment, and assuming that the inner Settlements are willing to share their precious zygotes. Of course, I will have to build gestation facilities as well as zoology labs. I don't understand why people are not satisfied with the holographic menageries. With pumped in odors, they smell as well as look like the real thing. But for some reason, people must touch the beasts. Before you know it, they will want to bring pets. I am forced to concede to the public's wishes because in order for the settlement of the Jovian sphere to succeed, I must convince the populace to migrate."

Dane said, "I would think they'd flock to live in the largest construct in the history of mankind."

"Reason tells you so, but emotion dictates otherwise. I have had to hire architects with a flare for space-wasting artistry, to garnish the residential regions with playgrounds and amusement centers, to add woodlands and arboretums. If people could only guide their botanical predilections toward consumption instead of cosmetics, I would have more room for the kind of plants that count: for mineral extraction, distillation, and carbochlorination; for industrial machinery; for production equipment; for scientific research facilities."

"Brunel, you can't lose sight of who this Settlement is being built for. People, no matter where they live, are still people. By their nature — by *our* nature — they need certain settings and group activities the same way flowers need soil and sunlight. Being a more basic form of life, you can feed plants with nutrient solutions and artificial lighting. But you can't expect human beings to sleep in coffins, and live in boxes. People are not simply more complicated biological machines — they're living, breathing, growing, thinking, *feeling* organisms."

"Or unthinking, as the case may be. I am continuously frustrated by the illogical manner of human beings, and their whims and ways. Do you know, they even want to give the B-40 a name that does not define its parameters: the *O'Neill*, a useless sentimentality."

"But that's the kind of thing that makes a house a home, that makes a platform a community. If you want this Settlement to succeed, if you want to achieve your ambitions of life in the Jovian sphere, you have to factor in the human equation. Don't lose sight of the original purpose of living in space. It isn't an exercise in vacuum vapor fabrication, or a metallurgical experiment in torsion design. It's a way of expanding man's horizons beyond the bars of his crib. Engineering is not an end in itself, it's merely a means to an end."

Brunel sucked again on his foodtube. "You have not disappointed me — any of you. I can see that you are all thinkers, that you are all open-minded and strong-willed. I like that in a person. I am surrounded by so many sycophants, incompetents, bunglers, and fools, that I am often lonely for the company of intellectuals and perfectionists like myself. You are, perhaps, somewhat too passionate for one of my sensibilities, but that in itself I honor as an acceptably human trait."

Dane winked at Fred, and exhibited a quirky smile. "I like you, too. So, now that we've cleared the vacuum, tell me a little about your Galactic Odyssey starship."

Brunel continued eating. "It is nothing innovative. It

is simply a larger and faster version of previous models, with a few modifications."

"Your idea of simplicity is not the same as mine."

Brunel ignored Dane's statement while he typed thoughts and ideas on his lap pad. For the moment, he was lost in the intricacies of his own mind, without the impingement of external stimuli.

Fred tapped his temple with his index finger. "He'll be back."

"Fred, does this happen often?"

"Yes, although he's been more communicative today than I've ever seen him. I think the involvement with new and powerful personalities came as a shock. He's stifled from working with people who tolerate him without interacting. He gets along much better with electronic circuitry."

"That's not very healthy," Barbara said.

"No, but it's productive. You see, his mind works differently from ours."

"I'll say. He's more eccentric than Hidalgo." Dane made reference to the asteroid whose inclination to the plane of the ecliptic was forty-three degrees, and whose eccentricity was point six three. "Can — can he hear us?"

"Every word," Brunel said abruptly. He rotated his chair and faced his companions. "Excuse me, but I cannot spend the entire rev at idle chatter. Everything you need to know is in the Operating Manual on disk."

"How about a quick overview?"

Brunel scowled, glanced at Barbara, rolled his dark eyes, and sighed. "I am certain that a man of your experience will adapt quite readily. Without making radical alterations in the basic design, I have merely added refinements that increase the GOmod-1's safety, comfort, and overall performance."

"Such as?"

Brunel took another draught from his foodtube. "If you insist. Since the basic model is intended for unmanned flight, I installed self-analyzing circuits throughout, and automatic rerouting backups. All components are fully modularized for remote replacement. Programming instructions are quadruplicated and shielded, so there is no possibility of magnetic data misalignment such as what occurred to you and Fred and Professor Mettleson."

"Please, call me Barbara."

Brunel harrumphed. "Also a derivative of that classic flight is interphasing between the stardrive and the inertia pump through the shield circuits. During real-time, power can be easily diverted for increased protection from cosmic radiation, heat, even gas clouds if the speed of the vehicle and the density of the matter is less than output demands. Your solution to the approach problems of that neutron star was little less than ingenious. I have taken that genius and have implemented it in the GOmod-1's defense network."

Dane smiled broadly. "I don't think I'm as brilliant as a first magnitude star, but I'll accept the compliment."

"Since the prototype is a fledgling out for its first flight, I incorporated a removable manual operation module in the hull. All acceleration couches are fitted with ergonomic monitors which calculate muscular stress points. The pilot's viewscreen is implanted with neurosensors and handeye manipulators: you merely look at the function on the screen which you wish activated, press the engage button, and the computer does the rest. It is much faster than manual input." Brunel paused to take a drink from his straw. "Must I continue?"

Dane pursed his lips. "Brunel, you've aroused my curiosity. I can't wait to get that baby's pulse beam burning through the cosmos. Not only that, it'll be a pleasure to work with my old team again. Fred doesn't seem to have changed a bit, except for his hair color. And Sandy is merely a reflection of her mother in both brains and beauty. When do we hop?"

"I appreciate your enthusiasm. But you are jumping the jet a bit. While Fred has helped me in the design and construction of the GOmod-1, and understands its systems better than anyone other than myself, his skills are needed elsewhere. He cannot afford to be away from his construction duties for the extended period of time that this flight will consume."

Fred stepped forward to tap Brunel's lap pad. "I have prepared the list of eligible systems specialists."

Brunel prevented his finger from keying the codes. "That will not be necessary. I cannot allow anything to go wrong with this flight. Too much depends upon its success. The flight engineering officer must be intimately acquainted with every aspect of the GOmod-1, including its functions, capabilities, and, of course, emergency repair. There is only one person who is competent to fill such a position."

Brunel paused, and tilted his head to grasp the straw between his lips. He emptied the foodtube of its contents. "*I* am that person."

Chapter 12

"The advance of science and technology is cumulative, and each advance tends to encourage a more rapid further advance."

— Isaac Asimov

"This is damned foolishness: theological nonsense leftover from the retarded era of Catholicism." Brunel whizzed about his private study in his airchair. He switched on a bank of monitors and keyed instructions through his lap pad. "With man's rational approach to life and his place in the Universe, and with a realistic outlook based on logic and intelligence instead of fear and belief, he no longer needs the irrationality of religion. Why, then, must we inflict upon ourselves this ancient ritual of confession?"

Sandy floated alongside the upright aligned kitchen equipment. She took a foodbar out of the dispenser. "It has nothing to do with divinity, or the nature of the soul. Those conceits are long since dead and — "

"Not on Earth," Dane interrupted. "They have more orthodoxies than you can count with a mainframe."

"I mean among the Settlements. First of all, you have to give credit to the ancient Catholics for their prescience in comprehending the relief of the heart that is afforded by the outpouring of pent-up and often unrecognized emotional distress. Confession is the great catharsis, especially when shared with people who have the same susceptibilities."

"You feel good, and you make others feel good," Dane agreed. He floated slowly around Brunel's private suite, noting cases full of engineering disks, and the strictly utilitarian furnishings. "Surely you haven't forgotten the joy of human companionship. Don't you remember the sense of rapport you had with your children's mothers?"

"That was purely a sexual drive, a pain as necessary

of release as the pain of hunger." As if to drive home his point, Brunel reached out with his lips for the ever-present straw, and sucked a greenish-red liquid out of the foodtube that was tucked into his jacket pocket. "I cannot create while aching with the distractions of physical discomfort. For example, in opposition to accepted standards of consumption, I begin lunch immediately after breakfast, and continue it until immediately prior to dinner. By keeping a constant trickle of food circulating through my system, I can concentrate on the tasks at hand. Sex was the same way: a mechanical function for which I found relief as soon as the urge became apparent."

Sandy shook her head sadly. "Then you missed the most important joy of sex: the mutual satisfaction and closeness, and the sympathy of love and friendship. On whatever level a particular encounter occurs, the positive rewards of emotional bonding far outweigh the physical satisfaction. Although, that's not so bad, either."

"Brunel, remember that you're a man, not a machine." Dane pushed himself off a horizontal wall-pad, and joined Sandy next to the countertop. He held tightly onto her hand. "Caring is part of humanity, and that's what an encounter session is all about. It puts you in touch not only with your own feelings, but with the feelings of others with whom you're about to spend a great deal of time in close confinement. People do it all the time. And they enjoy it not just because of the pleasure that they transmit to others, but because of the catharsis that comes from the release of their own subconscious inhibitions. It's for your own well being, as well as for the well being of your companions. Exploteam has developed stringent guidelines through decades of research. Without complete honesty and understanding among team members, a starhop could meet complete disaster not because of mechanical failure, but because of a weakness in the human component. So I'll tell you again: unless we have this encounter session, unless we bring into the open your real motivation for taking this hop, I won't go."

"Brunel, I'm afraid that that goes for me, as well," Sandy said. "Stellar evolution may be an exact science, but human interaction is less than predictable."

"Once we board that starship, we're more than three individuals doing their jobs — like three programs in a computer sequence. We become a unit, a team, a family. You can't ship out with strangers whose personalities are masks: cover-ups for what they don't understand of themselves. *That* is real foolishness: the termination of personal growth."

Brunel raised his voice, but from the other side of the low pressure room only the harshness was evident. "I am an engineer, and only an engineer. Everything I do is a consequence of my work. And my motivation is exactingly simple: how better to accomplish my chosen assignments. I have neither the time nor the inclination for psychoanalysis in any of its forms. Now, if you will excuse me, I have projects that need my attention, and I have some thinking to do before we go."

"Brunel, you must not be paying attention. We're not going with you unless you encounter with us."

"Then I will go alone," he bellowed. He zipped forward in his chair to a point only two meters in front of them, and stopped on a credit. "The GOmod-1 is *my* creation. I built it with *my* funds. I do not need a pilot because it is fully automated. I do not need an astro because I can drop off probes."

"Then why did you ask us along?"

"Added safety. More expertise. Certainly not necessity. You have both overrated yourselves if you think that I cannot undertake this venture without you."

Sandy said, "Now you're beginning to sound like a walker. As soon as your insecurities are challenged, you get your hackles up and take a defensive posture. Why don't you face the situation? You want to take this hop for reasons that are buried in your subconscious, and you can't let your conscious self know what those reasons are because acknowledgement of what you perceive as a human fault is too painful for you."

"Young woman! I have had more experience at self-awareness than you in your brief life span can possibly imagine. I am an engineer. I build things. That is what I do. And that is *all* I do. I do not waste time on companionship, or relationships, or any of the baser human endeavors. The GOmod-1's central computer is large enough to handle all my programs, so I can take my ongoing projects with me. Dane can fly us there, you can conduct your studies, and I can continue to put my ideas on disk. It is as simple as that."

Dane disagreed. "No, Brunel, you're wrong. It's much more complicated than you will admit. I have no doubt that you can take the GOmod-1 out on your own. If I didn't think the ship would work, I would never have agreed to fly it. But if you want to stretch the envelope, if you want to put it through a real test, you'll need more than automatic programming. In that respect, my presence as pilot is necessary. And Sandy can certainly make more creative analyses than a roboprobe. Therefore, — "

"I don't give a wit about this stellob, or any other object in the Galaxy. I chose it only because of its distance, and the chance to prove the GOmod-1's worth."

Dane continued undaunted. "Therefore, there's more at stake than a simple test hop. And among the three of us, there are more important questions to be answered than our understanding of your purposes, *your* understanding of your purposes, or your understanding of ours."

Brunel backed away. He maintained an elevation so that his head was level with Dane's. "Please do not talk in riddles."

"I'm talking about a mutual regard for each other. Sandy and I are already in accord — we've known each other for a long time."

"My entire life," Sandy interpolated.

"But you represent an unknown factor to us — a radical and possibly dangerous element in this mission. Unless you cooperate, there's no point in continuing this discussion any further."

"Are you trying to threaten me?"

"No, I'm trying to bargain with you. You've got to open up. I've already explained to Sandy that I had no intention of making another long hop. With the Committee offer looking more attractive to my future needs, I'd have been willing to retire after one or two more shorties. But, there's an aspect of this mission that I find alluring: to get behind the controls of the starship of the future before I pass on the pulse beam to the next generation of starship pilots. Sandy?"

"My situation is a little more complicated. For one thing, I never had any intention of going to the stars myself. I'm a cube body. I planned to spend my life pursuing cosmology academically. As far as I'm concerned, a probe would have served my purposes adequately. But first hand observation is better than waiting years for data which may only tell me how to ask the next question or to develop the next experiment. This hop is a prime opportunity to advance our knowledge of the workings of the Universe in a very short time. Subjectively speaking, I can have answers to my queries in the next few revs.

"For another, I want to test my own inner strength. I feel that my development as a person would be enhanced by grappling with the terrors that an occasion of this nature presents for me. I'm like my mother in many ways, and I harbor some of the same fears. One that I'm facing directly is the horror of the vast, unknown interstellar spaces.

"When I was a little girl, sitting on my mother's lap and watching her viewscreen as she worked, I used to get chills on my spine when I saw compugraphs of stars and galaxies in all their splendor. I wondered how many there were, how far they extended. My imagination ran wild. Then she explained to me about pulsars, and I wondered how such a thing could come into being: how did they fit into the scheme of the Universe? But I could not understand. I could not grasp a picture of the whole, not even as a mathematical concept. The Universe seemed to go on forever, in complexity, in space,

in time. I used to go to bed crying. I guess I'm a romantic at heart, always thinking in terms of a beginning, a
middle, and an end. The thought of infinity terrified me.

"As an adult, even though I could not come to terms
with the images of my dreams, I at least accepted the
finitude of the human mind. In a way, this hop is the
culmination of all the years of dreaming. I want to listen to the music of the spheres, and put into perspective the mathematical precision of the Universe. I don't
expect to realize any of my childhood fantasies. But you
never know what you might find if you don't seek."

In order not to lose any work time, Brunel typed vig-
orously on his lap pad. Display screens lit up with
megabytes of data, synthesizing programs that he was
writing and editing. His mind had the curious ability to
think in various directions at once, enabling him to
carry on conversations while cogitating problems of a
completely different nature.

Brunel sipped from his straw. "All very interesting,
but I do not see the purpose of it. Your dreams are not
my dreams, and mine are not yours. Our visions of the
future are idiosyncratic. I want to spend *my* time real-
izing my goals. I have no interest in yours."

"It's not necessary that you do, as long as you
accept that I have as much right to achieve my ambitions as you have to achieve yours, and that, while my
purpose for making this hop is exclusive of yours and
Dane's, it deserves at least as much respect."

"You already have my respect. What I want to avoid
is interference. Every project that I have ever undertak-
en has met with bureaucratic backwash. People who
cannot think with my grandness of scale try to put limitations on my engineering enterprises. I am constantly forced to make idiotic concessions to two-dimensional minds. This very Settlement is full of the vacuity of
those moronic thinking processes.

"I wanted to incorporate completely separate, non-
rotational endcaps, to facilitate the docking of ships.
'It's never been done before,' they cry. 'What if the seals
don't hold?' Instead, I am forced to design a complicat-

ed arrangement that warps ships into a loading chamber. This changes nothing of my original concept: it still requires sealed mating surfaces. Only the scale is different.

"I want to extend the midpoint power nodes the entire length of the cylinder, to be used as weightless machinery spaces. Keep it only partially pressurized, inhibit convection, and fires will snuff themselves in their own smoke. 'For esthetic reasons, no workspaces must show above the inner lining. We do not want to obstruct the upside view.' Appearance is more important than safety, spectacle more demanding than symmetry of design.

"At least let me install industrial vacuum chambers in the z-gee hubs, for crystal growth and the production of ball bearings. But the docking chamber is in the way. They will not let me add a false inner endcap to house foundries and workshops because it will interfere with freight and passenger facilities. Instead, freefall factories must be constructed in space, and the workers shuttled to and fro in buses.

"I want to recycle stray ions that are generated by the plasma shield. They say, 'With all the mass available in the asteroids, we have no need for bulky, space consuming matter collection equipment'." Brunel shook his head. "Their vision of the future is myopic. The asteroids that are both leading and lagging Jupiter's orbit will someday be mined away. *I* am thinking not just years ahead, but decades — centuries. The Trojans cannot last forever, so I make plans for the future: the most audacious scheme in the history of mankind. Soon, this platform and the other that has already been started at the Lag, will be relics of the past. When my Jupiter Project gets underway, all other construction in the System will be as miniscule and as evanescent as a castle in a child's sandbox."

As he stopped to input some recently formed ideas, Dane and Sandy exchanged raised eyebrows. Dane waited patiently while Brunel played his fingers across his keypad.

"Brunel, what can you possibly have in mind that is more grandiose than the *O'Neill*, or the GOmod-1? I haven't read anything in the newscomps about it."

"Bah, I design perfection, the Committee miscegenates my ideas. I talk about the System of the future, the reporters think I am spouting fanciful fiction. They can conceive of nothing that they cannot see. But this time I work without Committee approval. I do not need their paltry appropriations. From my investments, I can capitalize my own venture into the Jovian sphere. This is where I make my reputation. This is where I go down in history. Brunel will be a name to stand on its own, not in the shadow of my father. I will change the course of human history, despite simian opinions to the contrary."

Dane again raised his eyebrows at Sandy. To Brunel, "We're open-minded. Why don't you explain it to us?"

Brunel jetted his airchair around the room and glanced at the various viewscreens that occupied most of the wall space. He made a few notations while sucking on his straw. He finally hovered in front of them, drifting slowly. "Do you know of the Venus atmosphere siphon?"

Sandy nodded. "You designed magnetic ion pumps that could draw free atoms from the upper regions of Venus's atmosphere, to be used as mass material for inner orbit Settlement construction. Isn't that where you . . . "

"Lost my legs? Yes. But the Committee fared worse than I: they lost their heads. While I was recuperating, they withdrew financial backing because they thought that the concept was 'too farfetched in light of modern technology.' The fools!" Dark eyes stabbed at Dane like coalescing nebulae. "And this is the Committee you wish to join. Bah!"

Dane squeezed his hands together and floated along with Brunel's trajectory. "Maybe it's for reasons like this that I should accept its leadership. Or, maybe you should consider applying yourself. The members, as you know, wield quite a bit of power — "

"I care nothing for power, other than that which I can capture from the sun. Once my ideas are developed into hardware, there will be more solar energy for power conversion than can ever be used by the System. Consider: the sun radiates more than two billion times as much energy as the Earth intercepts. Only a very little more strikes the solar panels of all the Settlements in the System. Then, microwave conversion utilizes only a narrow band of the electromagnetic spectrum. I propose to capture *all* wavelengths of light, as well as every bit of radiated atomic matter. Instead of building my Settlements from asteroidal ore, I propose to use as my construction material — the planet Jupiter!"

In the stunned silence that followed, Brunel again swung around the room and checked ongoing calculations that were being flashed across multiplexed monitors. Sandy plucked the last of the foodbar into her mouth, but stopped in the middle of a chew. Dane took a sip of water from a tube; his mouth was suddenly very dry.

Sandy mumbled, "Fred did say something about rejuvenating the atmosphere siphon, but I thought he meant — "

"Yes, dear sweet Fred. He talks more than he should, and constantly grates my nerves with his witticisms: a knack which he said he picked up from our illustrious pilot." Brunel gestured to Dane as he paused in front of the dispenser and exchanged his empty food-tube for a full one. "But, he does have his uses, and I do not know what I would do without him. He is my closest associate."

"Why don't you tell *him* that?" Dane winked. "I'm sure he'd like to hear it. From you."

"I do not discuss anything with my employees, but work."

"But, your lifestyle admits to nothing *but* employees."

"Exactly, and I wish to keep it that way. Friendship implies pledges which need to be repaid, and I want no debts. I pay for what I take. I expect others to do the same."

Sandy swallowed her food, and dabbed her lips with a chemical cloth. "Since this project is one of your goals, and seems to be very important to you, perhaps you should explain how you plan to — transform history." She pushed the cloth into a disposal orifice, where it was sucked through vacuum tubing, through micro-eliminators, and eventually evacuated in the form of emulsified polymers into the boundless void of outer space. Automatic waste elimination was a key feature in Brunel's concept of Trojan Settlements, as he expected eventually to be able to obtain an inexhaustible supply of raw elements from the largest planet in the Solar System.

"My dear, in your case it will be a delight." He touched some keys on his lap pad. "And I will record the event so that you can replay it for your mother." Brunel stationed himself in front of a camera and programmed the lens for tracking. He glided back and forth across the suite as a man with legs would have paced. "I am certain that you have the vision that my critics lack. Just because this platform and its twin, each with one hundred sixty thousand hectares of inner surface space, will relieve overcrowding on the Earth sphere Settlements, and will fill the needs of humanity for the immediate future, they see no reason to experiment with alternative forms of spatial architecture. I have answers for questions that they have not even conceived."

Dane sighed heavily at Brunel's preamble, wondering when he would finish building himself up long enough to get down to the facts.

"The newscomps think that my Jupiter Project involves the establishment of mass drivers on the satellites, constructing even larger platforms to house entire populations. Such puerile notions I leave to engineering quacks of lesser imagination. They think that by refusing to finance the completion of the atmosphere siphon, the idea will die on the drawing screen. I do not forget so easily. I continue to work on it on disk until now the first construction phase is about to begin.

"Consider Jupiter: more than three hundred times the mass of the Earth, a seething globe of metallic hydrogen that is too large to have the stability of a planet, yet too small to trigger the fusion reaction that would make it a star; a hydrodynamic atmosphere of aerosols and hydrocarbons; the greatest source of recoverable matter in the System, and which I intend to tap with the Brunel siphon.

"I use the planet's radiation belt to fuel the ion field, the same way a ramjet utilizes the free hydrogen of interstellar space. These high-energy charged particles induce a current like the flow of electricity, siphoning off the outer layers of the atmosphere into an accelerator. But I do not merely take this mass for immediate use. Instead, I propel it along Jupiter's orbital plane, creating a pipeline which eventually stretches completely around the sun. Now I can build Settlements anywhere I like along the Jovian sphere by simply tapping into the never-ending mass supply: the Brunel pipe.

"Because of the square cube law, increasing the diameter of a cylinder only marginally increases its surface area in relation to volume: a waste of free oxygen. Instead, I build hundreds — thousands — of B-10 platforms with stationary endcaps, but whose perimeters are immense particle accelerators. The extreme radius of the vacuum chamber, and the angular velocity of the relativistic particles, produces a gyroscopic inertia which stabilizes the platform without the use of a drive system.

"Solar panels are antique. Each of my new platforms utilizes ramjet principles: a collector head assembly and magnetic torus which directs particle flow from the sun into a compression node. I have only ten percent efficiency in prototype design, but eventually *nothing* will pass by the collectors: neither particles nor electromagnetic radiation. I save it all.

"I do away with plant life entirely. The unwilling

tools of mankind once converted the sun's energy through photosynthesis: to oxygenate the air, to be eaten as food, to be burnt for fuel. The Brunel System runs directly on every bit of sunlight and solar wind, through direct fusion into the heavier elements. The new Brunel Settlements will live indefinitely, and with machinelike precision."

Triumphantly, Brunel thrust his airchair overhead. His eyes, however, were fixed on a point in space at which no viewscreen offered data. It was not until his head touched the padding that he took notice of his position. A touch of the attitude jets brought him down to eye level.

Dane said with what he hoped was a disarming voice, "It sounds like a Brunel pipe dream." He was quick to add, "But one that could work."

Sandy squinted, lost in thought. "I can't see that it violates any physical principles. There's no reason why, theoretically at least, it can't work." To Brunel, "I assume you've got all the calculations on disk. Have you computed a time table for fabrication and production?"

"I have already set the jets in motion. Construction techs are now being hired to erect living quarters and the ion generation equipment. But it will be several years yet before the Brunel pipe becomes a reality."

Dane clamped himself to a wallgrip. "Brunel, I must be missing something here. You're about to start the biggest engineering project since the parting of the Red Sea — and you want to leave it? How does this tie in with embarking on a three year galactic odyssey?"

"Very good, Dane. I see that my faith in your ratiocination has not been misplaced." Brunel's thumbs played idly with the lateral jets, causing the airchair to pitch and yaw nervously. "Always I am surrounded by Greek thinkers: those who believe that to reach a point, you must first travel half the distance, then half of that, then half of that, until eventually the halving process brings you within sight of, but out of touch with, your goal. Instead, I jump the whole way in a single bound.

Everything I do is with purpose.

"You are young, both of you. You cannot understand what it is like to enter old age. I do not have many decades left to me. Yet, I have so much to accomplish, so many dreams to fulfill. If I had my youth, I would live unconcerned by the pressure of time. But I am old, and I must plan my remaining years prudently, with as much foresight as I exhibit in my inventions. I cannot be satisfied with just seeing my projects begun, I must be there at the completion. I must stave off the encroachment of discontinuance. I must buy some time."

Dane's eyes widened with sudden enlightenment. "So you want to go into a time stasis where you will age only a couple of months during the next three years, by which time — "

"The project will have begun to produce results. You are astute. The engineering, the conceptualization —" Brunel tapped his temple with a crooked finger. " — is done. My presence is superfluous during the construction phase. Fred is a capable enough engineer to handle the rev-to-rev minutiae. I want to be here to see the finished product. Then, the mass production of the Brunel gyroplats can begin, from the material siphoned into the Brunel pipe, and I can take off again and return later, to see my System begin to take shape: an entire ring of self-sufficient gyroscopic platforms in the orbit of Jupiter."

"My compliments, Brunel. It is indeed a magnificent prospect for the ultimate colonization of the solar system."

Sandy said, "I've heard so much of your engineering genius, but this surpasses everything. What ideas! What — ambition!"

"The ideas come from my head. The ambition comes from my heart. Ever since I was a boy, I have been subjugated to and driven by the fame of my father. It is not just that he was a great engineer — he was the *greatest* engineer. They say that it was only a one in a million chance that he stumbled upon the principle of the stardrive, but that is not true. Selkirk Brunel was the genius's genius. He never stumbled onto anything that he was not diligently seeking. All my life I have been overshadowed by his name, by his fame. It has been a great burden, being known only as the son of Selkirk. Now, before I go, I have the opportunity to change all that — to make *him* the father of Brunel.

"I must live to see it happen. I must procrastinate my termination long enough to become the *ultimate* engineer, as I wish future generations to know and remember me. I want *my* name associated with the next stage in the evolution of the human race."

Chapter 13

"For all but a vanishingly brief instant near the dawn of history, the word 'ship' will mean — 'spaceship'."

— Arthur C. Clarke

Sandy lowered the wristrad on which she had just called her mother. "She and Fred are on their way — to help us celebrate."

Brunel jetted his airchair in a circle and halted in front of her. His thick, wiry hair clung to his head regardless of weightlessness. "I do not understand. You tell me that you will not go unless I submit to a prehistoric confession hearing — "

"We call it an encounter session."

"Whatever. Then you both change your minds and decide to go along. If you are that irrational, I am not certain that I want you on this flight."

Dane lounged against a ceiling pad. In a z-gee, unfurnished room surrounded by viewscreens, wall space was at a minimum. "*We* didn't change *our* minds; *you* fessed up."

Brunel's face screwed into a grimace. "What is the meaning of 'fess'?"

"Sorry, I've been watching old Earth Easterns — no, Westerns. They're movies from before the induction of holographic tech — Forget it. It's not important. I just meant that you finally unmasked."

"What the hell are you talking about? I do not wear cosmetic prostheses — except for these polymerized alloy teeth that — "

"Brunel, I'm talking about baring your soul, unveiling your feelings, letting us in on your secret thoughts and dreams, admitting to yourself as well as to us your hidden motives."

"I have never been unaware of my motivations. How do you think I could devise such a logical course of events if I did not fully comprehend *why* I was doing it? That does not make sense. Everything I do is planned, programmed, and engineered."

Sandy smiled, and intruded into the private dialogue. "Brunel, it seems as if we were wrong about you. Because of the image you project, both publicly and privately, we thought that you were out of touch with yourself. That's why we staged this session, to draw you out — "

"You *staged* it?"

"Actually, it was Mother's idea. You see, you had such a block about encountering with us — you still have this archaic notion of a closed booth, and confessing your sins, and cringing lest your mother spank you for being bad — "

"I did not have a mother. I was tubed. My father did not want our lineage to die out."

Dane smirked. "He would have been proud of your accomplishments in that respect."

"Anyway," Sandy continued, "An encounter is any heart to heart discussion between two, or among a group of, people. It's not like a test that you pass or fail. It's something you share. And you shared yourself with us. Now, I don't have any qualms about spending several months of subtime cooped up with you, because I understand you a little better."

"The same goes for me," Dane added. "I was intimidated at first by your eccentric personality. But as long as I know you as a person, and not the facade that you wear for the workers and newscomps, I think you're an all right guy. Welcome aboard."

Brunel stared at them both in silence, his dark gaze shifting from one to the other. His lips trembled for a moment, the corners upraised in a way that seemed foreign to Dane.

"Don't smile," Sandy taunted. "You might crack your face."

He did not. His face returned to its hardened mien, his eyes narrowed, his jaw outthrust. "Young lady, I will not be talked to like a child. And I will not allow this familiarity to continue. We are together because we have a job to do, and for no other reason."

Dane asked, "What's the matter? Are you afraid of falling in like with us?"

"What I am afraid is that your humor will become grating after a while. Worse, that is, than it has already."

"That's life in the big Settlement." Dane smiled, and winked at Sandy. "But you'll get used to it. My jokes haven't killed anyone yet. Besides, during slowtime, I spend most of my off-duty hours reading. I won't intrude if you wish to play with your programs."

"And I've got lots of journals to keep me occupied. By the way, Brunel, will it bother you to be with a sexually active couple?"

"I remind you that I am of true floater stock, and no stranger to the urges of the flesh. Fortunately, I was freed from the hormonal chains long before I lost the apparatus for its delivery. You may do as you please, as long as it does not interfere with the performance of your duties. I am counting on a successful mission. There is even the slim possibility that we may learn something useful from this proto-neutron star."

Dane said, "Any hop you return from alive is successful. My engines are warmed up, and my course is plotted. When do we leave?"

"The GOmod-1 is ready now. I trust you have accessed the SpaVeOpMan."

"That's another thing, Brunel, that I wanted to bring up." Dane brushed aside the reference to the Space Vehicle Operating Manual. "I don't care for your use of acronyms. GOmod-1 sounds too much like an engineering term, or a manufacturing designation, or a sexual appurtenance for producing gametes. I'd like to give her a name."

"You've already given it a sex. Why must people always apply nomenclature that has no descriptive foundation?"

"Without getting involved in sociologic notions, let's just call it human nature. Now, we don't have to crack a tube of champagne over her power nodes, but if you'll key in a search and replace function, I'd like to official-ly christen the starship of the future."

Brunel scowled. "I do this with great trepidation, only to demonstrate my willingness to cooperate." He entered the central computer through his lap pad. The proper code sequence would automatically change all references to the GOmod-1 to its new designation.

"I'm sure you think nostalgia is as useless as senti-mentality, but I'd like to recall the era of watersips, when a great engineering advancement was made that was far ahead of its time. Before spaceflight, the oceans of the world — "

The buzzer sounded raucously. Brunel said, "Enter."

The hatch unsealed, and swung open on silent pis-tons. Barbara and Fred floated into the room. Fred said "Close," and the latch slipped into its gaskets.

Barbara had her long hair swept to one side, and fastened with an ornamental broach representative of a star cluster: tiny, reflective pseudopearls poised on the tips of filigreed brass spines. As the great blonde tress-es bounced in z-gee, they stayed behind her line of sight. She hugged and kissed her daughter. "I'm so happy for all of you. I told you Brunel was not the mar-tinet that he appears to be." She rotated, and held her hand out to the engineer. "Brunel, my congratulations."

"I am given to understand that it was your machi-nations that led to this — " He glanced at Sandy. " — encounter."

"I can't take all the credit. Fred offered some insight into your character, and this seemed like the best way to bring you out of your shell."

"Fred!" Brunel spun his chair with mechanical pre-cision, and faced his chief engineer from a position that was slightly elevated. "Have you fomented this conspir-acy against me?"

Not to be outdone, Fred spun on his axis and changed his vertical attitude so that, without moving upward (in a room which had no upright alignment) he had to crane his neck chestward in order to peer at his boss. "Brunel, I did only what I thought was best for you. Sometimes you get so involved with your projects that you forget the most important part of being a person — involvement with other people."

Like a boxer, Brunel maneuvered for a position which could be construed as superior. This was not easy in a z-gee chamber. "I do not forget — I choose to ignore. I do not have time for useless — " He hesitated, and glanced at Dane.

The Exploteam pilot raised his eyebrows noncommittally.

"Although, sometimes, it does serve a purpose."

"You see, you *can* teach an old computer new programs." Dane winked. "And the better I get to know you, the more I think that you may be just right for this hop."

"I am not only just right, I am perfect," Brunel stated flatly. "Physically, without the impediments of lower extremities, I require less food and oxygen than the average person. Emotionally, since I depend only upon myself for fulfillment, I am as sound as a synthesizer. And mechanically, no one understands the GOmod-1's systems better than its designer."

"Which brings me back to the christening." Dane typed on the kitchen keypad, and removed five tubes of pink liquid electrolyte as they slid into the dispenser. He tossed the drinktubes to his companions. "I was just about to inaugurate the new era of spaceflight, in the same way in which the era of Atlantic Ocean crossings was inaugurated in the mid-eighteen hundreds by the launching of an improved design in seagoing vessels."

He held his tube out straight, vacustraw mouthward. The others followed his example. "Galactic Odyssey Model One, the first of a new series of starcraft which will vault mankind into the next realm of his exploration of, and understanding of, the wonders of the Universe, I christen thee — *Great Eastern.*"

Dane sipped triumphantly from the bulbous straw tip. Sandy, Barbara, and Fred followed suit. But Brunel paused with the straw on his lips, his fingers frozen over his lap pad, his eyes agleam with a light that could have outshone a nova. His usually angry countenance was betrayed only by his slack jaw, and by his momentary speechlessness.

When Brunel finally found his voice, it was cracked and halting. "Where — where did you — hear of such — a ship?"

The grin on Dane's face could have swallowed an asteroid. "Why, Brunel, I have finally gotten a reaction out of you. You're not a heartless machine after all."

"Where?" The drinktube slipped from flaxen lips and drifted gently away. "How could you know?"

"That you are a direct lineal descendant of the greatest engineering mind of the nineteenth century?" Dane took another sip of electrolyte. "I read a lot of old Earth disks. And while I was on Earth, I stocked my IDcard with hundreds of antique volumes. The magnetic alignments are off, and there's quite a bit of static, but they're still legible. So, when I received your transmission about test hopping the GOmod-1, I punched the search circuits for old navigational texts. Anyone brought up on Earth, with its paranoid predilection for conservation of the past, possesses multigigabytes of useless historical trivia.

"I recalled that at one time, steam was considered the most advanced form of watership propulsion. I was looking for the name of the first steam watership. It's the *Clermont*, which was designed and built by Robert Fulton. But during the course of my compscan, I came upon the name of Isambard Kingdom Brunel: your prespatial ancestor. He was the creator of what was then, and for half a century afterward, the largest moving manmade object ever built.

"Allow me to soliloquize. The *Great Eastern* was the ideal watership from the point of sheer power and bulkhead construction. She was propelled through the water by two enormous paddlewheels and a single screw propeller, and carried six masts with auxiliary canvas sails: the perfect combination of coal-fired steam and atmospheric wind. She is amazingly analogous to the GOmod-1, which is propelled through space by ion thrusters and fusion reactors, and to the stars by capturing free interstellar hydrogen in her magnetic sails.

"What's more, the *Great Eastern's* radical designer was your paragon: of equivalent stature, as extreme in personality, and as revolutionary in engineering skill. Everything he built was bigger, grander, and more outrageous than anything that had ever been done before. Scale meant nothing to him. According to the needs and technology of his day, he built trains, railroads, bridges, tunnels, and waterships. And, like you, he had an equally famous and engaging father who played a role model to be surpassed."

Fred drifted across the room and captured Brunel's errant drinktube. "Brunel, I never knew that about you."

"What are you saying? None of what he said has anything to do with me. It's all about historical personages who lived hundreds of years ago. They have no bearing on me. I made myself what I am."

Barbara smiled whimsically. "Oh, Brunel, you are *some* character. From the way you talk, you'd think you conceived yourself from nothing, then went on to create the planets and the stars and the human race."

"He *has* contributed a good portion of the latter," Dane said. "How do you manage to get your ego through the hatches?"

"Is this an example of what I will have to endure?" Brunel snatched the drinktube from Fred's hand. "Perhaps I *should* go alone. At least then I will be in good company."

Sandy joined the good-natured banter. "You need someone along to make sure that you don't get absorbed by your computer and integrated into its circuits. You might wind up becoming the link between us and the next order of intelligence: the logically thinking biological machine."

"It would certainly be a more rational existence

than what I am forced to abide."

"What would life be without emotion?" Sandy persisted.

"Simple."

"Dull."

"Boring," Barbara added. "The only variety would be the on-off positions of a binary digit."

"Besides," Fred said, "No matter how many data fields a computer incorporates, it will always be limited in its range of thought to what has already been programmed. It can neither conceive, nor imagine. It's a linear intelligence which can never progress. It can think faster, but without cognitive thought. The greatest advantage the human brain has over — "

"*Please!*" screamed Brunel. "Spare me your philosophies. Must I be continually subjected to this endless prattle? Why must people engage in semantics and useless conversation? What purpose does it serve?"

Dane said, "At the very least, communication is interesting. On the other hand, you just never know what serendipitous discoveries might come out of it. After all, the faculty of speech does more than separate us from the animals, it's serves as the medium for the solidification of ideas."

"That is it! I have had enough!" Brunel stretched himself in his chair. The absence of gravity makes a person taller by removing the pressure on the vertebrae. Years of weightlessness had lengthened his trunk. "The productivity of this grandiloquent diatribe has ended. I would like to make some last minute notations before we depart. Fred, I have some final orders to issue, if you will stay behind."

"Hold on a microsec!" Dane protested. "Aren't we going to have a farewell party, or a launching ceremony of some kind?"

"A useless formality without purpose. If you will excuse me, I have — "

"Brunel, sometimes you have to do things not for yourself, but for others. Okay, so we don't have to have a big social event with a grand send off, but we can at least acknowledge all those who poured their guts into building the — Hey, did you key in the *Great Eastern's* newly commissioned name?"

Brunel ground his teeth. The squeaking of plastic pierced the silence of the suite. "Dane, you seem to know the entire history of its namesake. Has the fact escaped you that the original *Great Eastern* failed to fulfill the goals that were established by its creator?"

"Nothing escapes me except your resistance." Dane softened his words with a wink. "If you were an electronic component, you'd be the perfect insulator. So, okay, the *Great Eastern* did not inaugurate the new era of passenger liner service as Isambard intended. She was a flop, a failure, or, to use old Earth vernacular, a white elephant. She lost money right from the start, and sent several companies bankrupt during the lifetime of her career. She was too innovative for her time, and people couldn't accept her. What does that have to do with the life of a red giant?"

Brunel spun slowly in his airchair. "I have an uncomfortable feeling about history repeating itself."

Barbara guffawed. "Coming from you, that's a ridiculous statement. You don't believe in connotations with the past. How is a name going to affect the performance of your ship?"

"I did not say that it would, but why name a spaceship that was perfected by genius after a watership of dubious renown?"

Dane said, "You're forgetting that the *Great Eastern* won the sovereignty of the seas in another way: by laying the first transatlantic telegraph cable, and bringing the continents of Europe and America closer together. Instead of carrying passengers, she redeemed herself by bringing on the age of information. The GOmod-1 could do no better than to herald the dawn of communication among the faraway stars, and by acting as the fastest transfer of knowledge in the history of mankind. Assuming, of course, that you believe in history."

"Come on, Brunel," Sandy pleaded. "Shake off the stigma of the past, and put your finger where your mouth is."

Brunel's face clouded, and his body jerked back in the restraining straps. His ominous eyes touched those of all the others. Tentatively, his index finger stretched out over his lap pad, hovered, then stabbed down suddenly. "I hereby christen thee — *Great Eastern.*"

Chapter 14

"Even the longest journey is begun with a single step."

— Confucius

"Good luck to you all. See you in a few years."

Brunel harrumphed. "Chance has nothing to do with performance. It is by proficiency, tenacity, and ingenuity that we accomplish our goals."

Barbara Mettleson's face continued to smile from all three of the *Great Eastern's* viewscreens. "Brunel, I hope you lose some of your iconoclasm on this hop, and come back with a better understanding of your place in the System. You push too hard for your own good."

"Without labor, there is no achievement. It is the lazy who are unsatisfied, because they only wish for what others are willing to work for. What I want, I go out and grab."

"Try not to grab too much, or this hot little stellob is likely to burn you. Honey, you take care of that lover of yours."

"I will," Dane and Sandy chorused. They looked at each other for a moment, then laughed.

"I meant that for both of you."

"You keep the System running till we get back."

"And Mother, if what we learn there doesn't conform to any known physical body, I'm going to name it after you: the Mettleson object."

"I'm not sure I care for the connotation."

"It won't be named after your shape," Dane quipped.

"In that case, it's okay. Just make sure it's worthy of me," Barbara said.

As the *Great Eastern* raced farther away from the platform, the time lag between transmissions increased until there was a noticeable delay between dialogue exchanges.

Fred's face swam into view. Despite his proximity to the projecting lens, comphanced achromatic prisms corrected planar distortion. "Brunel, I thought you'd like to know that the trash vaporizers have reached full potential. We're ejecting one hundred percent of our non-recyclable material into downstream orbit. In a few days, the trash buildup on the *O'Neill* will be over."

"Forget that. It is inconsequential. How is the efficiency rating of the wind catchers now that the power nodes are breeding?"

The *Great Eastern* flew on full automatic, making Dane feel like a supernumerary at the controls. However, he could not but marvel at the barely perceptible increase in speed that pushed them gently past the one gee mark. Logarithmic compfaced functions actuated incremental verniers with smoothness that was unknown in any spaceship he had ever conned.

"It has peaked out at thirty-one point seven two eight eight two one percent, give or take a millionth."

"You see!" Brunel shouted with glee. His voice was deep and resounding in full cabin pressure. Dane harkened back to how docile the engineer sounded at about three hundred millibars. "I have captured nearly one third of the sun's output. No more will its energy reserves be lost to the reaches of interstellar space." To the screen, "Have you started the exponential grids?"

"Yesterrev. I'm still experimenting, but initial results indicate an efficiency curve that could approach one hundred percent. I have no doubt that by the time you return, we'll have your latest program installed. If the catchers work as predicted, absolutely no molecular or photonic quanta will get past the magnetic focusers."

"Excellent." Brunel typed until the increased gravity got the best of him. "I cannot take this weight. Have we reached translation speed yet?"

Dane touched his offset keyboard. Figures and equations appeared in the lower right sixteenth of his screen. "Only one point five. We've got a long ways to go."

Brunel's acceleration couch was specially fitted to accommodate his airchair. "I do not remember this much stress during my physical."

"Don't worry. It gets worse."

Sandy typed on her keyboard, using only half the screen for communication visual. "Hang on, Brunel. We're approaching the heliosphere now. As soon as we clear the ripple tides, we'll go into top speed FTL."

"Then we'll see what this baby can do." Dane deployed the magnetic scoops and set the ramjet engine in motion. He looked at his screen. "Babs. Fred. This is the long good-bye."

Brunel coughed and sputtered. Still, his fingers found his lap pad. "Fred, here is a last calculation on the biomass potential once we get the slipstream going."

"It's logged." Fred looked down for a moment as the figures were collated telemetrically. "So long, gang. We'll see you in eternity. Oh, and Brunel. Congratulations. Wilma delivered forty-nine. Out."

The screen went blank. Dane checked their translation velocity. "Fred's still as sharp as they come. He knew exactly when we'd reach transvel."

Sandy handled the astronomical navigation. "The attic door is open." An interstellar hop left either through the roof or the cellar. Since all but the most eccentric mascons rotated in the plane of the ecliptic, the best way to avoid them was to leave the System by either rising above or dropping below the orbital plane of the planets. Comets maintained station far beyond the Plutonian sphere. "The Oort cloud is below us."

"Please. This is making me sick."

"Quit griping, Brunel. You'll get a lot sicker when we translate." It was equally important to be protected from fast-moving cosmic radiation and stray ions. "Repulser shields up."

Sandy rechecked her coordinates. The *Great Eastern's* computer had already locked them in to the one hundred seventeenth place. "Target is complocked. No astrophysical anomalies along our predicted trajectory

— at least, as long as we're in charted space."

"Hold onto your guts, people. This is where we prove Selkirk's Asymptotic Paradox."

Dane sent them into translation.

Nausea hit him in the stomach like a short-armed centrifuge. His heart and his intestines momentarily traded places; his peritoneum was a bagful of billiard balls. After a ten-cushion ricochet, his gizzard slowly settled down until it was nothing more than a beehive of angry drones all trying to escape at once. A thimbleful of bile surged up his throat, stinging. To avoid aspirating, he forced his glottis shut. Later, when he felt it was safe, be began to breathe.

The section of the screen that was still on visual was blank. Traveling faster than the speed of light, it was impossible for electromagnetic radiation to impinge upon the ship's sensors. This did not mean that the *Great Eastern* was beyond the laws of the physical Universe, only that all the frequencies of light were beyond the realm of interpretation in a slower-than-light context, and that the concentration of energy fields that were conceived as mass would be felt before they were seen: the repulser shields could protect the ship from fairly large-sized chains of interstellar hydrocarbons, but collision with a micrometeoroid the size of a pinpoint would go right through any manmade materials that were bursting through space at FTL velocities. If she ran into a star or planet, the *Great Eastern* would be instantly vaporized. But the probability against that happening was, in all senses of the word, astronomical.

"The early bird gets the worm hole," Dane choked, forcing a grin at the trite but traditional starship joke.

Sandy ran a napkin across her mouth, and spit delicately into the cupped cloth. She stuffed the residue into the disposal shoot. With a slurp, it was whisked into the trash storage compartment. "What's worse than finding a worm hole?"

"Finding half a worm hole."

Brunel struggled with his safety harness. "Dane, would you help me? My chair appears to be stuck. I cannot move." The thrusters exhausted ineffectually. The airchair rocked a bit on the acceleration couch, but did not float away.

Dane uncinched his restraining straps and tumbled out of the command couch. He alighted on the floor with the agility of a cat. "Brunel, the inertia pump is phased to offset our FTL speed by less one gee. You're being held down by the universal force of gravity."

"How do you expect me to move about under these conditions?"

"I'm sorry. Did you have somewhere to go?" Dane swept his arms around him, and indicated the viewscreens. "We're not within chairing distance of anything at the moment."

Sandy plopped her softsoled slippers on the padded deck. "I can run a plot, if you think — "

"Stop it!" Brunel shouted. His black whiskers bristled as his face contorted into a grimace. "I am not in the mood for humor."

"That's not inconsistent with your normal disposition, according to Fred and your psychfile. I thought you were going to try to be more agreeable."

"Young lady, I am not being discordant. But I cannot spend three years in one gee traction."

Dane's expression was one of guileful sincerity. "Oh, time goes by quickly out here. It'll feel like only a few weeks. A month at the most. Slowtime will be over before you — "

"Do *not* patronize me. Either of you. I have no time for it."

"Oh, I don't know. According to the equations, you have all the time in the Universe — and then some."

"*Enough!*" Brunel twisted sideways and wagged a shaking finger. "My arms feel like ingots of lead at the centrifugal perimeter of an endcap. How can I type under the constraints of such weight?"

"Did you expect us to live in freefall all the way?"

"Of course. It's the only medium in which I can move."

Sandy walked lightly around the couches, stopping

at Brunel's head. "Didn't you have any consideration for the rest of us?"

"You have two legs. You can get around in z-gee just as well as I can. Everything reduces to the lowest common denominator."

Dane frowned. "You do have a decimal point, there, Brunel." He shrugged at Sandy. "As much as I hate to admit it, he has logic on his side."

"Of course I do. Do you think I am fighting a silly contest of wills?"

"If that implies a recognition of emotion, I guess not."

Sandy compromised. "How about if we work out shifts? We can live on z-gee during your waketime, and go to half gee during your sleeptime?"

"Wait a minute," Dane protested. "He sleeps only four hours a rev. At that rate, our bones will decalcify to pudding by the end of the hop."

"Do I look decalcified?" Brunel shouted. "I've been living in full z-gee for years."

"You just admitted you can't hold your hands against a one gee force."

"Physical conditioning has no meaning for me. I work solely with my brain. But you can utilize the ship's exercise facilities if you wish." Dane shrugged, and rolled his eyes.

Sandy said, "Brunel, can you sleep in half gee?"

"I don't like it, but I will if I have to."

"Then it's settled. Dane, flip us into z-gee."

Grumbling, he slid into the command couch and pulled the keypad over his legs. He input instructions. Gradually, he felt the weight of gravity leave his body. There was no doubt about the initial relief from tension, but he knew the long-term effects of weightlessness. Already, as the Mettlesons had proved to him on the *Ellison*, his muscular and cardiovascular systems were substandard. "I'm going to have to do extra hard workouts."

"I'll be glad to help," Sandy smiled. "Your cube or mine?"

"That's the best offer I've had all rev." Without the restraining straps across his body, Dane floated up off the couch. He pushed the console away from his lap, executed a torque motion, and rotated deftly so that he faced Brunel and Sandy. "Brunel, we're on full automatic. Will you be all right out here by yourself?"

Blandly, "I have plenty of work to do, so you two go off and have your fun." He pulled the engineering keyboard in front of his lower abdomen, and started typing. His screen flashed with logarithmic displays and scrolling digital readouts. With a foodtube straw stuck in his mouth, he was in a galaxy all his own.

In the community cubicle, Dane and Sandy stabilized by the food dispenser and keyed their culinary desires. Dane had an appetite for solids. He ordered a mixture of textured vegetable extracts with a high grain content, highly seasoned and with the taste of lamb. "I think he's going to be a beam full of trouble."

Sandy requested a variety of flavored pastes. "Getting cold feet?"

"I've already put on extra socks. I can see through him like he was a black hole."

Actually, one could not see *through* such an intense gravitational anomaly. Theoretically, while an object opposite the line of sight of a black hole had most of its emissions swallowed in a one-way downward passage, enough radiation passing tangentially was deflected around it in concentrically, like the corona of an annular eclipse, that they met on the observer's side in an infinite number of focal points. The image created was seen just as if the black hole was not there at all. This made black holes effectively invisible. Speaking theoretically again (since no black hole had yet been discovered) it could be perceived by mass detectors - hopefully before a ship crashed into it.

"He *is* rather transparent, but that's to our advantage."

"The hop is hardly underway, and already he's trying to take over. I don't like it."

"You should tell him that."

Dane chewed as he floated against a wallpad. "I know. And I will. I guess I just have trouble being up front like a natural-born floater."

Sandy sucked her meal through a tube extension. "Give him credit for compromising. Let's see what he's doing." She pushed away from the dispenser and grabbed a wallgrip next to a compsole. She pulled out the keypad and interfaced with the main monitor. The small screen flashed with running mathematical equations. "Hmmnn, it looks like he's making mass catcher efficiency calculations. He'll be busy for a while. Let me see how my program's doing."

She touched a few keys. The screen cleared, then filled with chemical symbols. The readouts meant little or nothing to Dane, but by the element scan reproduced on screen she appeared to be collating data through spectroscopic analysis. She frowned, hmmnned, and seemed to forget about Dane being in the room with her. She scanned, typed, and displayed, caught up in the intricacies of her profession.

Dane floated behind her to another miniscreen and keyed in a recall code. He had had enough of work, and for the moment needed some mental recreation. He munched on his foodbars as he scanned some of his preprogrammed material. He clipped a lanyard to his belt, and hovered in a small arc in front of the flat screen. This was very interesting information . . .

"Sorry, pumpkin. I guess I got carried away." Sandy gave him a peck on the back of the neck, then gave him a kiss which lingered in the same spot. "What are you reading?"

Dane returned her kiss, on the lips. " 'Three Cases of Unsuccessful Corneal Transplant in Agricultural Farm Rodents,' by C. Howdie Rhuyn."

"Cute. Very cute."

"How about 'Twin Winds,' by Sigh Clone?"

"Clever, Honey. Is this how you spend your off-time?"

"Only when my lover is preoccupied with her work."

Sandy wrapped her arms around Dane from

behind, and snuggled up to him. "Mother downloaded the latest data on nebular hypotheses onto my files. We'll be in a good position to make observations of the Coal-Sack, so I need to bone up on what we already know about it."

The Coal-Sack was a concentration of nebular dust in the constellation of the Southern Cross, and so dense that it blocked out the stars behind it with utter totality. The area hid a huge area of the Galaxy's spiral arm from Earth's view. Like the Horsehead Nebula, and hundreds of others, the Coal-Sack was comprised of molecular litter that drifted between the stars: origin unknown. It was one of the great unanswered questions of modern astronomy.

Sandy rubbed her hands over Dane's chest. She released his lanyard, and pushed gently away from the screen. "What's this disk about? Seasonal noise abatement? Or soundless recoil devices?

"Now you're beginning to sound like me. No, *Silent Spring* is a twentieth-century book by an environmentalist named Rachel Carson. My sister dredged it out of the Archive circuits. You know how they are down there, documenting every insignificant iota about the past. This one's about insecticides — at least on the label. But it has more broad-reaching meaning than the killing of unwanted bugs. Of course, it's way out of date and no longer relevant. Its message was for the people of the time. But it's interesting how the many aspects of nature are so intertwined, how one thing depends on another, and how a whole building can be toppled by the removal of a single brick.

"I think Sis wanted me to see it as an example of the fix that the world got itself into when people didn't heed the warnings of disaster, despite the abundance of evidence. How did she say it? 'You can't see the forest for the trees.' Whatever that means."

"Kind of like, you can't see the Moon for the craters?"

"Something like that. Walkers think so differently, and always so secretively, it's difficult to know what they mean when their speech is couched in euphemisms. They attack life with the onslaught of a tangent. She kept asking me, 'What are you looking for out there in space?' I told her I wasn't looking for anything. 'Then you must be running away from something,' she said. 'No, I'm just doing — period. Is there anything wrong with that?' 'Then don't you have any goals?' she asked. 'I don't need to justify my existence,' I said. 'I'm doing what I want to do, and it must be a useful function because they're paying me damned well for doing it.' 'But don't you want to succeed at anything? For yourself? For your society?'

"You know what it came down to, as near as I could figure out? That you don't grow unless you're aware of your growth. That you can't realize your full potential unless you know your limitations. That you can't accomplish anything unless you first set goals to reach. That sounds like defeatism: if you achieve something serendipitously, it has no meaning. You must do everything with purpose. Sandy, is it necessary to be so directed in life that you can never have any fun?"

They bounced against a wallpad. Sandy slipped her feet into bungees and arched her spine so her back clung to the panel. "Do you want my opinion, or floater philosophy?"

"They're the same thing."

She rotated Dane in freefall so he faced her. She pulled him close until his body pressed against hers. She slowly unzipped his one-piece jumper. "I think — it's important to have a combination of both. People live for themselves, and societies survive on voluntary public input. Different people have different proportions of their sense of purpose, and those proportions vary during a person's lifetime. Ultimately, though, in a free society, the freedom of the individual is of supreme importance."

Sandy kissed him on the neck, on the clavicle, on the chest. "What we're taught in school is the baby-cuddling theory. If you hug your children when they're young, and whenever they need attention, they grow up with the faith that you'll always be there when they want you. But people who ignore their kids find that they become more dependent, and are always crying for more attention than those who are given it willingly. They need more because they have less.

"Society works the same way. You treat individuals with respect, encourage an environment in which they're happy, and they return with dividends whatever investment the society has made. Oldtime sociologists recognized the unrest in militarily occupied territories, because people ruled by others never had a stable society. They were always protesting, and were always prepared for war against their aggressors. Throughout history, uprisings were the eventual result in countries that were not self-governed."

"Sandy, I didn't ask for a college course. A simple yes or no would have sufficed."

"But short answers are seldom instructive." She pushed the jumper back over his shoulders, and pulled it down to his waist. "Now, let's play a game in which I give you lots of attention and try to make you happy."

Dane closed his eyes, hungering under the tingling of her kisses. "Are you acting the role of society, or a mother?"

She slipped her own jumper off her shoulders, and moved Dane's weightless body down until his face brushed her bare breasts. "They're the same thing."

Chapter 15

"Not only is the universe stranger than we imagine, it is stranger than we *can* imagine."

— J.B.S. Haldane

With gut wrenching precision, the *Great Eastern* emerged from the limbo of alter space-time into the physical reality of matter and energy: the flow of entropy perceived by the human consciousness as time. The blackness of the viewscreens in the command module burst into visual brilliance. Stars shone as brightly and as colorfully as a deep purple, sequin-covered cloth that was illuminated by a continuous burst of stark, white light.

Dane delegated the navigational duties while he concentrated on flying the ship. "Sandy, how close are we?"

"Closer than I want to be." She telemetered the computations to a section of his screen. "I think we should have stopped three hops back."

"Come on, where's your spirit of adventure?"

"I just swallowed it."

Brunel kept both eyes glued to his engineering systems figures. "Why don't we just drop off a few probes and back off? This constant jumping into and out of FTL is upsetting my equilibrium."

Dane said, "I see you're equanimity hasn't changed."

"There's no reason to rub elbows with this thing. We have nothing to gain by entering the cloud field."

"Wrong, Brunel. *You* have nothing to gain, because your reason for being here is just to waste obtime. But the scientific purpose of this hop is to study this stellob and find out what makes it pulse. Now, I suggest you turn up the gain on the shields before we *really* start cooking."

Brunel made some adjustments to the magnetic

deflectors. The same principle that focused interstellar particles into the thermonuclear reactor was utilized to protect the living quarters by deflecting those same interstellar particles from the command module. "My latest design field-reversal generator will repel matter of nearly grain size."

"That's good, because we're about to put it to the test on this solar beachhead. Sandy, what're we looking at for dimensions?"

For four hundred ninety-seven days of obtime (but only weeks in subtime) Sandy had been the paragon of womanhood, but right now she was an astronomer from her baby-blue eyes to her pink-painted toenails. She was no longer a figure for minds, but a mind for figures.

"Extreme diameter is approximately seven hundred fifty million kleters, but the main cloud is only half that."

"What's that in AU's?"

"Oh, call it five to the periphery, two and a half across the central sphere where maximum shell density occurs. I can't get obs on the solar mass itself because of electrical interference."

An image of the Solar System took form in Dane's mind. With the radius of Earth's orbit as an Astronomical Unit, that put the dust ball somewhere around the orbit of Jupiter, with the thickest part just beyond the orbit of Mars.

"Most of what you see — or rather, don't see, since it's eclipsing the stars behind it — is moving at a speed of about two hundred kleters per second." Orbital velocity of the outer layer was fifteen times that of Jupiter. "In this case, I'm getting more accurate readings than we got from the remote probe. The dust is fairly tenuous along the edge, then it condenses to about point-zero-two millibars."

"That's so thick you can practically *hear* the sun shine."

Brunel grumbled pragmatically, "Don't be ridiculous. That's only one five hundredth the density of the

Martian atmosphere."

"Brunel, have you no sense of hyperbole? Besides, in outer space, that kind of precipitation is like an atomic snowstorm. Sandy, what kind of drifts are we talking about?"

Her screen was a dazzling array of scrolling data. "It's not all molecular hydrogen, as you'd expect for uncoalesced stellar matter. I'm getting readings on every element in the Periodic Table — stable elements, that is."

"What about mascons?"

"Millions. Billions. Not near the edge, but in where maximum density occurs. We're getting far too much backscatter for accurate counts or measurements."

"Is there any ecliptic conformation?"

"Not that I can tell. Distribution appears to be random but even. The computer is still calibrating the fine details on disk flattening and speed of rotation." She remained calm, clinical, and coldly scientific. "It's strange, but some of the numbers keep increasing."

"Lock-on trouble?"

"Insufficient data. Dane, as much as I hate to say this, since the radiation level is acceptable, I see no reason why we can't increase proximity."

"*Wait a second!*" Brunel screamed. As long as none of the equipment malfunctioned, he had nothing to do but stand by and observe. "Can't we dispatch an instrumentation packet instead?"

Dane's finger hovered over the enact key. With the EEG helmet on his head, he kept his eyes on the functions that he wanted to actuate. "We can, and we will. But the closer we get, the better our equipment registers. You know that."

"Must we go FTL?"

"Unless you want to take a month to get there — an obmonth. Maybe you could invent a realtime periscope that we could poke out of limbo, so we could see where we are without having to translate. It would be a great nausea inhibitor."

Brunel stared at his screen, his eyebrows raised.

"Not a bad idea, really. I wonder how one would go about it."

"I'll tell you what, Brunel. You work it out while we investigate the stellob. Now start swallowing."

Dane worked the controls. A moment later they winked out of realspace. All the viewscreens went blank as telemetered information quit registering. With all the atomic debris, there was ample fuel for shielding as well as for speed.

The *Great Eastern* entered the system at about ten p-sol. Interpolated navigational coordinates flashed on the command screen. Traveling at FTL allowed only straight-line movement, or what passed as a straight line between two points in a four-dimensional Universe. A few hours later, they popped back out of limbo. The big ball of dust filled the forward visual monitors with ebony that was nearly as black as that of alter space-time.

Brunel screamed at once, "What are you trying to do? Reduce us to protoplasm?"

"You keep your eye on the shields and hull temperature, and leave the flying to me. We're not cinders yet. Sandy, how's the instrument focus now?"

"Better, but there's still a lot of interference. Dane, this is amazing. The mass detectors register a central core about point-five solmass. A body that size has to be radiating, but nothing is coming through."

"Look at those density measurements now. If we get inside this cloud, we can *walk* to the sun. Okay, maybe swim."

Brunel shouted, "Dane, I do *not* appreciate your daring. This is merely a trial mission, not a last stand."

"I see the tendency to exaggerate is contagious." Dane flipped some of his screen sections onto visual, and cross-linked the external monitors. Looking aft, it became apparent that he had conned them *inside* the rarified outer strata. The Galaxy was a rippling, diaphanous curtain; individual stars were soft and twinkling with a luster that was leaden. "Sandy?"

"Loud and dear, Sweetie Pie. Input is on overload,

and going into storage. It'll take me revs to skim through it all. I'd like to drop some transponders so we can triangulate the data."

"Go to it. Brunel, is our nose being roasted yet?"

"Your reputation has always been tainted with a touch of eccentricity, but I did not think that you were insane." Brunel allowed his eyes to dart between Dane and his viewscreen. "Do not think that you are going to get away with this — insubordination."

"Brunel, didn't you hire me for this job because you trusted my skill and judgment?"

"I hired you because you are the best there is, and I accept nothing less. As the owner of the *Great Eastern*, I demand that you turn this ship around and take us out of a potentially hazardous situation."

"If it's too hot for you, I can drop you off in a survival sphere and pick you up on the way out. Otherwise, you just remember that the captain of a ship is the law, and I'm in command."

"You can't take over *my* ship. I *own* it."

"Your presence here does not abdicate my authority. Your official capacity on this hop is that of engineering officer. My position is superior to yours. When we get solside, you can protest your treatment. But my contract specifically delineates the chain of command, making you number two."

Brunel beetled his brow, and peered past Dane at the astronomer. "Sandy, are you willing to follow these madcap events?"

"Only to the horizon. Then I bail out before we run into the complete compression of time."

Brunel did a double take. "What is that supposed to mean?"

Dane answered, "It means that this ship is not a democracy. The two of you together can't outvote me. Brunel, I'm not trying to throw my weight around — easy as it is in freefall — but a ship in interstellar space cannot be bound by the vagaries of whim. Just because we're beyond the reach of civilization and due legal process, doesn't mean that we can act in a way that's uncivilized and illegal. We're all bound by the laws of space, natural and manmade. And unless my decisions are blatantly deleterious to the safety of the crew, and unless you're both willing to plead your claims to an Exploteam caucus, you can't relieve me of my command without serious repercussions."

Dane took a deep breath, but cut it short when Brunel opened his mouth to respond. "Now, I've put up with your idiosyncrasies halfway across the Galaxy — and without complaint. I'm sick of your whimpering about the partial gravity, the limited computer time, the lack of memory space, and the intrusions on your buffer when I'm using the mainframe circuits to take navigational fixes. So let's get one thing geodesic: there's more purpose to this mission than meets your optical scanner. You want to lose time, I want to test fly, and Sandy wants to study this stellob. None of these goals are mutually exclusive. And as long as we're here, we *will* do our best to accomplish all three. Is that clear?"

Brunel's jaw dropped, and the ever-present straw fell from his flaxen lips.

Dane tried to run his fingers through his hair, but encountered the EEG helmet and nearly ripped out the electrodes in his exasperation. "Brunel, why do you always do this to me? I hate getting excited like this. I hate the feelings of anger. Why are you always so difficult?"

Brunel worked his mouth for several seconds before any sound emerged. "It is my nature?" he asked, his voice rising in uncertainty.

"Then change it. Brunel, we've got to communicate on an adult-to-adult level. I don't want to have to treat you like a child in order to get through your hairy cranium. It's not fair to either of us."

Brunel was silent, ruminating.

Sandy fractured the crystalline water. "Dane, I think we're all a little on edge, so don't feel bad about it. And Brunel, you've got to remember that you're part of a team. You can't just think about yourself all the time. You have to help us."

The engineer did not utter a word.

"Brunel, talk to us," Dane pleaded. "Open up. If you're angry, say so. But don't keep your feelings in, or they'll just continue to build like pressure in an air bottle. Don't let it explode. Crack the valve and vent it slowly. Now, please, for your own sake as well as for the sake of the team, what are you feeling?"

The corners of Brunel's lips quivered. The tension on his face relaxed. The knot in his forehead and the wrinkles under his eyes faded. "I feel pretty good." He almost smiled. "I am beginning to believe that this constant communication is as therapeutic as you say it is."

Sandy asked, "Would you care to elaborate?"

"No. But do carry on your activities. While you are conducting your studies, I have calculations to make."

"Is this your way of blocking us out?"

"On the contrary, I am just staying out of your way."

Dane exchanged looks with Sandy. "Okay, Brunel. That's fine with me. But while I'm flying this ship, I'll need you to monitor the mechanical functions. That's your job."

"Oh, I can handle that along with my other work. My mind moves along many parallel tracks."

"If that's a way of saying you have a split personality, I'm willing to believe it. Sandy, are you ready?"

The astronomer glanced at her screen. She was all business. "The transponders are away. We're also detecting some ionization on the starboard nacelle. Our post FTL trajectory has us entering the cloud layer at a perpendicular. The lateral buffeting is heating up our leading flank. I suggest we either increase power to the shields, or program a course that matches the rotational vector."

"We'll do both." Shrinking the magnetic collectors of a ramjet does not decelerate a vehicle because of fuel-feed loss, but it does prevent it from going any faster. "Brunel?"

"I heard, and I am altering the focus nodes."

Dane fired the attitude jets and gyrated the ship

along the complicated axes of pitch, yaw, and roll. This did not alter the angle of approach. A ship sticks to its bearing unless power is applied in a new direction. Then it tacks along a course that is the vector of its forward momentum and its newly imparted angular motion: a long, slow curve.

(Also, when dealing with the tremendous distances of interplanetary space, hours pass between deciding on a course of action, taking that course, and discerning the result. With pilot's license, some compressibility of dialogue will abbreviate the extension of time.)

"Stand by. I'm going to light the fire."

Dane funneled hydrogen into the nuclear reactor, and phased the magnetic couplers so that they allowed the larger molecules to pass through unimpeded. Inside the hull, with instantaneous calibration of the inertia pump, and backfed timelag between intent and execution, gravity flux was not felt. With sails spread, the *Great Eastern* luffed along the outer reaches of nebulosity as she continued to delve deeper into the area of increasing density.

"Honey Buns, if I'm going to obtain any useful information out of this dust bowl, we're going to have to get way inside it, where I can collect readings from the sun."

"I thought you were the one who wanted to stop three hops back?"

"The initial fear has worn off, and my curiosity is getting the better of me. I'm — I'm thrilled — at the prospect of what we may find in there. And look at these readings. Absolutely no radiation of any kind is escaping the peripheral cloudbank. We're safe in that respect."

"But I don't like the idea of hitting a brick wall at planetary speed. It's not good for my rheumatism. Brunel, how's the — "

"Ionization is dropping. I have the shields wound up to full excitement. As long as you stop bucking the current, and keep the ship scudding in this maelstrom, the *Great Eastern* can handle it. I designed her for just such a contingency."

"That's great." Dane meant Brunel's assignment of gender to the spacecraft as well as the information that he had to impart, but decided not to mention it. "Okay, tangential velocity is nearly matched. How fast can we head into the wind?"

Brunel's fingers flew along the lap pad. "It depends on relative density. At this magnitude — "

"Dane, the density is increasing exponentially. But according to data correlated by the remote probes, in another half AU it reaches maximum. Then, it — " She typed for a moment, staring at her screen with wide-eyed exaltation. "Then we won't be able to see out any more — at least on visual. I should still be able to detect our transponders on high frequency."

"Are we detecting anything from inside?"

"No electromagnetic radiation at all escapes from the central star, except at the poles. Other than the neutron pulse, the debris field must capture all rays and particles that are radiating outward from the core. Dane, we've got to find out how this dust cloud was formed. It just — it makes no sense at all, either mathematically or astronomically."

"All right, already. I get the point. You want to go in. And I'm game just to see what this baby can do. Brunel — "

"Hull sensors indicate that the rate of impact is still within acceptable safety margins."

"If that's your way of saying it's okay by you, then let's do it. I'm cutting off the automatics and taking control of the ion thrusters. I need to *feel* my way in."

"Penetration is one of your strong points," Sandy said. "I have full confidence in your ability to get through a soup of simple organic hydrocarbons."

Dane eyed her askance. Then a thought occurred to him. "Hey, is that possible? With the heavy element concentration and the polymerized chains, could this dust cloud be some kind of stellar sea, with life forms adapted to an ecosystem in rotating freefall? If solar radiation is being soaked up by the inner surface, this might be a system-sized ocean, full of plants and animals."

"How wildly imaginative," Brunel commented, with deep intonation. His fingers stopped in mid-flight, and for a moment, he stared off into a blank corner of his screen. "Do you know, we might make a discovery of some importance after all. Yes, you have my whole-hearted assent to proceed."

"Terrific. You get delusions of grandeur, and all of a sudden it's okay to risk our necks."

"I did not mean it quite like that. I cannot afford the loss of any more hardware."

Dane smiled. "I know. I'm just easing my anxiety with a little humor."

"Very little," Sandy added.

Dane readjusted the EEG helmet, and melded with the machine. As he glanced over the thousands of scrolling figures on the navigational screen, each screen flashed as if it were touched by the fire of his eyes. Dane was overcome by the thought that one did not merely fly the *Great Eastern*: one became the brain of the ship, with the external sensors becoming one's eyes and ears. This noble ship was not flying through space, *he* was.

"Okay, let's put some kindling into the stove and stoke the fire. It's a long way to hell."

Chapter 16

"In order to attain the impossible one must attempt the absurd."

— Miguel de Unamuno y Jugo

Hull sensors counted the rate of molecular impact. Dane kept the *Great Eastern* thrusting into the gas cloud at maximum allowable speed, just short of burning up. The cooling system was already working overtime.

"What's the sizing?"

Sandy tapped a key sequence. "A few stray particles as large as point zero zero zero zero one centimeter. Everything else is on the atomic scale. We may have lost the first coat of paint."

Brunel broke in brusquely. "Paint does not bond to a properly machined surface. The *Great Eastern's* hull is anti-ionized with localized dissembler capacitors that — "

"Brunel, don't be so literal. She was only using a figure of speech. Sandy, how's the radiation level?"

"Still zero."

Except for the exterior temperature, and the incoming data flooding the memory banks, the visual impact of entering the fringes of the stellob's cloud layer was almost like FTL limbo. They could see nothing other than the glow of St. Elmo's fire sparkling off the engine nacelles and accumulator heads.

"The angle of incidence has just changed a degree," Brunel said. "Dane, check your orientation. You must have let the roll wander."

"I did not," he replied, with sudden venom. "I know how to control the three simple ship motions better than that." To Sandy, "We're out a whole degree?"

"One point three eight four, roughly." Sandy had set her program for selective retrieval, and was a little behind on skimming pertinent data. "I don't see any alteration in the ship's attitude — at least, not in relation to the external star field. Brunel, how did you — "

"Temperature fluctuations on the fuselage and trunnions. Some surfaces are heating, others are cooling. The obvious deduction is that the rotating cloud is contacting the hull surface at a different angle. Ergo — "

"Dane, he's right."

"I know he is, damn it. I can feel the changes." Dane's fingers flew across his keypad as his eyes picked digitized commands on the viewscreen. Flying a starship was like balancing a razor blade on its edge. Once out of control, its vertical alignment deviated with ever increasing acceleration. "But *how?*"

"It's not your fault. Look at our coordinates." Sandy took command of the lower left sixteenth of Dane's screen, her allotment of central control, and showed him the figures. "Our orientation hasn't changed."

Dane stared at the computer screen. "Then how is it possible — "

"There's only one other explanation: cloud spin precession."

"That makes even less sense. What could make — "

Brunel shouted, "Decelerate at once. Too much heavy particulate matter is getting through the shields."

Dane looked at the heat equations that Brunel was displaying for him. "Shortening sail, pronto." He cut back the thrusters and retarded ion fuel. "Sandy, give me a vector analysis. I've got to catch up with this cloud before it sandblasts the hull to tissue paper."

Her screen filled with numbers. "Dane, I don't like this. Maybe we should back out before — "

"No. We're going on with it. Just — Brunel, patch the ion beam into the shield circuit."

"It is already done."

There was something about Brunel's unemotional efficiency that rubbed Dane the wrong way. Granted, a good engineer should be able to anticipate a pilot's orders, but he should not implement procedure until told to do so. Preempting control could be dangerous.

The pilot might have a number of alternative actions from which to choose. If he and the engineer were out of synchronization, even though the pilot could override any command, the wrong action, or the time loss before execution of the proper action, could prove fatal.

"Brunel, don't do a thing unless I tell you."

"Logic predicts your conduct. Under the circumstances, you could not do anything other than — "

"Just let me make the decisions!" Dane focused peripherally on the giant viewscreen, now parceled into sixteen separate sections. He did not consciously let his eyes rest on any one segment, or equation, but instead worked on a subliminal level which, in conjunction with the EEG probes and optical scanning feedback, allowed him to fly almost as easily as he could think. His concentration was multiplied by the ship's neural augmentation circuits. He could *feel* the hull heating up as if it were his own skin.

"Lamb Chop, you'd better ease up before you burn yourself out."

"I'm trying!" The stress was evident in Dane's voice. His body tingled synergistically with the starship's electrical circuits. Her sensors were nerve endings, her cameras his eyes, the sensitivity of her instruments perceived as pain. Every subatomic particle that slammed against her hull plates was a searing pinprick on his skin; the touch of every molecular chain was a knife wound. The ship was a personification, an extension of his senses. He no longer needed Brunel's engineering reports — he could *taste* every mechanical movement, every external stimulus. The electron flow was his blood. The *Great Eastern* was alive! "I'm rotating, but I'm still heating up."

"The cloud orientation has gone another degree plus out of phase." Brunel said calmly, with scientific detachment, "Could this be the convection zone of a dying sun? Or supergranular cells?"

"The temperature would have to be in the thousands of degrees, and we'd be bombarded by X-rays from the radiation zone. We're registering close to absolute zero."

"Fascinating."

The pain was increasing. The only way to alleviate it was to turn away from the incoming matter, to flow at the same speed with the circulating cloud. In order to do that he had to halt his sunward approach and increase his orbital velocity. But that meant taking power away from the shields. And that meant that he would incinerate before he could match speed. Brunel had designed the *Great Eastern* in such a way that Dane did not have to cheat the central processing unit with patches, as he had four decades previously, upon entering the neutron star field with Fred and Barbara. But he still had to calculate the power sharing. He allocated as many megabytes as possible to the task.

Sandy called out, "I'm registering mascons all around us. Dane, be careful."

He did not answer. He was concentrating too hard on being a starship to communicate with living organisms.

"What is he doing?" Brunel asked gruffly. "The shield power is fluctuating like a high frequency sine wave."

"Dane, ease up, or the physical tension will knock you out."

Sandy flashed the ergonometer chart onto his screen. Pictured in color were his body and all its stress points. The EEG helmet transmitted his brain wave pattern and highlighted hyperactive activity, while the neurosensors built into the command couch registered muscle strain.

A part of Dane's brain — his organic brain — saw the weaknesses in the human corporeal components. Tissue and muscle fibers were woefully inadequate alloys in starship mechanics. The nagging cramps and aches hindered his ability to intensify his energy on flight controls and auxiliary subsystems. With his newfound enhanced perceptions, his physical being was a slow-reacting, twinging ancillary member whose stability augmentation needed major overhaul.

"Honey Love, you're as tense as a ten-gauge wire."

Dane ignored her. He could not understand the malfunctions occurring in the blob of protoplasm that was the actuating center of the control system. The image on the screen showed a mammalian form that harbored a vague familiarity in his altered memory chips. Areas stained red coincided with internal pain that was backfeeding through interfaced amplification circuits.

"I do not know how he is doing it, but he is counterphasing our directional components." Brunel stared at the screen with eyebrows pinched. "He is decelerating our penetration into the solar disk, matching speed with this pseudo photosphere, and keeping the heavy elements from getting through the screens. Somehow, he is using three times the power that this vessel is capable of generating."

"Dane! Stop! You're tearing yourself apart."

Sandy watched the ergochart increase the warning signals on Dane's two-dimensional screen representation. The nerve endings in the spine glowed dangerously, and red lights shot up the cerebral cortex like thrusting daggers. The muscle groups in the lower back surged spasmodically.

"According to the couch monitors, I would say he is flying by the seat of his pants," Brunel said.

"Stop it!" Sandy shouted at the engineer. To Dane, "Pumpkin, listen to me. Use your mind to run the ship, not your body."

But Dane's mind *was* the ship, and his body a useless impediment. He exalted in the pure freedom of flying through space, of absolute control of his subfunctions, of the instantaneous response that devolved from pure thought. The body lying on the couch was merely a holographic computer simulation.

"However he is doing it, he is bringing the ship under control."

"But look at the readings. He's killing himself."

"If he does not parallel our flight path with that of the rotating dust cloud, we will all die."

Sandy pleaded, "Dane, please come out of it."

He wished the organic modules would power down their acoustical circuits. They were distracting him. Input data was hitting him at an enormous rate: the *Great Eastern's* entire memory network was his to access, and information flowed through the lattice of his brain with ever increasing speed. He chafed at the sluggish switching capability of the synaptic process. The biological neurons suffered as their axons and dendrites went into sensory overload.

"Dane! Talk to me!"

Brunel said, "I believe we are out of immediate danger."

"Shut up, you beast! I think he's hurt."

"His eyes are a little glazed."

"Look at the chart. Every nerve ending in his body is exploding."

The *Great Dane Eastern* was more sensitive, more aware, more alive, than he had ever been in his life. The merging of mind and machine, the splicing of external stimuli, the converging of electrical flux, had altered his spatial perceptions. The entity that he had become was greater, much greater, than the sum of the individual parts.

Unlimited access to incoming data flooded him with images, ideas, concepts, possibilities, and surrealities. He saw the Universe in its entire electromagnetic spectrum, throughout the length and breadth of space and time. He did not need to scan, he did not need to vocalize: his data banks interfaced directly with his cerebrum. He/she was beyond the realm of normal communication.

Multiplexing amplifiers discharged at an enormous rate. The melding of mechanical and biological neural circuits met infinite resonance, the syncopation of events between them reached perfect harmony. He/she saw the bright, fundamental ball of light that was the almighty directive power behind the guidance of the Universe. He/she could almost divine the purpose —

His/her reverie entered an abstract arena beyond

comprehension. He/she could not absorb all the data, could not separate the chaotic order from orderly chaos. The harmony of the stars was within the realm of reason, but slightly out of focus — if he/she could only sharpen his/her concentration . . .

Input exceeded the capacity to store. The organic data bank overloaded. The neurons fibrillated. Then came the utter and final oblivion of power failure.

****

Dissolution persisted through an uncounted, and uncountable, period of time. There was nothing but darkness: a black, hollow pit of emptiness. Nothing existed in the Universe. Nothing, that is, but the pure thought form that was *Great* Dane *Eastern* Gerrace. No! Dane *Eastern*. Still not right. *Great* Dane. Or was it, Dane Gerrace? Somehow, that dangerous thought, that sequence of sounds, had a familiar ring to it.

From somewhere, matter appeared in the Universe. It coalesced into a central point. Its compression created heat, created energy. This bulging ball of ylem became visible through its own interaction. It burst outward in all directions, separated into swirling clouds of atomic gas that condensed into galaxies, clusters, stars, and planets. The cosmos was born in front of his very eyes.

The islands of cosmic dust began to assume form. Some were coruscating lights, and indistinct. Others were flowing patterns. The first celestial body that acquired recognizable definition was shaped in a way that disturbed his inner workings, that awoke vague, deep-seated feelings, that reminded him of a long ago biological existence.

The pink ball was surrounded by gleaming filaments. "Dane. Wake up." The ball opened in the middle and discharged vibrating atoms. "Wake up, Dane." An articulated extension stretched toward him, and closed tensors on his nerve endings. "Baby Cakes, come out of it."

"Sandy?" The sound came out garbled, muted, distant — like the hiss of air through a ventilator port.

"You see, as long as the Medwife's life support functions register normal brain waves and healthy physiological signs, the patient *must* be viable."

"Brunel, I don't *care* what the machine says. I want him conscious."

"Viable or vegetable, it will awaken him with the proper injections when it deems his condition stable."

Sandy leaned into the clear plastiglass casemate that was the Medwife: an automated medical facility that monitored, mended, and administered appropriate pharmaceuticals. The pungent hygiatmosphere lingered in the enclosure.

Dane felt a sting on his thigh. Disorientation began to leave him, like cobwebs melting off gray matter. He came suddenly to full awareness. "How long was I out?"

"Hours," Sandy whined. She placed her head on his chest, and nestled in the black, curly hair. "Oh, Dane. I thought we were going to lose you."

He shook his head, pushed her warm body gently away, rolled onto his side, sat up, and kept on going. He reached back for a handgrip, and pulled himself back to the edge of the Medwife. "This ship isn't big enough to get lost in."

"Your intolerable drollery alleges to your return to normality." Brunel sucked a mouthful of liquid out of the container that was tucked into his jacket pocket. "I will have to redesign the Medwife's applications to incorporate customer improvement rather than simple healing."

"Brunel, either I've been reborn into a parallel dimension, or you're gaining a sense of humor."

"Apologies. I was swayed by the emotion of the moment." Dark eyebrows arched high. "Even though the medical readouts present your condition with fifth place decimal accuracy, I will be so redundant as to inquire into your health."

"After being juiced by the *Great Eastern's* neurocircuits, I feel like a new man. I got into a mindmeld with the CPU. Sandy, touch me so I know I'm a man and not a mechanical construct."

She did as instructed.

"Not there!"

Sandy snickered. "Your responses are normal. You're still a man."

"Okay, that's enough. May I have a fresh jumpsuit, please?"

Brunel jetted around the cabin and collected the appropriate clothing from the laundry dispenser. "Do you know that you were completely uncommunicative during the final episode? What caused your blackout?"

Dane floated off the padded Medwife gurney. He shrugged into the one-piece uniform and donned stippers. "I had an out-of-body experience, aided by your neurofeedback system. Brunel, have you ever tested this device?"

"*This* is the test run, remember?"

"But, didn't you ever conduct space trials, just to see how the subsystems would function?"

"Tests need to be passed. Engineering is an exact science. Whatever I build works to perfection."

"Except that the self-analyzing circuits extended control into my cerebral cortex. One microsecond I was flying this ship, the next it was flying me. Now that I can think about it with detachment, it was scary. But at the time it was — exhilarating. The sublime interaction between mind and computer, generating an ensemble that could visualize the fabric of the Universe. My god, I was inside the crystal lattice. My brain was digitized, and I could handle the cybernetic functions as if they were my own."

Sandy's voice was full of concern. "Are you sure you're all right?"

Dane looked down at his hands, watched intently as he contracted them into fists. "I think — I think I'm all back together. But, I don't know. I have a feeling that part of me is still circulating through the mainframe — and that a portion of the data bank has been downloaded into my brain. I seem to be able to sense things, to know they're true, without having any knowledge of how, or why."

"You experienced the mental aberration similar to drug-induced mind expansion. Do not confuse such erroneous notions as the nonexistent altered states of consciousness with what they really are -- pure imagination."

"You make me feel so much better," Dane scowled. "Whatever happened to me seemed real at the time. Brunel, you need some kind of governor on the biofeedback circuits, or I'm likely to get swallowed by carnivorous neurotransmitters. How did I get out of that heterodyning hegemony, anyway?"

Sandy floated to his side and steadied herself by holding onto his knee. "I broke the contact by ripping the electrodes off your head. I had no idea what was happening to your mind, but the ergonomic chart indicated severe physical trauma."

"You had already stabilized the ship, so it was safe to relieve you of the controls."

"I'm touched by your concern." To Sandy, "What was going on with the cloud orientation changes?"

"Different ecliptic planes. Dane, this stellob is constructed like an onion, each peel equivalent to a distinct rotating cloud zone which has its own ecliptic, and its own density pattern. Each zone is one point three eight four six one five four degrees out of alignment with the next. We went through twenty-seven layers before you brought the ship under control, and they were all angled by the same amount. If that progression continues to two hundred sixty separate strata, it could form a complete shield around the central star."

"It sounds crazy."

Brunel said calmly, "No, just out of our experience."

"No, Brunel. It's impossible, " Sandy said, nearly shouting. "The only thing that makes sense is that the speed of revolution of each succeeding inner zone increases."

Dane shrugged. "The inverse square law of gravitation. The planets — "

"*But* — how can a series of cloud layers all form in their own ecliptic planes, each exactly the same angular distance out of phase with the others? We're seeing something that doesn't fit any known, or predicted, cosmological principle — which, in fact, opposes all the laws of physics. Whatever the Mettleson Object is, it can't possibly exist in this Universe."

Dane stared at the nonsensical data on her screen. "It's also been proven that bees can't fly."

Chapter 17

"There are no enemies in science, Professor, only phenomena to study. We are studying one."
— Charles Lederer

"It's beginning to come back to me." Dane lay on the command couch, fingers on the keypad. The EEG helmet floated alongside. Whenever the electrodes drifted too close, clutching at him like predatory pincers, he shoved the device away. "When I was in this — imaginary dream state, or electronically induced condition of consciousness, I was in charge of the ship."

Sandy looked at him askance.

"I really was. Okay, maybe I wasn't in conscious control, but on a subliminal level, I was telling the computer what to do."

"That isn't what you said before."

"I know, but I was just coming out of it then. I was still groggy. It's — a confusing and exhausting experience. The drain on my mental reserves was incredible because I was forced to think faster than I ever have before — matching speed with the computer. Anyway, I knew what I was doing. I was maneuvering this ship like no ship has ever been maneuvered. What a performance."

Brunel stopped typing for a moment. "She has the most powerful and most responsive fusion drive train of any ship in the System — or out of it. The magnetic collectors have a field that is three times larger than any previous starship. And the CPU operates at over seven bips."

Dane recalled that the *Phantom Jackal* could handle two point five billion instructions per second, and he thought *that* was fast. "It's a good thing, too. No other ship could have gotten this far inside the cloud radius so fast. It would have taken weeks with normal shield power. Anyway, I was able to function at electronic speed with laser beam accuracy. What you saw as a sine wave between power potentials was a three-way alternating energy division. I swear, I don't know how I did it. On a scale of microseconds, I diverted power from the focusing nodes first to the forward thrusters, then to the shields, then to the lateral thrusters, then back to the shields. And I did it so fast that I turned the ship in an arc while protecting the fuselage from molecular friction — like an electron orbiting a proton, it gave the appearance of solidity. It was a fantastic feeling of absolute, utter control."

"Excuse me, Honey Bun, but throw your screen on full visual, and take a look at the sun."

Dane executed the command. A dull, yellow light appeared in the middle of his wall monitor, no brighter than a candle in a coal bin. It was ringed by a diffuse, rainbow-hued halo. Light thrown forward reflected off intervening dust, highlighting the larger motes so that they sparkled like gemstone facets.

Sandy's screen was full of scrolling chemical formulae. "We're getting much more than simple free elements in here. I'm getting resolution on thousands of minerals, alloys, plastics, polymers, and complex hydrocarbons — the kinds of chemical combinations that you wouldn't expect to find in nature. Since nothing else adds up, these readings fit right in. Don't ask me to interpret the meaning."

"Odd. Most odd." Brunel sucked on his ever-present straw. "Dane, I have installed the output restriction that you requested." He dispatched the hastily written program to the pilot's screen, and used his remote cursor to indicate the user functions. "This filter will prevent all data from backfeeding from the logic circuits through the EEG probes, unless specifically requested. I have created an applications potentiometer which can be calibrated only by the user."

"You mean, I can regulate the data load as I see fit?"

"With infinite precision. You can fly the ship on peripheral input, or, if you require more control for refined spatialdynamic tactics, you can allow data entry bit by bit. As an added precaution, I have devised a system purge which will cut in automatically if the stress monitors reach the approximate level of prognosticated fatality."

"Hey, why use a small word when ten large ones will do?"

Brunel pierced Dane with rapierlike eyes. "The principle criterion of communication is not simplicity of expression, but specificity of meaning without the possibility of misinterpretation."

"Another round goes to the engineer. Brunel, can you be a little more definite. Do I die before or after it separates me from the computer?"

"I have not worked out the final details. This is only a rough schematic . . . "

"Then how about if we refine it a bit." Dane rolled his eyes at Sandy. "Can you program it so it will cut me out of the circuit *before* I byte the dust?"

"Hmmnn." Brunel tapped away on his lap pad for several minutes before replying. "There are factors of uncertainty involving your physical and mental stamina. However, I feel certain that disjunction will occur immediately prior to the cessation of cerebral activity — but you will have to experiment to be certain."

"I hate on-the-job training. Okay, I'll take your profound word for it. Will I still be able to perform the triple alternating bypass maneuver without having an electronic orgasm with the black widow subroutine?"

"More than likely. I will need time to perfect the program."

"You let me know when it's ready. In the meantime, I'll fly this baby on manual. Sandy, is there anywhere you'd like to go?"

She filled her screen with menus. "Within scooting distance, I have over a thousand possible targets. But let's stick to this peel." She scrolled until the coordinates were all columnized in order of ascending proximity. "Let's see, I've got about three hundred mascons in range of our sensors, but none are within optical scanning distance."

"Are any of them more intriguing than the others?"

Sandy slowly shook her head. "There's not a textdisk case among them. The size is asteroidal, but the mass is negligible — almost as if they were hollow. High metallic composition. Dane, I've got to see one of these things close up. First, we've got a stellob that couldn't form this way, and can't have gotten this way after formation, now we've got mascons that don't fit any category at all."

"Could they be bubble bodies? Like molten blobs of solar material that were expulsed by the sun during eruptive prominence, and later cooled into empty globules."

"Kind of like stellar soap bubbles? Hmmnn. I suppose it's not impossible. We certainly haven't seen all the kinds of astrophysical bodies that exist in the Galaxy, and every hop returns data on totally unexpected phenomena. I could run an algorithmic prediction program. But as long as we're this close, we'd probably be there before the program finished running."

"Brunel, do you have any objections?"

"None. I am sketching out this FTL periscope idea of yours. Using the Selkirk equations, it is possible that such a device can be constructed."

"Good. You keep working on it while we play around with the mascons. If anything interesting comes up, I'll wake you. Sandy, take your pick."

She touched her keypad. Instantly, a set of navigational fixes flashed onto Dane's screen. "Head in this direction."

Dane typed the numbers into the CPU. When he took the helm, it was difficult at first to get used to the sluggish response. But he was not yet ready for another bout with the neurotransmitters. He conned the ship digitally through the thickened dust storm. It was slow beaming, but it insured his schizophrenic separation from the computer's overpowering feedback amplifiers.

"I'm getting abnormally high albedos, on the order of point six three."

Dane pursed his lips. "Nine times as bright as the

Moon. Even in this gloomy sunshine, we should see some mascons soon. Sandy, could you be picking up luminosity rather than albedo?"

Sandy clucked her tongue against the roof of her mouth. "Temperature is pretty close to absolute zero — what you'd expect from a cold body in space. An object emitting its own light would have to radiate heat. No, it's definitely reflected sunlight."

"It would take a planar surface to bounce that much light."

Sandy agreed. "Like a smooth metallic crust that might at one time have been molten."

"Or a crystal face. You know, I'm having a crazy idea. Suppose these mascons are some kind of super geodes — like those rock balls they have in the Earth museums, with the crystals growing inside? We can call them stellodes."

"They're not igneous, so the analogy doesn't hold true. But it's an interesting idea."

"How about if we find crystalline life forms? This solar fog is dense enough to be called atmosphere. Maybe we've got a bunch of miniature worlds flying through this soup, with intelligent crystals living on the surfaces. Think of it. They could draw energy directly from the sun, and feed on minerals in the soil. Their blood could be a flow of ions. This entire solar system could be one gigantic bed of crystals."

Sandy smiled. "A highly imaginative concept, but not too likely."

"You're just envious because they might have more cleavage than you. But think of the possibilities. Radio waves are transmitted through crystal sets. Our computers are constructed of crystalline solid-state semiconductors. Not only could crystal life forms communicate among themselves through their own framework, each one could be a miniature computer — a crystal clear intellect."

"Kind of a brain with a transmitter. How unique," Sandy said sarcastically.

"We might soon be making contact with diamonds

and rubies, a society of living transistors. The mind boggles."

"Yours does, anyway."

"True xenomorphic structures, each housed in its own crystal lattice. You could recognize individuals by their impurities. And great communities could live together in a polycrystalline mass."

"An old salt of the sun."

"Sandy, you're not taking me seriously."

"Sweetie Pie, no one could, or she'd soon find herself in a solution of hydrated carbon. Nevertheless, your theory does have certain symmetry to it. The Greeks would have called it the Music of the Squares."

"All right, that's enough."

"If you think you have trouble with two-faced people, imagine trying to understand a multifaceted emerald."

"I said, that's enough! I'm sorry I brought up the subject."

Sandy kept her serious mien. "Why don't you gaze into your crystal ball, and tell me what a nice whorl like that is doing in a phase like this."

"Cut it *out!*" Dane's shoulders rippled as he tried to shrug off her cutting remarks. "Now, can you put something on my screen that isn't a bunch of equations? What do these mascons look like?"

"Can do, Honey Love." Sandy typed instructions and hit the transfer switch.

Dane's full screen illuminated like a multicolored Christmas tree: millions of pinpoints of light with no more form than a child's connect-the-dot drawing. He had to let his mind drift and his eyes go out of focus before he could visualize the computerized imagery. The bursts of light flickered on and off with the rapidity of slow-cycle alternating current.

"Hey, Sandy, can you just pick out one mascon and lock in on it?"

"Sorry, Pumpkin. I was rambling through the data banks for correlations."

"Just give me the one whose trajectory you want to

match, and I'll take it from there."

Sandy scrolled through her menu. "That two three two nine five slash four zero eight eight looks promising. It's representative of the bunch."

Dane issued instructions. "Got it."

Because it had to create a three-dimensional, artificial meridian, the gyronavigator took a long time to interpolate the relative position of the designated mascon with respect to the *Great Eastern*. A computer issued instantaneous responses only when it was given problems for which the answers had already been programmed — that is, when it had the data on file, and all it had to do was locate and retrieve. In this case, it had to synchronize all the course changes made by the starship since entering the dust cloud, with the azimuth of the star field that was last imprinted on its autopilot circuits.

"Have you looked around you lately?" Dane sequestered a corner space on the screen for external visual. "It's as dark as a pocket out there, and getting worse as we near the mascon."

"Yes, ambient light is extremely dim. It's on the positive side of the magnitude scale."

"You can damn near measure it in lumens." While no stars were visible as points, other than the nebulous, central sun, the entire cloud glowed like mist seen through a diffuser. As the *Great Eastern* closed on the mascon, it seemed as if some cosmic god were playing with a dimmer switch. "It's eerie."

"All systems functioning." Brunel's screen was filled with tensor equations that described stress on the pulse field and acceleration potential for the ion thrusters. "At this speed, you can plow through a comet with shield power to spare."

"Brunel, I didn't know you were here."

"I have never left this couch."

"I meant mentally. I thought you were deep into the calculus of your atmosphere siphon project."

"Contrary to belief, I do take breaks from my work — when I have a program running calculations necessary for further progress. Sandy, have you been able to ascertain the shape of the mascon which we are approaching?"

"Not yet, but I'm getting approximate dimensions through the backscatter. Let's call the diameter a hundred fifty kleters."

Dane held the helm steady. "Are you receiving telemetry from the sun?"

"I haven't been paying attention, but yes. It's more massive than Sol — according to gravitational effects, nearly twice as much. I'm still getting rapidly changing figures for density, but it's not a lock-on problem. My impression is that the core is condensing while the interplanetary rings are shrinking."

"*That's it!*" Dane bellowed suddenly. He ran his fingers over the keypad with lightninglike speed. "When I was under the electronic influence, matching velocity, one of the most difficult procedures was compensating for acceleration. I didn't have a conscious awareness at the time of what was happening — I just did it. Then, I forget most of what I had done when my neural circuits overloaded. But you've just sparked my memory. Look at this."

He flashed some figures on his screen, then transmitted them to a section of Sandy's monitor.

"May I see that, also?" Brunel asked.

"Of course." Dane sent the data to the engineering screen for easy viewing. "You see how our speed is increasing? That's what really sent me over the brink. I had to throw an acceleration constant into the formula, otherwise we would have kept falling behind. Each cloud layer, or peel, is not only rotating at a separate velocity, it's accelerating at a different rate. I had to program the thrusters to compensate accordingly as we passed through each successive peel."

"A first class job of navigational skill. It shows that my faith in you was not misplaced. You have my compliments."

Sandy cross-linked data into the banks. "Hot Pants rides again. But seriously, Liver Pill, I can't make any sense out of this. Interplanetary bodies accelerate only during the perihelion approach of an elliptical orbit. According to my preliminary computations, these cloud peels are seventeen decimal places close to perfect circles."

Dane shrugged. "An eccentric system without eccentricity. Chalk it up as another idiosyncrasy of this crazy stellob. Anyway, you can see that our base course includes all these variables, while our overtaking course is extrapolated from our position with respect to those variables."

"I am happy that you are piloting this ship," Brunel said, with a touch of gravity. "To be fair, despite the genius of my design, I do not think that she could have done it on preprogrammed automatics."

"I'm not sure who you're complimenting, Brunel, but it doesn't really matter. Synergism between pilot and ship is an old story. With the *Great Eastern*, the effect is carried out to the nth degree. Together, this gal and I could plumb the depths of a black hole, and come out on the other side of the Universe in one piece."

"Please don't try it while I'm aboard," Sandy said. "*This* body is partial to tidal effects."

"I can't see any stretch marks from here."

Brunel said, "If you two will cease the banter, you will notice that the proximity alarm has just been activated."

"Put us on visual, Sandy."

Dane allowed three-quarters of his screen to project external compugraphic imagery. In the murky shadow of the cloud within a cloud, a splotchy configuration was taking shape. Even with optical and electronic image enhancers, the overall pattern was vague, and the contours uncertain.

"It's not spherical," Sandy commented dryly.

"Doesn't surprise me. That would have been too normal for this system. Could it be a planetesimal?"

"The thought had crossed my mind, as well as the computer's deduction circuits."

Brunel, for once, was neither eating nor working.

Unmoving, he watched as the digital animation display filtered out the intervening dust motes and intensified the outline of the mascon. "The ends are too blunt for a small planet."

"No, you don't understand. According to the planetesimal hypothesis, all the planets and satellites were formed by the gravitational aggregation of planetesimals: small bodies thought to orbit a star in the beginning of its life cycle. What I've seen so far appears to conform to that hypothesis. We have a star that is seemingly condensing from interstellar matter, still surrounded by the original cosmic dust, and full of innumerable smaller bodies. The evidence we have so far indicates that this stellob is the formation — the actual birth — of a solar system."

For the next several minutes, Dane concentrated on three-dimensional guidance controls and match acceleration tasks. Gradually, the planetesimal grew in definition. When it came into full view, compugraphics showed that it was tumbling slowly. Dane swung the *Great Eastern* in a broad arc that partially circumnavigated the curved surface. It appeared longer than its width.

"It is somewhat cylindrical," Brunel observed.

"Ratio four to one," Sandy called out.

The sun caught the terminus of the elongated dimension. As the object spun through space, the dim rays of the sun cascaded garishly through the filmy mist and spilled onto the foreshortened end. What appeared was a perfectly formed crescent, with a circular configuration spreading from the inside of the arc, while in the other dimension, the curved surface extended almost to the limit of visibility, with the upper and lower lines almost converging to a point.

"Oh my god," Dane breathed. There was not a sound in the cubicle, and not one finger touched an input key. The icy chill that coursed along his spine sent tongues of frosted tingles. Every inch of skin erupted in nervous, trembling goose bumps. His scalp crawled. "It's a Settlement."

Chapter 18

"With a very high intelligence would also go higher moral values because, without these, intelligence is self-destructive."

— Arthur C. Clarke

The platform was old.

Its surface was sandblasted to a bright metallic finish by the abrasive effect of interplanetary dust. It was also pockmarked from collision with millions of micrometeoroids. The cylinder was not intact, but ripped open in great sheets that exposed the interior to the cloud-filled vacuum of space. Its guts hung by tatters of twisted metal. It no longer had function, just a vague, barely contiguous form.

The Settlement had been dead, and its inhabitants extinct, when man's ancestors were still gathering roots in the Olduvai Gorge.

"Hang on, people. We're pulling up stakes." Dane unscrewed a bright red cap from the control board, punched a finger into the well, and primed the tactical emergency evasion program. The entire control room lit up with red warning lights and flashing strobes. Sirens wailed raucously.

"Dane! Don't do it!" Sandy shouted over the clamor.

One slight touch on the heat activated sensor, and the CPU would take over the ship. The teep was designed to take evasive action by shooting a computerized back azimuth at maximum allowable thrust for the quickest possible translation into FTL. One of its purposes was to enable the crew to get home in case the pilot became incapacitated.

"You know Exploteam's prime directive: 'any contact with alien life of an intelligent nature is strictly forbidden.' This is a scouting expedition, not a diplomatic mission."

Sandy culled through programs with blinding

speed. The memory bank was jammed with incoming data. "We can't leave now. This is *important*. It needs to be studied."

"We've got all the preliminary data we need to make a report." But his finger hesitated. Not that there was anything irreversible about touching that button. Dane could disconnect the recall program any time he wanted. The difference was that, while any one of the three could activate the teep, the countermand was coded to Dane's living thumbprint. "It's up to the Committee to evaluate it."

"We haven't seen any aliens yet."

'Yet' was an awfully big word. "That cylinder sure as hell isn't a naturally occurring phenomenon."

"Granted that it's an object of intelligent and unknown manufacture, but there hasn't been any actual contact."

"And there isn't going to be." Dane's finger millimetered closer. "Visual observation in space is almost like a French kiss."

"Dane, please be reasonable. Sighting the remains of an ancient civilization doesn't constitute physical liaison. There's been no reciprocal observation."

"That's exactly what I want to avoid."

"She is right, you know." Brunel stared at them both. His eyes shone with a light that Dane had never seen before. The straw had slipped from his mouth, and the foodtube was drifting slowly among the interstices of the control cabin. "This is an entirely unprecedented event, and I will not allow you to jeopardize the opportunity of further investigation. I forbid you to touch that button."

"Brunel, maybe it's slipped your mind, but we've already had this discussion. For your benefit, I'll repeat it. *I* am in charge here, *I* make the decisions, and *I* will do what I have been trained to think is right."

"Must you persist in this silly contest of wills? I am not interested in abrogating your delusions of authority. I am simply telling you what is a reasonable course of action under the circumstances. Look at these readouts. Ambient internal temperature of the cylinder, including that from solar heating, is two degrees above zero."

Dane knew that he was speaking in degrees absolute.

"Whoever engineered this magnificent structure did not intend to occupy it in that kind of cold. Neither is it emitting E-M radiation — it is not broadcasting on any wavelength."

Dane's finger never twitched.

"Chicken Livers, think of the philosophical impact that this will have on humanity. Think of what it must mean — not just in terms of our place in the Universe, but our direction for the future. The mere existence of another intelligence, our sharing of the Galaxy with another race, will have a profound effect on all human events. It will unseat our entire concept of the cosmos. To leave now, without at least a cursory examination of the cultural artifacts, will give us too little information on which to base any logical deductions concerning their beginnings, their growth, their — eventual demise. All we'll know is that something out here killed them off, and it'll throw the System into chaos. We're not only facing dialectical destruction through ultimate iconoclasm, we're repudiating our own immortality. Our society might not survive the impact if we bring back a bankful of agonizing suspicions without any credible consolations."

Dane scowled. "You're making an assumption that further discovery will be advantageous. Suppose we find something that we don't like?"

"The first criterion of science is to abolish prejudgment. The second is to entertain only positive thoughts. To a thinking, rational being, full cognizance is more desirable than partial knowledge. Enlightenment can't come from half truths."

Brunel broke in. "This is a discovery of incredible proportion. *We* have made it, and *we* must take credit for it. To depart now, without assembling the material that will ensure our names in the history disks, would be a sacrilege to human endeavor."

"Do you need special thrusters to boost your ego?" Dane glanced from side to side, from Brunel to Sandy. He was afraid to let his emotion run away with him. "Doesn't anyone care about personal danger?" He received two blank stares. "How can we be absolutely certain and one hundred percent positive that we won't meet a surviving recluse?"

Sandy said, "Our instruments are registering no physical movement, and no chemical reaction. There aren't even signs of photosynthesis. Whatever happened here, happened a long time ago."

Dane's goose bumps had long since grown to moguls, which the aura of rationality surrounding the arguments of his companions did little to dispel. As almost the head of the Committee, if in offer only, he felt that he had the prerogative to arbitrate the case. And since he was a risk taker at heart, he knew which way his inclinations would swing. Besides, there were no directives against the investigation of dead civilizations.

"Okay." Dane keyed off the annunciators. The control room returned to womblike darkness, the only lights being those emitted by the viewscreens and panel switches. His voice sounded loud in the sudden silence. "We stay."

Sandy and Brunel both cheered; for the engineer, that was decidedly out of character.

"*But*, we restrict our reconnaissance to this one particular alifact — I don't want to run into a construction gang in some other part of the system. They might have laws against trespassing. *And*, we limit our time, collect our data, then skedaddle."

Brunel's eyebrows arched. "Skedaddle?"

"An old Earth colloquialism that means 'get the hell out.' Agreed?"

Sandy nodded. "I think that's fair. Brunel?"

"I agree with everything except the word 'alifact.' I suggest that 'xenofact' more properly describes an artifact of alien manufacture."

Dane sighed, and rolled his eyes. "Have it your way."

"And, since they might not have had hands, we should use the word 'xenofacture' to describe their production process."

Sarcastically, "Any *more* objections?"

Brunel pursed his lips, glanced at the overhead for a moment, and recaptured the errant foodtube. His deep, base voice lilted questioningly. "Chicken Livers?"

Dane stabbed a finger at Sandy. "I'm innocent."

"A quaint phrase of endearment that I picked up from my mother." Sandy tilted her head. "With all due respect, it's not intended for great-great-grandfathers."

"I consider myself spared. Dane, I propose that you motivate this vessel to within close scanning range of this fascinating piece of architecture." The engineer looked up at his screen. "It may be large enough to house a million people — beings, but what a waste of breathing medium. I have already determined that many small cylinders are more economical with respect to internal surface area than one huge monstrosity. Perhaps that is where this vanished race erred."

"I'm sure you could have taught them plenty." Dane screwed down the red cap, canceling the teep. He initiated docking maneuvers, and began to bring the *Great Eastern* on a matched trajectory with the alien cylinder. "Let's hope that we can learn something from them."

Sandy played with her keyboard. "With your permission, I'm detaching probes *now*."

Two instrumentation packages deployed from the cargo bay. They immediately telemetered positive function signals, and awaited further instructions. Dane tripped the relays that would allow them to perform independently of the mother craft. He left one in stationary orbit, and dispatched the other toward the surface of the platform where magnetic grapples would hold it in place.

"Two three two nine five slash four zero eight eight, you're a way out baby. I hereby christen thee — *Kuttner*. And Brunel, please don't tell me about useless sentimentality. I'm just a natural born romantic."

"I'll second that." Sandy transmitted kisses from her screen to Dane's, and winked at him. "But for now, let's stick to business. How close can you take us to — the *Kuttner*?"

"You're in for a surprise, Honey. The epidermis of that thing has some pretty big cavities in it. Big enough to drive a ship through. I figure, as long as we've knocked on the door, we may as well go inside."

"That is preposterous!" Brunel spat so violently that his foodtube shot away from his mouth and slammed into his viewscreen. He captured it on the rebound. "We can obtain sufficient telemetry resolution without joining the platform's molecular structure."

"For a guy who strives for communicative exactitude, you're gaining quite a penchant for hyperbole."

"Not only is the cylinder rotating, it is tumbling as well. The slightest docking error will smash this ship against its superstructure. Our shields are effective against atoms and dust, not massive bodies or compact amalgamated metals. The tensile strength of our hull is negligible against high impact with dense obstructions. Once the integrity of the ship is compromised, our — "

"All right, Brunel, you've made your point. I understand the risks." Dane commenced the initial maneuvers. "What happened to your faith in my spaviation ability?" All of Dane's space aviation experience went into his keypad. Without the aid of the EEG helmet, he continued to scan the navigation screen as he talked. "Don't answer. The question was rhetorical. Besides, I'll do all the vector matching from a distance, and zero in only after we're stationary with respect to the *Kuttner*. Watch."

Dane warped the *Great Eastern* alongside the immense bulk of the ancient cylinder. He paralleled its solar revolutionary path with ease. More difficult was matching trajectories with the end-over-end longitudinal component. Nearly impossible was stabilizing an orbit that kept the *Great Eastern* hovering motionless over a specific spot on the cylinders broad, broken surface. Since the mass attraction between the *Kuttner* and the *Great Eastern* was negligible, the orbit was maintained by constant computerized side-thrust course corrections that forced the starship into a circular pattern whose single locus was the cylinder's midpoint.

"Hold onto your seat, Brunel. We're going in."

"I am semipermanently bonded to my chair, so your declaration is totally without meaning. Besides, I am pulling in enough matter to power the inertia pump." Usually, only at FTL speeds did a starship move through enough space to collect sufficient fusionable material. "It is calibrated to equalize instantly and perfectly all the ship's thrust capabilities."

"Brunel, you're as literal and logical as a ten-frame computer."

"Thank you."

"It wasn't meant as a compliment."

"Logic and clarity are the ultimate concerns of the engineer."

"What about deductive reasoning?"

"There is no deduction in engineering, only calculation."

The *Great Eastern* converged on the alien cylinder as if a towing cable was drawing it in. The ship was miniscule by comparison. A ragged opening in the outer skin appeared as a monstrous, dark maw that was ready to swallow the starship and its awkward looking, projecting drive appendages.

Thick dust clouds created a halo effect around the *Kuttner*. The tiny particles were magnetically and gravitationally bound to the cylinder, and glowed with the light of ionized gas. Dane switched on the ship's outboard lights to supplement the faint illumination.

Sandy skimmed through the information that was being telemetered aboard. "Spectroscopic analyses indicate some mineral compositions and free metals, but most of the cloud consists of polymerized chemicals and organic hydrocarbons, with a high proportion of amino compounds, sugars, acids, enzymes, even simple proteins."

"Sounds as if you're describing some kind of living solar broth."

"Nothing is alive, but they do represent the basic chemicals of life. It's difficult to reconstruct the original formulae. Sunlight has caused so much molecular decomposition."

"Could that be all that's left of our alien counterparts? Maybe their bodies have disintegrated over the millennia."

"It's difficult to imagine that much chemical breakdown from living biomass, especially since solar and cosmic radiation is so effectively shielded by the cloud layers. I'd have to say that it was processed material."

Dane kept both eyes on the screen, splitting between a visual representation of the space-worn platform and navigational functions. The astronomical gyros emitted a constant flux of coordinates. "Like food?"

"Could be. But I was thinking more in terms of — waste matter."

"Doesn't make sense. They'd have had eliminators that could handle — "

"Would you please keep your mind on the controls!" Brunel filled his screen with mechanical systems checks and electronic sensor data. "You've got enough routines running to choke a bypass circuit."

"This isn't easy, you know. I can't fly this ship without cooperation. Sandy, can you cut back any of the astrolog? We need more working memory."

"The transponders are still giving me quirky readings. Whenever I triangulate a navigational fix on the sun, the distance measurements come out wrong. The odd thing is that the differences are incremental in a time-frame orientation. Dane, I've *got* to figure out what this system is doing to our instrumentation, because somehow it's altering our data."

"Okay, if we've got computer errors I want to know about it. Sorry, Brunel, but you'll have to wait until I can cut out the drive motors. That will free some buffer space."

"I can't just sit here and daydream. I've got work to do."

"How about diverting more of your attention to reality, instead of to your creative engineering problems? Once we get inside this thing you'll be busier than a rock collector in the Asteroid Belt."

A huge, black pit lay before the *Great Eastern*: the cavernous opening through which Dane was steering the starship. The torn fabric of rectennas and heat radiators were recognizable despite their alien design. The frameworks of solar power cells were all that remained of the power collectors. Large support towers protruded spaceward from massive foundations, but whatever they had supported had long since been sheared off by unequal torque stress.

The outer skin was worn to eggshell thinness, exposing rigid metal cross-members. The three-layered bottom was compartmentalized. The perimeter of the hole was not rent inward or outward by explosion, but honed to flat, bladelike thinness as if the cylinder had been dragged along a sandy beach until the outer layers wore through. There was no sign of violent destruction.

"It looks so fragile," Sandy said.

The starship passed through the yawning aperture, and into the dirty, dark, dust-filled oblivion inside.

Chapter 19

"The Redman did not alter the face of the earth but left it very much as he found it. And this it is that constitutes the fundamental difference between civilization, so called, and savagery."

— Max Schrabisch

Dane flipped his screen to three-quarters visual. "Unless those slots are vertical louvers, these guys were as tall as three-meter bean poles."

Brunel said, "They undoubtedly evolved on a low gravity planet."

"Makes it easier for building cylinders, because they don't have to spin as fast to create artificial gravity."

"Not only that, but the relatively rarefied atmosphere of their home world might account for their lack of concern about platform diameter. They would need less gas to fill the void, so they could afford to be less economical. Nonetheless, it still seems like an unwise allocation of space."

The *Great Eastern's* docking lights were intended for visual reference only. They were inadequate for exterior Illumination. The thin, garish beams were barely bright enough to dispel the insipid gloom of the spacious cylinder.

The platform's interior structures were neither lofty nor graceful, but short, squat blocks without windows — more like rows of coffins than living quarters. A repetitive, unchanging grid pattern of roads and pathways separated buildings that butted upward — or inward — like the planar sides of crystal growths whose surfaces were toneless, monotonous shades of gray.

"The design isn't as alien as it is — utterly designless." Sandy used her screen to peer through side-scan optical viewers. "Everything is the same, in all directions. It's so boring."

"Complete modularized construction, as one would

expect from a race of such great engineers. Form and function foremost, utility epitomized."

"Their work is so plain," Dane said. "They didn't even use wall panels to cover cables and wiring."

Sandy agreed. "Where is their *art*?"

"Why would you limit access with useless facade? It only makes repair and renovation more difficult." Brunel's voice was touched with marvel. "Pure intellect needs nothing but knowledge to satisfy its directives. Art is a human vanity."

Dane said, "People aren't machines, that can be turned on or off by the flick of a switch. They need the stimulus of variety."

"Only because they have been trained by their culture to think so."

"Wrong, Brunel. Man's art goes all the way back to cave wall paintings. You think all the following generations have been deluded by a conspiracy of artists? Art is basic to our nature, an expression of creativity. Without it, we'd be nothing more than self-programming calculators."

Brunel was coldly scientific. "Instead, we are cursed with emotion, blinded by attacks of unreason, afflicted with mental diseases brought about by an irrational mind in a perfectly rational Universe. Can't you comprehend the unadulterated symmetry of their architectural scheme? Think how much further we might have advanced by now had we not devoted so much time to wasteful pageantry. These beings, on the other hand, thinking more linearly, have repudiated the hypocrisy of gloss and glamour for the more fundamental magnificence of useful, constructive achievement. They may very well have discovered the doctrine of cosmic dialectics."

Dane was silent for a moment, his mind racing. He was not sure that he agreed with Brunel — except that his hypotheses seemed to fit together so neatly. It could explain so much. Yet, the engineer's theoretical ramblings did not resolve the problem of the aliens' eventual extinction. How could a people with a technology so advanced, have died out?

Or had they reached a state where corporeality held no meaning, where they had no further use for the impediments of physical structure? Perhaps they had shrugged off their material encumbrances and evolved into completely ethereal beings, on an altogether different plane of existence. Perhaps this burnt out star system represented nothing more than a byway to transcendental freedom, like the abandoned nest to the fledgling.

Sandy typed furiously on her keyboard. "I've got the central hub on radar, but I don't see any command post."

"It will be there," Brunel said confidently. "It is the logical progression. They and I are in full agreement, because we ascribe to the order of logical development."

Dane decelerated the ship until she was barely moving. Tracking monitors flashed proximity warnings across the bottom of his screen. "Brunel, can you cut your logic circuits for a spell? The backfeed is giving me a headache."

"I detect anger in your voice."

"I don't need you to tell me that."

"But, Dane, it was you who told me to always release my feelings. To quote you exactly, 'The articulation of ideas into words helps to coalesce otherwise diffuse thoughts.' You said that it was good for the team. I am only trying to do what is best."

"You always have a few ready words for — oh, Brunel, I'm sorry. You're right. I guess the strain's getting to me."

"Quite all right. I accept your apology. Sandy, I believe that indentation in the endcap will be the computer complex. The configuration is dissimilar to mine, but it makes sense to have all the heavy machinery and delicate hardware at the z-gee position."

Sandy said without inflection, "You're right again, Brunel. But I think I'll prove you wrong when you try to interface with their storage files. In pre-Settlement times, countries on the same continent couldn't even cross-reference another country's data banks because their computers were programmed in different languages."

"I did not say that we would be able to interpret at once the meaning behind their machine code, only that it can be translated through a logical binary progression by our kiloframe computers back home. Natural law does not change anywhere in the cosmos: E-M radiation propagates one way only, electrons always flow toward a positive pole, and those rather stupid mechanisms that we call computers rely on universally basic principles. If any data still exists in their memory banks, our own CPU can synthesize it for storage purposes. I can initiate an interpretation program immediately."

Dane said, "Maybe we'll be lucky and loop into a digitized Rosetta Crystal."

"Your thinking is always so planar," Brunel commented dryly. "Sandy, may I help run the telemetry scan? I would like to deploy a probe through that opening."

"Why don't you take over for me? The external probes are broadcasting data that need correlation." Sandy executed a two-key command that put Brunel in tactical control.

Microthrusters propelled the instrument package away from the *Great Eastern*. Brunel held rein on the inertial guidance systems. He directed the probe through the aperture and into the lightless room beyond. Infrared scanners cast an eerie, flickering glow on the screen. A complex array of interlocking panels occupied a chamber that spread outward in three dimensions beyond the limit of visibility. The one-meter-thick partitions looked like gray pegboard. Out of some of the holes protruded thin, pencillike cylinders.

"Those tubes must be communication modules, the equivalent of our data disks. You see, there is nothing so alien about their psychology. They follow the dictates of pure ratiocination."

"A biological machine — your perfect counterpart."

In awe, Dane watched the images that were imprinted on his screen. With the ship stationary, he was temporarily out of work. "I wonder if these people developed neurocircuits more advanced than the *Great Eastern's*? Maybe they transfused their neural patterns into their computers, like exchanging their anatomical remains for an integrated crystal lattice. They might still exist as digitalized cybernetic simulations, zipping through the database as information bits."

"Your imagination never ceases to amaze me."

"Sometimes I chew off more than I can byte."

Sandy groaned. "We may not have to worry about biological contamination, but you're enough to infect any central processing unit. Brunel, don't let him get near the interface amplifiers."

The probe locked its sensors onto what Brunel thought were readout devices. Through a gamut of electronic manipulations, the transponders began reacting to magnetic pulses. But the symbols that scrolled across the viewscreens were unrecognizable garbage.

"Hey, anybody see any doorknobs? They must have had some kind of non-automatic override to get into their buildings."

"You think of the strangest things," Brunel said.

"Then think about this: over all those hectares of surface area we passed, we saw no parks or playgrounds, no sculptures, no murals, no windows, nothing that would indicate any inclination toward pastime or esthetic theme. If these guys had no art, if they had no concept of conceit or pretense of emotion or even the slightest predilection toward ostentation, they might not have left any pictures of themselves. How are we going to know what they looked like?"

"The body is not important. It is the mind that makes us what we are."

"You're wrong. The mind gives us the capacity to think, to create, to contemplate. But the body is more than a taxi to carry the brain. The body is responsible for maintaining singularity. The body ensures separation from the masses. The body preserves individuality.

Without a physical encasement, and the adoration of its structure, there's nothing to prevent the personality from being absorbed by a more powerful influence. The body — "

Sandy said, "Dane, I think you'd better look at this."

"Don't interrupt me when I'm on a roll, pitch, and yaw. The body encapsulates the brain, and holds it inviolable from the lines of magnetic flux that flow throughout the Universe. Otherwise, all our thoughts would run together. Instead of distinct units, each with its own hopes, dreams, desires, and points of view, we would become one massive interwoven biological analogue. If you don't know what I'm talking about — " Dane grabbed the EEG helmet and held it out to the extent of its wire connections. " — put this on your head and let the computer suck your brains out. Then you'll understand how much you cherish that synaptic process known as consciousness."

Brunel's mouth was ajar. "I certainly did not mean to imply — "

"*Please!* I need your attention. Both of you." Sandy clapped her hands, then quickly returned to her keyboard. Her screen was full of equations. The CPU ran column after column of numbers, taking up all sixteen sections of the viewing monitor. "Something is happening here that I don't understand."

Dane immediately dropped his conversation with the engineer. "What's the problem?"

"I don't know. Or rather, I'm afraid I *do* know. If my interpretations are correct — " She typed quickly, and scanned the incoming data. "The readings from the remote probes are correlating."

"That's what they're supposed to do."

"No, I mean, the probes that we deployed outside the cloud, before we entered the solar system, are corroborating specific data with the probes left outside the cylinder."

Dane frowned. "Which data?"

Sandy looked at him with wide-open eyes. "A geometrical progression with respect to tangential verity of

the cloud layers and the distance from the sun. If — "
She turned toward the screen and typed furiously. The
figures disappeared, then returned. "Oh, no. If this
means what I think it means — "

Dane squinted at the engineer. "Brunel, do you
know what she's talking about?"

Brunel devised his own equations, siphoned off the
astronomer's screen. He did not reply, or give notice
that he had heard Dane's question.

"Can someone please tell me what the hell is going
on?" After a long silence broken only by the tapping of
fingers on heat sensitive keypads, he said, "If you people don't start talking to me, I'm pulling this ship out of
here."

"Pull it out, Dane," Sandy said frantically. "Do it
now."

Brunel spoke matter-of-factly. "Yes. I see what you
mean. I will run a projection . . . "

Dane put the thrusters on line. "We're about to lose
a probe."

"Forget it. Just get us out of here." Sandy was
almost panic-stricken.

"We can still receive input remotely. Even now it is
filling our memory banks with alien data." Brunel was
all business. "I think a retreat at this point might prove
advantageous."

The *Great Eastern* backed away from the inner surface of the endcap, pushing through the thick cloud of
dust like an arctic icebreaker. A wake of rippling, film-
like mist churned in the starship's backwash. Each
mote sparkled iridescently in the docking light beams,
causing an overall evanescent pattern that surrounded
the hull with dancing rainbow swirls.

"We're moving," Dane announced, since no movement was felt within the energy field of the inertia
pump. He was getting used to the unending fuel supply
that was usually unavailable at less than FTL speeds.
"I don't understand you people. First you beg me to
stay, then you cry for me to leave. Is someone coming
after us?"

"I wish that's all it were." Sandy floated lightly under her restraining straps. "Brunel, do you concur?"

"Unfortunately, I do. I have not yet predicted the time to ultimate collapse, but I urge a departure with extreme celerity. And, in case we do not make it out of the inner system, I am opening all circuits between the *Great Eastern* and our outer system probes. At least then, the information we have so far gathered will not be lost during vaporization."

"Hey, am I still a member of this team, or not?"

"Sorry, Honey Bun, but you just concentrate on getting us out of here."

"I can float and chew at the same time." His fingers flew across his keyboard. "What gives?"

Before Sandy could open her mouth, an awful, grating, rasping sound vibrated through the starship's hull. Dane's viscera tingled in protest, and shocked him into momentary inaction. Wide-eyed, he stared at the various monitors that were telemetering external data. He saw nothing wrong with the *Great Eastern's* airtight integrity. And while the trunnions and nacelles appeared to be maintaining contiguity, enormous unknown stresses were being exerted upon the starship appendage configuration.

"What the *hell*?"

Dane doused the docking lights, and switched to all-around visual. Pickups from the optical scanners blacked out his screen: the visible frequencies were opaque. But the infrared bands were emitting considerable amounts of energy.

"It's heating up out there."

"It'll get a lot hotter before long. Hot Pants, I think it's time to regain to your reputation and — skedaddle."

"This baby can only skedaddle so fast. The *Great Eastern* wasn't intended to be an atmosphere ship. We're buffeting a bow wake that's holding us back by some principle of aeronautical physics that they don't even teach any more, except in history class. Hell, I don't know how to fly an airplane."

Although he could not feel the battering because of

the inertia pump's instantaneous response, the instrumentation was registering random g-forces that made no sense to him. He had never conned a ship in anything but the vacuum of space. He guessed that Shirley and Rhonda, the transfer shuttle crew, could teach him a few tricks right about now. He wiped the visuals off the monitor, and concentrated on navigational fixes. He had to retrace the starship's route in order to relocate the entry hole in the platform's hull.

He focused the scanners to search for reference points. The alien landscape was so redundant that recognition was difficult even for the shipboard computer. Outside, shock waves racked the thick, dust-filled cloud that enveloped the *Great Eastern.* Billions of microcollisions reverberated throughout the hull.

"It's getting rough out there." Dane frantically processed information through the guidance controls. "And I can't seem to lock onto our reciprocal course. It's as if the platform has — jogged in orbit."

"Are we lost?" Sandy wanted to know.

"No, I'm just a might confused. Brunel, you'll have to sing out if we've got any mechanical problems. I'm pretty busy."

"We have not experienced any difficulties which I have not been able to correct."

"Just let me know if any components are about to malfunction. Sandy, this cylinder is about to shake itself apart. What's going on out there? Tell me."

"I forgot all about the conservation of angular momentum."

Dane rolled his eyes. "What's that got to do with anything?"

"Remember that I couldn't understand why I couldn't get an absolute fix on the diameter of the cloud? The numbers kept changing?"

Yes."

"You said that when you were locked inside the computer, you detected the acceleration of each peel?"

"So?"

"Aside from perihelion approach, there's only one

way a revolving astronomical body can increase its velocity: the closer two bodies are with respect to each other, the faster they revolve around their common center of gravity."

"Sandy, I had elementary physics in grade school. What's the point?"

"If the orbital speed of a body, or group of bodies, is increasing, it stands to reason that the radius of the orbit, or orbits, is decreasing. Those are the two points that the computer just correlated. That's what's happening in this system. Dane, the cloud layers are contracting, spiraling into the sun. And we're being swept along with the contraction."

Dane stared at her blankly. "Okay, I get the picture. Cloud friction is causing heat, and contraction of the system is increasing orbital velocity peel by peel. Mascons and particulates get closer. I guess if you work it out mathematically, there's a terminal point of contact at which every bit of matter falls into the sun. So how many million years do we have before this happy event occurs?"

The groaning outside was now audible. Even as Dane typed instructions for data display, the air was filled with high-pitched screeches and deep, lumbering peals of thunder. Angry squeals of pain emanated from without the starship's hull, and were transmitted through its solid bulkheads as the form of molecular vibration detected by the human auditory system as sound.

Dane cut the modulation circuits as a terrifying chill coursed along his spine. "What are we hearing out there?"

Brunel said calmly, "I think you should activate the mass proximity alarms. I would do it for you, but I know how you detest individual initiative."

"This is no time for games, Brunel."

"I suggest you switch to compugraphic simulation. It is getting brighter outside."

"How can it — " Before he completed the thought, he was ogling at the impossible visual display.

A bright ball of light, larger than the angular size of the sun, permeated the incandescent clouds that engulfed the starship. Even as he watched, the platform's inner surface, over which he had been piloting the *Great Eastern*, fell away as retreating blips on the radarscope.

"Ionization is so great, I doubt that our signal is getting through. We may already have transmitted our last message."

Sandy interpreted the digitized data. "The cylinder has just broken apart under gravitational stress and tidal forces."

Unable to speak, Dane conned the ship out of the fractured platform. According to the computer graphics that were taking form on his screen, the cylinder was hinging open like a gigantic egg over a frying pan. The *Great Eastern* was a yoke that was falling out of a cylindrical metal shell, and dropping into the sun.

Sandy could not keep the excitement and fear out of her voice. "What we're observing is not the birth of a solar system, but its death. And if you don't want to die with it, you've got to outrace a collapsing neutron star."

Chapter 20

"The mind is a construct of the brain. Change the architecture of the brain, and you change the attributes of the mind.

— G. G.

Sound is not transmitted through vacuum. But the solar dust was so concentrated due to the rapidly shrinking cloud spheres, that Dane heard the *Great Eastern* rasping through space like an Earth aircar in a smowstorm. The magnetic shields operated at full emergency power, but the larger particulates were punching through the deflectors and impacting against the starship's hull with a constant, bone-chilling squeal.

"That wasn't so bad," Dane breathed confidently. "Only twenty-six more peels to go."

The *Great Eastern* escaped from the rupturing *Kuttner* only to find herself in a condensing, cyclonic dust bowl. Gusts of solar wind, at hundreds of kilometers per hour, smashed the starship from every angle. Warning alarms broadcast on all channels.

Sandy transferred numbers to the pilot's screen. "We're losing space, Hot Shot. The clouds are being sucked into the sun faster than we're flying away from it. It's like walking two kleters per hour on a conveyor belt rolling toward you at four. Can't you go any faster?"

"I'm pedaling as hard as I can."

Brunel's voice displayed no awareness of the danger of their plight, but for once no foodtube straw was tucked in the corner of his mouth. "The shields are generating every available erg, and we are still overheating."

"If it gets any hotter we'll be baked lasagna. You have any time predictions, yet?"

"No one has ever observed a star going nova."

"How about a guess?"

Sandy said, "The terminal velocity of neutron collapse is the speed of light."

"Doesn't give us much leeway. If we go FTL in this gas cloud, we'll vaporize instantly. We'll have to pussyfoot out of here at sublight speeds. All right, get ready. Here comes the next peel."

Dane rolled the *Great Eastern* as the sensors registered the next cloud's orientation. Brunel displayed computer graphics on the engineering screen. Out of the corner of his eye, Dane saw the digitized onion with all its layers, and the central, pulsing solar body — a transitory phase in stellar evolution of which they might soon become a part.

Brunel said, "According to my calculations, our chances of outracing the gravitational influence, before we are ripped apart by tidal forces, are almost negligible. Disassembly should be quick even on the atomic scale. It will not occur as fast as electron flow in an electrical circuit, but it should take less time than nerve impulse transfer from axon to dendrite."

"I'd rather not think about it." Dane's mind whirled as he manually keyed the helm. He was finding it impossible to activate the controls with the agility necessary to coordinate the starship's roll, speed, and shielding, with incursion into the accelerating cloud layers.

"We have just wiped out the primary backup on the deflector circuits," Brunel enunciated clearly. "I suggest that you don the neurosensor coupler."

"And have my mind devoured by your computer. No thanks. I'd rather have a mind of my own."

"Dane, you know I love you," Sandy said softly. She could not reach him from her couch, but imploringly, she extended one pearly white hand. "You mean more to me than anything. I would die if anything happened to you. But you have to do this for — for all of us. I know the computer link was a frightening experience. I know it almost wiped out your mind. But we'll all be dragged into the sun if you don't integrate with the CPU."

"And if I do, I might get trapped permanently inside a silicon memory chip. I don't want to become an integrated circuit."

"I guarantee that my governor will disconnect you before total assimilation," Brunel stated flatly.

Dane watched his monitors. It had been so much easier flying into the cloud, when he was using the EEG and the optical actuators. Now, he felt the starship slipping out of control. The *Great Eastern* was slingshotting within the cloud layer, utilizing the accelerating speed of revolution to vector away from the dense core, and spitting out into the next layer like an electron from a particle accelerator. Since each succeeding outward peel spun slower, the sudden headwind threatened to burn the ship to a crisp if she did not decelerate. Yet, she had to keep climbing up the treadmill at maximum allowable speed, or be gobbled up from behind as she was drawn into the gullet of the collapsing core.

Sweat beaded on Dane's forehead as the internal temperature increased painfully. His fingers could not move fast enough over his keypad; he could not fly the starship at optimum efficiency. "Can we expect any help from time dilation?"

"If we get close enough to the core to experience relativistic effects, we won't be in any shape to appreciate it." Sandy watched her screen helplessly. At this point, further calculation was academic. "Sweetie, you're reaction time is not fast enough get us out of here without the neurotransmitter circuits."

Brunel said, "We are about to blow some more deflector circuits. We are running out of backups, although for a while, I can patch in some auxiliaries to share the load."

"I'm about to lose my mind." Dane grabbed the EEG helmet and hastily attached the probes to his skull. "If we get out of this alive, promise me you'll send love programs to my database every once in a while. I can use the input."

****

The burning! The heat was intense. He could feel it

on his skin/hull as friction ate away at his outer molecular structure.

With the insight of electronic/neural circuits, his comprehension of his surroundings was no longer bound by simplified graphic displays. He sensed the entire solar system at once, through his eyes/sensors, through his ears/probes, through his nose/gauges. He swam with huge paddles that were magnetic collectors; he kicked with ion thrusters; he breathed through matter accumulators. The deflector shields were protective clothing.

When he flexed his muscles, his fusion reactor converted matter into energy and propelled his body/hull through the dust-filled medium. When he cringed in pain, his plasma flux lines increased the density of his protective electron cloud. His brain/CPU coordinated the movements of his body/hull.

Dane forgot about being a man. He soared through space like a prowling eagle gliding on fierce feathery wings across the clear blue sky of ancient Earth.

He possessed a power — an atomic power — that enabled him to vie with the forces of the Universe. He was nature's latest, greatest creation: the culmination of millions of years of biological evolution, the accumulation of thousands of generations of human knowledge, the ultimate combination of man and machine. He was as far removed from the caveman who wielded a sharpened stone, as that cave man was from the amoeba.

As a chemical unit, he had had to rely on sluggish biological nerve impulses; as a cybernetic organism, it could respond to stimulus with practically instantaneous speed. Vaulting through the precessing, madly rotating cloud layers was child's play. Escaping the fusion furnace of the sun was a game of catch-me-if-you-can. The man/machine had infinite control over its functions; its only limitation was natural law. In exchange for this almighty, godlike power, it had to make only one sacrifice — its identity.

The Dane machine no longer existed as separate entities that were temporarily bonded by encephalic electrodes. It was a consolidation of analytical abilities:

the cognitive awareness emanating from the convoluted gray matter of the cerebral cortex, and the vast storehouse of data that were magnetically aligned in the central processing unit. It called itself Danine.

As the stellar object contracted and the multilayered accretion disk fell back upon itself, Danine flitted through the spiraling cloud zones with simplistic ease. It spun perfectly with each succeeding peel, braked just enough to prevent itself from burning up, applied every bit of power that it could generate as it banked through the dust. The collapsing neutron star was not even a challenge to its skill. There was no force in this galaxy or the next that was its master. It was invincible.

It was also insane.

And it knew it.

It was racked with inner conflicts, torn between the desire to roam freely throughout the cosmos demonstrating its awesome capabilities, and its deep-seated need to regain its self-control. A machine has no consciousness; it cannot act in any manner for which it is not designed, or programmed. Mechanical parts have no will. But a chemical unit, by the very nature of its uncertainty, exercises choice in its actions. It may make decisions that are erroneous, or unreasonable, but that is a small price to pay for independent volition.

That is the cardinal difference between machine intelligence and true sentience.

Danine, as a construct, despite the physical powers that it could harness, could never experience option, originality, or spontaneity, as long as it was a prisoner of cold, unmoving, unfeeling, predetermined logic. An infinity of and/or decisions premeditated an eternity of sameness and synonymity. Purpose came from self-awareness, but pleasure came from creativity, from surprise, from wonder, from love, from lack of mental restraint.

Danine could realize satisfaction, but it could never know happiness.

The part of Danine that was the Great Eastern *did not know enjoyment. The part of Danine that was Dane*

Gerrace could not survive without it. For him, there was more to existence than flying. With great conscious effort, Dane fought to retract the essence of his being from the analogue synthesis that he had become. With control of the ship at the end of a thought, he flipped switches, disconnected circuits, overloaded breakers, shorted diodes, and burned out resistors: whatever was necessary to preserve all that was unique and idiosyncratic about his identity, no matter what the consequences.

To an emotional, contemplative, mortal creature, dissolution was far more desirable than total assimilation.

Dane exercised this choice.

****

Electrons dashed along printed circuits, spinning in unison, flashing brilliantly but momentarily like meteors in the nighttime firmament. The Universe was vast, dark, and everlasting. Somewhere, in the middle of existence, a gray dimness developed. As the blackness receded, as the brightness grew, the madly whirling electrons faded from sight. The purple velvet sky twinkled with first light, the land shimmered with dawn, the sun peeked over the horizon with a comforting yellow glow.

Shadows took shape. From far away, as if on a nearly airless world, a vaguely familiar voice called to him. "Dane," it whispered, like the Siren calling to Odysseus. "Dane. Can you hear me?"

Seen through a milky film, the Siren appeared to float effortlessly before a backdrop of glittering, colorful dots. Gradually, the scene resolved itself into a frightened angel surrounded by green and red stars. "Sandy?" His voice was harsh and cracked, his throat parched.

As if understanding his predicament, Sandy placed a straw between his dry lips. "Drink this."

He sucked gratefully. The cool liquid enlivened his mouth, coated his throat, filled him with energy. "Am I alive?"

A broad smile split her face. "You tell me."

Dane glanced around at the compartment, noticed

the annunciator lights behind her. His voice was less raspy. "If I knew, I wouldn't ask."

"How do you feel?"

Dane thought for a moment, his mind a montage of fleeting images. "Like a burnt out capacitor." He reached out with an arm that barely responded to his command, as if it belonged to someone else. He placed his hand on the soft skin of her face. "You're real."

"Last time I checked," Sandy laughed. "But I feel more alive when you touch me."

Dane worked his stiff lips into a grin. "You always say the right thing at the right time." Then the awful memories of another life, another time, clouded his mind. "The ship? Did we make it?"

Sandy ran her fingers through his hair, and brushed the tousles off his forehead. "Yes, we made it. *You* made it. You brought us through."

"But, I thought — I remember cutting out before — I couldn't stand it any more. I was being absorbed — "

"Brunel's governor worked, but almost too late. The inhibitor circuits blew out twice, and he had to replace the module manually when he couldn't patch in a back-up."

"But we were still in the cloud — "

"We had two peels to go when you conked out. Brunel took over, and brought us out the rest of the way."

"Brunel?"

"We had no choice. We were afraid the teep would-n't work fast enough, and with the whole system col-lapsing behind us, we decided that someone had to take control of the ship. Naturally Brunel, being com-pletely familiar with the systems and computer func-tions, was the logical choice to take the helm."

"Did he — did he use the helmet?"

Sandy nodded. "He's okay, though. He survived the experience much better than you did. I guess because his brain is so rationalistic, so systematic, that merging with a computer was more like talking to himself."

Dane laughed out loud, although the chest heaving

was painful. "And argumentative. He probably had that computer running scared, and chasing its own logic circuits."

'I don't know. He's been catatonic for two revs."

"Two *revs*! How long have I been out?"

"Two and a half. I've been alone, taking care of the bodily functions of two grown men."

Dane cocked an eyebrow. "Which functions — of which men?"

"Honey Bun, if you're going to show jealousy at this stage of the game, we'll have to talk through another encounter session. Besides, Brunel's still in the Medwife. His condition was so unstable that I had to leave him under constant medical attention."

"Then how can you say he's okay?"

"He's just suffering from exhaustion. His brain waves are normal, so I know his higher functions are still in working order. It was strange, though. For the longest time, after he donned the helmet, he showed no ill effects. He answered questions just like he always has. He talked in that same unemotional monotone . . . " She shrugged. "He didn't seem to be — taken over, if you know what I mean."

"Believe me, I do."

"Even after we were in the clear, even after we translated, he stayed in the circuit. He was completely relaxed. His ergonomic chart showed no physical stress. That's when I really got worried. It was too — unnatural. I didn't like it. But when I tried to unplug him, he protested. He fought me off. Dane, he was *enjoying* it."

"Probably the first orgasm he's had in years. At last, he's found a partner suitable for him."

"That's what I thought at first. But then he started to struggle. He started to resist. I don't know what was going on in his mind — or between the two of them. Then he lost consciousness. That was when I pulled the plug — the whole thing, right out of the bulkhead connector. I floated him into the Medwife, but had to disengage him from the chair in order to fit him under the glass. It was pretty gruesome at first, because he's — his lower body is so broken up. I had to connect him to the Medwife evacuation tubes, and clean up the mess. Then I realized — it was no different from changing a baby's diapers, and dabbing its little behind. I even began to enjoy it."

Dane's eyes widened. "What kind of abnormal psychology is working here?"

"No, it was nothing like that," Sandy laughed. "In many ways, Brunel's just a big baby — like most men."

"Present company excepted."

She winked. "Like most men. But it did start me thinking — about babies, that is."

"Oh?"

"'I've been toying with the idea for quite a while. But I've always put it aside because — because I was involved in my work, because I hadn't accomplished anything in my life."

"Babies are accomplishments."

"I know that, but that isn't what I mean. I meant in my chosen field of endeavor. Not that you can't raise a family and have a career at the same time. Everybody does it. It's just that, I wanted to wait until I could concentrate my focus a little more — not just have a baby for its own sake, but to spend time with it, to enjoy it.

"Dane, I don't know how it was for you back there. I know you were pretty busy flying the ship. And Brunel had his engineering tasks to keep him occupied. But I had nothing. No matter what happened, there was no way that I could help. I just stared at the figures on the screen. I had — too much time to think. Too much time to — be afraid. And I was. I was terrified. We were so close to death that I could feel it. And I didn't like the feeling.

"I had to go on this hop, to give it a chance. Now I know what it's like, and I know I can do it. But I don't want to go on another one. I could never face the possibility of being lost forever, drifting about hopelessly until our stores ran out. Now I understand what Mother went through. It's not the kind of life for me. I want to go on with my studies, my teaching, my life. And I want to have that baby. And Dane, I would like you to sire it for me. If you don't mind."

Dane's jaw dropped. Without the help of gravity, this took a conscious muscular effort. "This is quite a shock. I've never been *asked* before."

Sandy tilted her head. "I know. But don't think that I want you just for your genetic material. I — I really do love you. I always have. Ever since I was — a little girl. Mother used to show me your picture, and talk about your hop together. And of course, you stopped by between hops whenever you could — to visit mother, and to bring me toys and candy. This isn't just puppy love, although it was at one time. Or love of humanity, which we all experience all the time. This is something different. Something that I can't explain. It's a feeling that makes my heart flutter, and causes a lonely ache in my chest. I guess what I'm feeling is being in love. It's a quantum difference from any other kind of feeling." Sandy batted her eyelashes, knocking out teardrops which, in z-gee, did not roll down her cheeks, but clung to her eyes and lids by the surface tension of the concentrated saline solution. "So, what do you think?"

Dane planted his elbows in the mattress. He did not bounce away as he had expected, because the restraining straps held him in place. Since he could not float into Sandy's arms, he pulled her into his. "I think — " He was so choked up that his voice returned to its prior cragginess. "I think I'm in love with you, too. I always have been, ever since I first met your mother. You and she are alike in so many ways. I feel as if I'm getting a second chance to make up for the one that I threw away with her."

"Mother loves you, too. I think she'd be happy if you would . . . "

"Yes, I think she would." Dane kissed her long and hard on the lips, felt the softness of her embrace. Minutes later, he said, "Sandy, I know this is going to sound like my old Earth heritage speaking, but — has it occurred to you that I'm twice your age?"

She brushed him aside with a feminine wave of her hand. "Oh, Dane, you think of the silliest things. But, yes, it did occur to me. And while I was by myself during the past two revs, I checked into your biofile and ran a few computer calcs. I added the subtime from all your hops and subtracted the total from your obtime, and — guess what?"

"I don't like that mischievous twinkle in your eyes."

She rolled her head and said perkily, "It turns out that in terms of objective biological age, I'm older than you."

Dane drew her close and kissed her again. "You've got an answer for everything, haven't you."

"Only when it comes to computers. I still don't have an answer from you. About whether you'll sire my baby. Will you?"

"Can we start now?"

"Do you think you're up to it?"

Dane placed his hands on her shapely derriere, and pulled her tight against his body. "What do you think?"

Sandy rolled her eyes. "I think I know how you *really* earned your reputation as Hot Pants."

"Then I'll go you one better. I'd like to be more than the sire of your child. I'd like to be its father. I'd like to watch him — or her — grow up. I'd like to exert a little influence on the next generation. Do you think you could stand to have me around all the time?"

"I'd love nothing better. But what about your — flying?"

"I'd much rather mix my genes with yours than with the ships of the future. Besides, I'm pretty certain that I can swing a solside job. Babs has been pushing me in that direction."

"You can do anything that you set your mind to." Sandy ran her hands up and down Dane's chest. "Honey, when you were under the influence, did the computer rearrange your neural circuits?"

"No, only my priorities. It just made me realize that I have capacities that a machine doesn't have — can never have. Being dehumanized and digitized by the

Great Eastern's CPU didn't change me as much as it compelled me to appreciate the magnificence of this grand, gracious gestalt that we call humanity."

"Pumpkin, realization is change."

"I prefer to think of it as growth. Speaking of which — " He pulled her close again.

Sandy's kisses lingered on his lips. "You recover quickly."

"Just to make sure that I'm fully recovered, why don't we do something about this baby situation?"

"It's not the right time, but we can always practice."

"Practice makes perfect."s

Chapter 21

"Our intelligence has recently provided us with awesome powers. It is not yet clear that we have the wisdom to avoid our own self-destruction. But many of us are trying very hard."

— Carl Sagan

"When did he finish the periscope?"

"You know Brunel. He always has ten projects going at the same time. That's the way his brain works. All I know is, while I was waiting for someone to wake up, I spotted it on a functions menu."

Dane walked lightly under partial gravity. "Did you try it? Did you see what happened to the Mettleson Object?"

"No, silly. I mean, yes I tried it. But you can't look back with it. I mean, you can look back, but you can't see anything new. As long as we're traveling FTL, E-M radiation from the M-O can't catch up with us. We can only see it the way it was when it emitted the observable light."

Dane zipped shut the front of his jumpsuit. He shook the cobwebs out of his head. "I don't know where my mind is."

"I do." Sandy pulled her jumpsuit up over her hips as she padded alongside him. Her breasts bobbled despite the half-gee drag. She shrugged her arms into the sleeves, and covered her breasts just before entering the Medwife chamber. "Are you sure that some of you isn't still locked up in the CPU?"

"Not the part that counts. You're not making much sense either."

"I'm not used to jumping out of bed in the middle of —"

Dane halted at the hatchway, one hand on the manual hydraulic override. "You know the first thing he's going to say?"

"Yes, but there's a limit to how long we can keep floating."

Dane pressed the automatic switch, opened the hatch to the Medwife chamber. "Hey, Brunel. Nice to see you up and about."

The engineer lay under a sheet that was wrapped around his abdomen. Horizontally, his sharply truncated figure assumed a more garish aspect. "How do you expect me to move in this abominable gravity? Where is my chair? Why are all the computer terminals out of reach? How do you expect me to survive without intellectual stimulation? What makes you think . . . ?"

Dane stifled Brunel's chatter by slamming down the Medwife's glass lid. He leaned close to the intercom and spoke in a smooth, controlled voice. "You were so much more pleasant as a cold, logical engineer, without inflection. Please don't revert to your old form of irascibility."

He switched off the speaker when Brunel started to shout, and turned to Sandy. "He's as fit as a feedback. That means we'll have to run the CPU through a psychoanalysis test. I hope it's salvageable." He made a pretense of looking at his wristrad, ticking off the time. When Brunel's dark eyes softened, and his grim lips bit down hard, Dane pulled up the plastiglass seal. "Are we feeling better, now?"

Brunel pushed himself up onto one elbow, and struck out with his other hand for Dane. "What is the meaning of this outrage?"

"My, but you're a short circuit." Dane jumped back out of reach. "I know it's no fun being cooped up in a glass jar, but it's the best treatment for electrode amalgamation. Why don't you just relax, and tell us all about your encounter session with the *Great Eastern*."

Brunel opened his mouth wide, but uttered not a sound. Slowly, eyes glazed, he eased his upper body down onto the foam pad. "It was the most exhilarating experience I have ever had. All the data I could possibly want was right there — not just at my fingertips, but at the mere cogitation. It was total thought control."

Dane said to Sandy, "What did I tell you? No computer is going to get the best of Brunel."

Sandy glanced over the biomonitor readings. "Everything looks normal."

"Of course I am normal," Brunel shouted. "Why should I be otherwise? I — " His head lolled, he ogled at the overhead. When he looked at Dane, his eyes were alight. "It has just come to me. The feeling — " He stopped and thought for a moment. "The computer almost won. It nearly absorbed me. And at the time, *I wanted it to*. For one wild microsecond, for the span of time between the crests of two high frequency cosmic waves, I almost let it." Brunel stared intently at Dane. "*You* were my savior."

Dane winced at the incredible psychic onslaught. "I wasn't even there. It was Sandy who pulled the plug."

Brunel surged up on one elbow again and rolled over on what was left of his hip. His free hand swung in the air like the baton of an orchestra conductor. "No, it was *you*. Your identity. All the components of your personality were — still are — imprinted on the *Great Eastern's* memory banks. A part of you has *become* the *Great Eastern*, indelibly, for all time. All your feelings, all your emotions, all your hopes, desires, and innermost secrets and fears, have become a permanent part of this ship. That was what saved me — because I became part of that as well. For the first time, I was able to understand your — your selflessness, your compassion, your — love of humanity. It drove home to me what it is to be more than an isolated individual, a naked intellect, but part of a network, a society of living, caring people. All my life, I have repudiated emotion as a weakness. Now, through you, I understand it as a strength — as *our* strength as a race. Because *that* is what the aliens did not possess.

"They were impassive, and impersonal — like a vegetable intelligence might be. They had no love, and no imagination. They were strictly engineers, reorganizers and users of natural law with no concept of the higher planes of character. That was their downfall. It takes a flare of — of irrationality — to supersede the limitations of logic, to dream, to envision concepts that do not come from experience, that cannot evolve from common sense, but which fall in the realm of fantasy. That is what makes us different from *them*. That is the noble quality that we possess — that allowed my father to visualize the Selkirk Drive. He refused to accept the dictates of logic. Instead, even though in purely mathematical terms he knew that matter could not achieve faster-than-light speeds, he ignored the postulates of physics. He had the imagination to embrace the absurd.

"*They* did not have that capacity. *They* built bigger, and larger, and more. They had fantastic inventions. They had machines that could perform countless tasks. They strived for mechanical perfection. I saw it all. I saw how they installed a diffusion beam above their living surface: it prevented their atmosphere from leaking into the immense inner space of their cylinders. They were highly skilled engineers, but they could not see into their own future. They were so — shortsighted . . . "

Brunel gasped and fell back, his chest heaving.

Sandy placed a hand on his forehead. "Brunel, you're getting too excited. Perhaps you should rest — "

"*No!* I am fine. I am — tired — is all. The drain — My mind is so filled with — data." He closed his eyes. Gradually, he got his breathing under control.

Dane said, "All that's gone now, anyway. All their artifacts were destroyed — "

"It makes no difference!" Brunel flared suddenly. He calmed down quickly, and went on with a new inner serenity. "Artifacts are not important. They are clutter, the useless impedimenta of the past. What matters is information. When I was united with the — data matrix — when I was privy to the computer's translating circuits, I *became* one of *them*. Their language was a simple, orderly mathematical progression that was easily deciphered. In seconds, I knew everything about them — how they were born, how they lived, and how they died.

"Their solar system was perfectly engineered. They established a circle of Settlements around the sun, using the material that was siphoned off a gas giant for mass. When the initial sphere became overcrowded, they constructed another in a closer orbit, offset in order to catch a different circumference of solar output. *They generated an artificial ecliptic.* The only occulting occurred at the two points of intersection. What beautiful simplicity! Once the project was conceived, it was continued until the entire star was enveloped by proliferating Settlements, rings within rings like encircling gimbals, capable of supporting a stellar civilization whose population of platforms was counted in the *trillions.* Their biomass grew to incredible proportions. But it did not matter, for they captured every wave and particle that their sun produced. Nothing escaped the encapsulating sphere of Settlement rings!"

Brunel remained outwardly calm, but the biomonitors registered extreme stress. The Medwife activated its healing circuits. As long as the lid was open, the medicated vapors were locked in their pressure bottles.

Dane pulled the glass barrier part way down. "Brunel, I think you need some more rest."

"I cannot rest. I can never rest. There is so much to do."

"That can come later. You'll have time to build all the Settlements you want."

"Not build! Educate! We cannot afford to make the same mistake that *they* made. With so much energy at their command, they became extravagant. Unused material that slipped through their solar scoops was decelerated to less than escape velocity, and fell into close solar orbit. Stray ions from flux shield production were emitted into the system. They atomized their waste and dumped it into space. The byproducts of their industry were released wantonly. They treated their environment as an infinite vacuum. Eventually, their atomic refuse became a shroud. They could not leave their system, so they choked in it. The aliens were a parasitic growth that not only killed themselves off, but asphyxiated their solar system as well. *That* is what we must prevent. That is what we must teach our young. That we are not an astronomical cancer that kills stars. We are the lifeblood of our System. Whether we become leukophytes or phages — is up to us."

The last of his energy spent, Brunel collapsed into coma. Dane hurriedly closed the Medwife lid. The medical analyzers reacted immediately by releasing the proper prophylactic recipes into the atmosphere.

Dane clicked his tongue. "He's as warped as a naked singularity. I hope the psychprobe can put him back together again. What do you say we get back to — " Sandy had a faraway look in her eye, as if she were studying a quasar through a worm hole. "Sandy?" She did not respond. "Sandy? Are you okay?"

She shook her head, and shifted her gaze to Dane. She stuttered, "He may — be right. It all — makes sense in — a crazy kind of way."

Dane grimaced.

"Think about it. You had access to the memory banks. Didn't you see any of what he was talking about?"

"I was pretty busy flying — " But the thoughts were coming through, fast, in a flood of alien data that had a ring of — truth. Or was it illusion?

"It's all true, isn't it? I'll have to run some calculations in order to work out the formulae, but I can see how it could have happened. No matter or radiation escapes, so it continues to accumulate. Cosmic radiation hammers in from all sides, shrinking the heliosphere. It forms this huge cloud, like an accretion disk, that overbalances the system. The sun keeps sweating protons, getting smaller. The dust bowl keeps getting denser. Eventually — "

Dane nodded frantically. "Eventually, it condenses into an ever-thickening, faster spinning cloud. It starts to contract, spiraling sunward faster and faster, drawn by the gravity of the star, until — "

"Until the entire solar system shrinks into a tiny, rapidly rotating body. When mass reaches criticality, it explodes. After the accretion disk is blown off, what remains is a homogeneous ball of — pure neutrons."

Dane saw it as clearly as if he were watching a compugraphic. His mind was flooded with images, a juxtaposition of his own mental thought processes and the CPU simulator circuits. What Sandy had deduced from intuition, he saw as computer enhanced, absolute, undeniable fact.

If the resultant neutron star happened to have its magnetic axis directed toward Sol, it was detected as a pulsar. Every flashing beacon in the sky was the tombstone of a long extinct race. Every supernova was a visible, cosmic death knell.

Sandy was still talking. "Our bodies may consist of heavy elements that were created by an ancient species that failed to invent the stardrive."

Dane heard, and absorbed the information. But there was something else on his mind. If all this were true, then what the *hell* was the Coal-Sack Nebula?

Epilogue

"All of life is like a plant coming to flower. And isn't it just possible that in spite of earth's insignificance, it actually is the birthplace of intelligence? Our space ship wouldn't be an invention in that case. It would be more like a natural growth — a seed pod like a bit of thistledown ready to be tossed on the winds of space and carry the spirit of reason."

— David Duncan

Barbara Mettleson floated in front of the communication console aboard the *O'Neill* and read the first transmission from the *Great Eastern.* " 'Mission accomplished.' That has to be from Sandy: a straightforward reply that is stated with typical reserve and modesty."

" 'With a bang,' Fred Malkowitz read. "Dane, undoubtedly."

The viewscreen flashed in large letters, "Tell the System."

"Brunel," they said simultaneously, then laughed.

Fred raised an eyebrow. "They don't seem to have changed."

"You can never tell. An awful lot can happen on a hop. Look how it influenced our lives."

Fred nodded, and pursed his lips. "I guess, being that far away from home, experiencing the solitude of infinity, it has to affect the psyche in some way. Dane is the only person I know who could keep going back out there, could keep facing the unknown. It never seemed to frighten him at all."

"He's a rare man. A good man." Barbara's lips curled slowly into a smile. "And a malleable man. In the purest sense."

Fred raised an eyebrow. "Are you ever going to tell him about his daughter?"

Barbara sighed wistfully. "I would like to. But despite his ability to adapt, despite his intellectual capacity to understand, there are some ideas that his upbringing would not allow him to accept. Raising a child is like baking a cake: the recipe calls for the ingredients to be mixed in exact proportions, in a certain order, at specific times. After the cake is removed from the oven, it's too late to add a forgotten ingredient. It can never then be cooked in, only layered on top."

"And Sandy?"

Barbara wagged a finger in the air. "That girl of mine is quite a conniver. I never intended that she make this hop. She outwitted me. I may have pulled a few strings in my time, but she yanks on stainless steel guy wires — and gets away with it."

Barbara touched a few keys, and switched the viewscreen to full external visual. Somewhere out there, among those sharp pinpoints of light that glistened in the farthest reaches of the Galaxy, the *Great Eastern* was nearing the end of a long and fruitful space voyage. The inaugural data that were even now being telemetered solside presaged tremendous changes that were in store for humanity.

"Sandy never believed that sperm bank story. She knows that I would not leave to chance something so important as flesh and blood. She has always sensed intuitively who her father is. Her love for him is as strong as mine. But what she wants from him is different than what I wanted for myself. And she knows better than I how to give him what he needs." Barbara tilted her head thoughtfully. "The only thing that bothers me is: did I finagle her into hooking him, or did she finagle me?"

"Why don't you ask her?"

Barbara grinned mischievously. "Because I might not like the answer."